Dedication:

To the golden age of boyhood, ages 9-10. I also dedicate the book to boyhood memories which all men retain of that time and the things we did and probably shouldn't have, during that trying time of life. I strongly believe youth can be robbed, which can mold behaviors that follow a person into adulthood. The sad story of girls in this book represents the failure of adults to treasure and preserve that time when a young girl blossoms into womanhood.

I remember my pleasant experiences while working in Mississippi with friends in Columbus, who were in the car business. Their gracious acceptance of me is a cherished memory I shall always treasure.

This book is retro-Annette. This story, along with Cheerleader Bluz and Le' Mustang Bluz, takes place after Bitcoin Bluz and before Dixie Bluz. These stories feature a younger more fearless Annette.

Enjoy this saturnine yarn. Patrick W. Emmett

The Finger Bone Club Bluz

An Annette Dupart book

By:

Patrick W. Emmett

Prologue:

Mississippi is officially known as the Magnolia State. The blossoms of the Granda Flora Magnolia trees issue a fragrance that floats on slight breezes that lift and drift on gentle eddies of air and bring a pleasant aroma to the olfactories of every living creature. The unique scent greeted humans who set foot on this land millennia ago as it does today.

In the South, a faint memory exists of gentlemen in white suits and ladies who floated like flowers on a glassy pond wearing multi-colored crinoline dresses. That memory continues to influence a culture of grace and manners. This faux culture of the past was built upon the backs of other human beings and like the fragrance of the Magnolia flowers, it's fingerprint still resonates among those who live on the land.

Yet today, you can still see gentlemen and their ladies, dressed in white, perched on front porches in rocking chairs. They wave fans cooling themselves in the shade of those Magnolia trees. The fans move pollen rich air. Sweet tea and lemonade quench thirsts as friendly faces wave at their neighbors and tell stories of days gone by. Sometimes, they slowly sip bourbon or the beverage known as Southern Comfort on ice.

It was into this mix of nostalgia and sins of the past that I stumbled into a rushing current of theft, betrayal, and revenge, which festered into a boiling point around me. The sublime facade of young boys riding bikes in parks in the summer and pretty girls playing hop scotch, would fail and turn a community against one another. I am a woman in my late 20's, yet murder and the willful destruction of a 60-year-old business was laid on my plate for me to figure out. Oh, the sweet fragrance of Magnolia!

Table of Contents

Chapter: 1

It was a late May, Saturday morning, when seven boys rode their bikes across town and parked them beside a huge live oak tree in a park at the center of Columbus. Some folks said the tree was over 400 years old. Around them, girls were playing hop scotch and mothers were nursing babies. The boys played together and attended school since they were in kindergarten. Billy, the oldest by five months, said, "This won't do! Man, we gotta find a better place to meet. There are too many people in the park. How can we be a secret club if everyone knows who we are and sees what we're doing?"

"Yeah, but where? There's no place in town we can go without being seen." Lawrence said.

"We need someplace like way out in the woods. Someplace where we can meet and hide stuff, you know?" Mark said.

"I've heard of a place, but it's not close," Pete said.

"Yeah? Like where?" Billy demanded.

"South of here, four miles or more, in the nature preserve, just south of the Luxapallia Creek, in the swampy area where no one goes." Pete drew a map in the dirt using a stick.

"Lot of land south of here, man," Oron said.

"And a lot of wetland." Robby chimed in.

"My dad says Luxapallia is a Choctaw Indian word that means flying turtle. No one goes in there," Mark said.

"Well, my dad said he and my uncle went in there years ago to hunt deer. He said there's a piece of land down there with an old building on it. He said some fur trapper built the place a long time ago. He warned me to never go there," Pete said.

"Why is that?" Billy wanted to know.

"Because some 'hooch maker' took over the place before the Tennessee-Tombigbee channel was built. They said he put out all kinds of traps for the revenuer men."

"Traps? Like what kind?" Robby wanted to know.

"I don't know for sure, but I heard, snake pits, booby traps, and bear traps." Pete said.

"Cool! Do you know how to find this place?" DeShawn asked.

"I think so. Dad warned me that a friend of his almost lost a leg in a bear trap while hunting turkey there years ago. He said it's very dangerous. It's near where Luxapallia Creek and the Tennessee-Tombigbee channel meet." Pete said.

"Yeah, and I heard some Confederate gold is buried down there somewhere, too. Maybe that's why someone put all of those traps out." Oron said.

"You say, four miles from here? That ain't so bad. We can be down there and back home this afternoon, easy," Mark urged.

"I can't be late. I have piano practice at three o'clock," Robby said.

Billy said, "Okay, let's take a vote. All who want to go find that house for a club house, raise your hand." Every hand went up.

"Then, it's settled." Billy said. "Let's go!"

"How do we get there?" The boys wanted to know at once.

"Follow me." Pete said.

Chapter: 2

"Wow! That place is really cool! How do we get over there?" Mark asked.

"We'll need a boat or canoe," Pete said.

"I don't know, look around, there must be something. And watch for snakes! If you see one, yell out," Billy said laughing.

Ten minutes later, Lawrence shouted, "Boat! I found us a rowboat. Over here!"

Billy warned, "Don't turn it over yet. Wait and we'll do it together. Could be snakes under the boat or even a gator."

Mark snorted a laugh and said, "There ain't any gators around here. My dad says they don't come this far north."

"Maybe, but let's not take any chances. We do this together. Okay?" Billy urged.

The boys lifted the boat together and they quickly dropped the boat when a rabbit darted out from underneath, startling the boys. When they saw what it was, they all began to laugh. Still laughing they put their backs into flipping the boat over.

Only four boys could cross the water in the small rowboat at a time. So, Billy, being the oldest and strongest, volunteered to row the boat over twice.

Once all seven boys were on a small wooden dock, they stood in awe looking at the old, yet sturdy wood building in front of them. "Wow!" They all exclaimed. "How cool. Come on, let's go inside," Robby urged. He led the way, and they entered the two room building. "I bet it's been here at least a hundred years."

"It's solid enough. Look at the size of those timbers. This place was built to last. I wonder if the roof leaks?" Mark asked.

"I see spiders, but no snakes," DeShawn observed.

"My uncle says, 'Just brush them spiders off before they bite'," Lawrence said laughing.

"It don't look like anyone's been here for a long time. I don't see no food cans or even trash," Billy said.

"You know, I think this would make one really cool club house," Billy stated.

"It's cool, but where's the bathroom?" Robby asked.

The other boys looked at him in disbelief. Robby said, "What? I gotta take a leak, okay?"

"Alright! Sure!" They said putting their hands up in surrender. Oron said, "Outhouse. Didn't that dad of yours ever teach you anything about living in the woods?" Pete asked.

Robby didn't admit his dad left him and his mom. He said, "Not about that. I'll go outside and look around for an outhouse."

"If you don't find one, just use a tree, but watch the ground for snakes and bear traps," Billy warned.

Robby didn't believe him. He went out the door onto a wooden porch and looked left and right. He stepped down to walk toward the back of the building. He was being careful, looking for snakes. Trees sprouts and deadfall limbs were everywhere. He decided if there were snakes, he couldn't see them because of the leaves. He didn't want to step into a bear trap, however.

He moved slowly and peeked around the corner of the building. He saw no additional structures. He heard something move in the leaves and he jumped to his right, tripped and fell into a large hole about a foot deep. He lost his glasses in the leaves. He panicked and rolled over, thinking a snake was near him. He felt around and didn't feel or see a snake. So, using his hands, he searched the leaves for his glasses. He found them and as he slipped them on, an object on the ground came into focus.

He couldn't tell what it was at first. Then he picked the item up and inspected the thing in his hand closer. He said, "It's a bone. It's two bones connected."

He still had to pee badly. Not being able to hold it any longer, he stepped out of the hole, walked three paces, undid his fly, and sighed with relief as the yellow stream spattered on sodden leaves. "Whoa! I needed that." He searched the ground once more and saw no more bones, no outhouse, and no Confederate gold. When he entered the house, Pete said, "Man, you were out there a long time. I thought we would have to send the Marines to find you."

"Ha, ha! Very funny. There is no outhouse, but I did find this." He pulled the jointed bones out of his pocket and the boys gathered around. They all oooed and awed, passing the object around.

Lawrence asked, "Did you see any more?"

"No, I looked. You can look for yourself, but watch out, there's a deep ditch out there."

Robby said, "Look, it took some time for us to find this place. It'll be easier the next time, but I really need to get back for my piano lesson."

"He's right! Let's go back to the boat. What a find! I can't wait till we come back here," Mark said.

Billy said, "We'll bring candles and sleeping bags."

"And food, too," DeShawn said.

Chapter: 3

Robby was at school when his mother began a search for the key to wind up the vintage Wittner Metronome she found at a garage sale. Robby used it while practicing his piano lessons. A community concert was planned in a few weeks. Robby was scheduled to play a Bach piece, and she wanted to make sure he had the correct timing.

Robby was an average boy in every way, but he was gifted when it came to playing the piano, a prodigy, his mom believed. Still, he loved to run and play ball with his friends. Lately, he and his friends from school enjoyed taking extended bike rides. She felt it was good exercise, and the boys liked each other's company.

"Now, where did he put that key?" She mumbled while searching on his desk and through every drawer in his room. She saw the old wooden box given to him by his grandfather. She opened it and was shocked by what she saw. Inside were two bones held together by a ligament. "Now, where did he get that?" She said.

She carefully picked up the object and inspected it. "Oh, goodness! This looks like a finger. Where on earth did, he get it?" She sat on the bed with the bones in her hand and debated what to do with what she found.

Her brother was the Sheriff's Deputy Investigator. He would know what to do. She took the finger bones and wrapped them in tissue. Before she shut the box, she saw the metronome key and pocketed it. She called and left a message for her brother.

Her brother, Mike, came by her place later that afternoon. "Okay, let's see what you've got, Sis."

She showed him the bones, and he said, "Yep, looks like a finger, alright. Did he say where he found it?"

"I haven't asked him yet. He's due home around 3:30."

"I'll take this to the coroner's office and let them have a look at it. Then I'll need to speak with Robby."

"He isn't in any trouble, is he?" She asked worried.

"No, no. Don't worry. We just need to know where he got this… finger bone. That's all."

"Okay, I guess. I don't want to upset him before his recital. He's worked so hard on those piano pieces."

"Let me find out what we have, first. Are you doing okay? Bring the kids and have supper with us."

"I'm working long hours at the beauty shop, Mike. Today was my day off. I'm trying to make ends meet, but it's hard paying daycare for Dotty and all."

"Suzane and I want you, Robby, and Dotty to come over for dinner tonight. Is that guy, Baker, still bothering you?"

"You know," she reflected, "he keeps coming by at odd times. I'm not worried so much about me. I just don't trust him around Dotty."

"I know him. He's married with three kids. He shouldn't be coming around here at all. I'll have a talk with him," Mike retorted.

"Thank you, Mike. That'll make me feel much better."

Mike took the tissue wrapped finger bones to the county coroner and explained where he got the finger joint. They promised to call him later. He told Sheriff Turnbull what he found. Turnbull said, "Okay, we need to talk to the kid to find out where he got the bones. Then, we need to check all unsolved disappearances in the county and try to make a DNA match."

While the finger was processed at the coroner's office, a reporter for the *Columbus Sun* newspaper was wrapping up a story about a tragic car accident where four people died on the highway. She heard technicians talking about a mysterious finger bone. That weekend, there was a front-page article with a banner line that read, "MYSTERIOUS FINGER FOUND." In that article, the reporter speculated that the finger was found in the nature preserve along the Tennessee-Tombigbee channel. "Who did it belong to?"

Suddenly, the finger bone story created all kinds of speculation. Lydia Longsleep, a local attorney and female shaman for the local Choctaw Native American community, immediately filed a cease-and-desist order. She asked for the sacred remains to be returned to Native people. Across town, a Baptist minister claimed the finger must be from a Black slave, and he was claiming the remains for his congregation to bury.

There was even more speculation that the finger was from a dead Confederate soldier who died when he and others stashed gold somewhere in the area. The stories spread like wild fire! Sheriff Turnbull told everyone, "No one is getting the finger until we find out more about where it came from."

Chapter 4

When he found out, Robby was visibly upset at his mom for going through his things. And he was embarrassed admitting he and his friends rode their bikes to a forbidden lake south of town. Eventually, he confessed to his Uncle Mike exactly where he found the finger bones.

The coroner's office determined the finger and connecting tissue wasn't all that old. A search party was assembled by Sheriff Turnbull. Deputy Mike and a team of forensics experts went to the island and began to search for remains.

The Sheriff was aware of rumored traps on an island, so they took special care with their investigation of the building and the area around it. They found a hole, one foot deep and five feet long near the front porch. The Sheriff said, "We have what looks like a shallow grave. Because of possible traps and maybe several burials, I am asking for State assistance to accurately search the property for human remains using LiDar and metal detectors. The area around the oxbow lake is off-limits to the public until we can figure out what happened here. Set up road blocks and warning signs to seal off access to the oxbow lake from the nature preserve."

Over the next few weeks investigators discovered what appeared to be a shallow grave and 32 metal traps on the island. One grizzly discovery was a human leg bone still ensnarled in the teeth of a trap. An empty bottle of Southern Comfort whiskey was found nearby. The femur was sent to the lab in Jackson for DNA and fingerprint analysis.

Twenty-five feet from the cabin, where the leg bone was removed, traces of blue jean shorts, a blouse and bra were also found scattered in the woods. All human remains were removed and taken to the medical examiner, to be tested for DNA, and matched to known missing persons from the area.

After a week of work, LiDar discovered some disturbing images that appeared to be skeletal remains and a large object underneath. Heavy equipment was brought in from the levy side. Over the next couple of weeks, skeletal remains of two individuals were dug up. Deeper in the hole, they found an intact 1963 Corvette hard top with a skeletal body, hair, teeth, and clothing inside.

Deputies in the Sheriff's office began an in-depth study of all unsolved disappearances going back 10 years. Most were recorded as runaways or abandonment cases. A few missing persons were deemed suspicious deaths. One such missing person was Grace Dowd, a 15 year old Columbus girl who attended high school and was a popular local babysitter. Her high school yearbook picture showed an attractive brunette with piercing eyes and a wan smile.

When she disappeared, her boyfriend, Josh, was hauled into the Sheriff's office and questioned at length. Without a body and no proof, the scared high school junior was let go and no charges were filed. Her father had left the area three years earlier. There were no other suspects to be questioned about Grace going missing.

Samples from her hairbrush were saved to match DNA. Nothing ever developed by questioning neighbors, friends, relatives, classmates, or church members. She was known as a flirtatious young girl trying to act older than she was. Her case was never closed but with no leads, authorities simply stopped looking for her.

Law enforcement at the time suspected she ran away and left the county to find her father. Her mother sued the county for failure to find her daughter; the suit failed. The father was nowhere to be found, and the mother filed for divorce. A year later, she left, too.

It has been five years, and the tragic story of Grace Dowd's vanishing still resonates in the Columbus community. No one believed that anyone in Columbus could ever do serious harm to such a pretty, brunette, high school girl.

Now, five years later, DNA proved a positive match from the hair brush. Grace Dowd was officially declared dead. The coroner ruled her cause of death was exsanguination from evidence found at a bear trap, on sandy soil, near the Tennessee-Tombigbee channel at an oxbow lake. Sheriff Turnbull had a very cold case to challenge his deputies with, to find out what happened to Grace.

Chapter 5

The mystery of who the finger bones belonged to was solved but why was she on that land in the first place and what happened to her was open to wild speculation. The other bodies found on the piece of land revealed an even more sinister chain of events.

When heavy equipment was brought to remove soil and sand, a gruesome discovery was made. Two bodies were carelessly tossed on top of a 1963 two-seat Corvette that had once been red with a removable white hard top.

The skeletal bodies in the pit and in the car left little to identify the victims. DNA was unable to determine who the victims were because there was no match to any known victims. A good-sized diamond ring with a ruby center was found on a bony finger. The ring identified the victim as a local mobster and illegal whiskey runner, known as Fats Donahue.

Newspapers at the time recorded that Fats and his gang were notorious from the 1940's to the 1960's. Fats paid bribes and county officials let him run his business. He supplied moonshine and whiskey as far away as Jackson, and Mobile, all without tax seals.

Stories in the papers at the time, said people who cheated him were often found dead along remote country roads. Fats lived in a nice house near Gulfport and was fond of flashy cars and fast women. Yet, people admired the flashy gangster and his lifestyle.

One day, Fats was nowhere to be found. Everyone thought the anti-hero retired to the good life in Florida. Now he was found, with two bodyguards and a Corvette that only had 210 miles on the odometer. Military medical records identified the two men as brothers discharged after the Korean war. The last name, Butterfield.

All of the mysterious bodies found at the oxbow lake property brought more questions than answers. Who killed these men? Why were they killed and why bury that flashy new car? How could they dig such a big hole? And most importantly, how does that tie to the death of a young 15-year-old girl several years later?

Teams were busy digging up the car and discovering evidence while Sheriff Turnbull assessed the scene. He organized a search team with an admonition to watch out for dangerous booby traps. He said, "Photograph anything you find before you touch it, and number it with an evidence tent." He was certain there would still be some evidence to find and hopeful for clues linked to any remains that might uncover who committed these crimes.

Turnbull dismissed the Southern Comfort bottle by saying, "Hell, just about everyone around here sips on Southern Comfort now and then. That bottle has been out here so long, fingerprints and DNA won't tell us much."

He confided to Deputy Riley, "Something bad happened to the girl Grace before she fell into a bear trap. Now, I'm just guessing, but I think she was abducted and almost killed before she was tossed into that shallow grave over there." He said pointing.

"I think her killer thought she was dead. He dug that shallow grave and tossed her in. I believe she clawed herself out and frightened as a scared kitten, she began running. I believe she ran from her grave and into that damned bear trap. Then the critters found her and scattered what was left of her. Poor girl. Do I have proof? Like I said, I'm just guessing." Turnbull turned around and shouted at a deputy, telling him to be careful where he stepped.

Turnbull knew he had a long and difficult task ahead to piece together what he found and to link details that might reveal exactly what happened at this oxbow lake for two separate crimes. One of them a very old crime and the other, a fifteen-year-old girl, still haunting the memories of everyone in his community.

Chapter 6

My name is Annette Dupart. I am a certified public account, and I work for my cousin, Wolf LeDuc, at an automotive consulting firm in Germantown, TN. I help car dealers with complex accounting issues like depreciation schedules and tax audits. I also keep my eyes out for fraudulent activities that the dealer may or may not be aware of. I bring things to light so that corrections can be made to help the dealer fix things that could cost them penalties.

Today, I am on my way to Columbus, Mississippi to work on a requested accounting audit at Magnolia Fine Cars. I was told by my cousin, Wolf, to look for Bucky Chalmers. He's being charged back by the car manufacturer for submitting fraudulent warranty claims. Ezra Johnson is looking into those claims. He's the best in the business for analyzing warranty claims and helping car dealerships negotiate a fair settlement with the car manufacturer. I'm meeting him there. My job is to look for theft in the business.

Wolf warned me that Bucky said his business had more than one issue. He believed his financial statements were not correct. He wanted advice on how to restructure the business to make ends meet. He suspected employees were up to their necks in fraud. Bucky told Wolf he wanted help to find and root out the bad apples. I would be auditing the dealership accounting basket to find those apples.

Wolf told me, "Bucky is a 55-year-old man who has questionable health due to his lifestyle. He's overweight, fond of nose candy and blondes on the younger side. His wife of 33 years rarely comes around. She ignores his wanderings in favor of frequent ocean cruises and visits her children who live on either coast. Locally, she is chairman of the local Arts Council, a member of the Garden Club and the Ladies of Old Waverly Golf Country Club in the West Point triangle."

The story goes, Vivian and Bucky met at Old Miss. He was a second string quarterback, and she was an Old Miss cheerleader. She came from old Southern money in Hattiesburg. Old being money earned during the reconstruction. Bucky was a third-generation heir to Magnolia Fine Cars, so they both had money. Bucky's dad, however, never allowed him any important role in the business. After graduating college, Vivian and Bucky's two children ran far and fast to get away from Mississippi. Both live comfortable lives, with good jobs and families of their own. Now, Bucky had no successor for a business that was struggling to survive with lots of debt. Bucky needed help.

I was aware of news articles about bodies found in a nature preserve south of Columbus. Stories about gangsters being dug up and remains of some local girl found dead had everyone talking. While this was the stuff of sensational national news, I could have cared less while checking into my hotel room on Monday evening. That evening, my only concern was for a good internet connection, a working shower head and a soft pillow.

When I checked in, the desk clerk asked, "You must be that woman who's working with that black fella to save Uncle Bucky from what he calls warranty jail?"

Shocked, I asked, "Bucky Chalmers is your Uncle?"

"Oh, yes! Lots of family work for him. My daddy said Bucky could lose the car business unless someone can save him."

"I see. Has Mr. Johnson checked in yet?"

"Yes'm. Do you need his room number?"

"No, thanks. I don't suppose you could recommend a good place to get a steak dinner in Columbus?"

"Us locals like to think 'Huck's Place' is the best for steak. They serve great Cajun food, too."

"Cajun food, hmmm. I might have to look into that place. Thank you."

I ordered off the menu at Huck's Place. The gumbo was fair, but not like Mama's but the steak was excellent. They actually had a live band playing and the service was friendly. I'll go back.

The next morning, I woke up ready for my daily run, but I used the treadmill in the hotel workout room instead of running outside. The weather was good enough I just wanted to get an early start at the dealership.

When I arrived at Magnolia Fine Cars at 7:30, I was met on the parking lot by an eager salesman who assaulted me at my car. I asked, "Is it okay if I park in front here?"

"Absolutely little lady. Nice car. I bet we can beat Blue Book on this little beauty of yours."

"Oh, I see. Where do employees park?"

"You're fine right here. You looking to upgrade your Camaro for a new one?"

"Look, it's barely 7:30. My name is Annette Dupart and I have business inside. Thank you. What's your name, by the way?"

"Luke Chalmers. Here's my card. Here, I'll escort you inside."

"I see. You want credit for bringing an 'UP' inside, right?"

Luke smiled and winked at me. I said, "Let's go, Luke."

The receptionist informed me Bucky wasn't in. "Was there somebody else you wanted to see?" She asked.

"How about your general manager or office manager?"

"Well, we have Mandy Sue. But she won't be in till after 8:00. There's no general manager. Is there someone else who can help you? Is it sales or service you need?"

"No thanks. Here's my card. If Mandy or Bucky happen to show up, tell them they can find me in the service department." She studied my card like she didn't know what to do with it. Then the phone rang, and I was suddenly ancient history.

I found my way to the service department and looked for Ezra. I saw the service manager's office. The sign read, Blane Sloan. He was busy on his phone. He had a pile of paper on his desk, a foot thick. He kept waving away two technicians with one hand, who were standing in his doorway. I heard him say. "Go find Lance, ask him" I walked past the parts department. The sign read, Troy St. Clair. He was on the phone like every parts manager I have ever met.

I found Ezra sitting in the customer lounge tapping on his laptop computer. He looked up and smiled. "Hello, Annette! I see you found the place," he said smiling.

"Yes, I can see this is going to be a new adventure for me."

"We can't talk in here. Let's step outside."

When we were outside the shop he began, "When I got here yesterday, the service manager greeted me, then ignored me. It's been like today since the doors opened. The shop seems to be starved for certified techs. They have an unusual pay plan. Line Techs get paid by the hour for 8 hours at the dealership not for work completed. Wages start at $10.00 per hour. Only two techs get paid using the time and labor standards manual. In other words, everyone is an hourly employee, except for two certified technicians."

"Never heard of that before. So, what you're saying, there is no incentive to complete a customer's repair in a timely fashion or to move along to the next job. Do they all get paid the same?"

"Only the diesel technician and one master technician are certified. They each get paid a hefty wage. The other technicians, not so much. In fact, the best I can figure, the shop employs about 8 to 10 Hispanics who speak very little English. I'm guessing they're undocumented. I think they get paid in cash at the end of every week. I can find no paperwork related to these workers. I see no way to document them for taxes or track how they get paid."

"So, the shop is cheating the IRS as well as the state. It'll be interesting to see how their accounting system is set up. Bucky sent Wolf and me a copy of last month's financial statement. He said none of the numbers look right to him, just numbers on a page. I'll dig into the books to see just how they arrive at those numbers."

"Well, I called the factory people. They are coming here with an audit crew to dig into false warranty claims. They should be here in the next three weeks. That's why I'm here, to spot flaws and submit corrections. Wolf said, "you'll figure out the accounting system and will search for shortages of working capital."

I checked my watch and said, "It's after 9:00. Time to go see if Mandy Sue is in her office yet. Bucky hasn't come in yet, too."

Chapter: 7

I walked to the accounting office and found a woman who looked younger than me. She sat in an office behind a huge desk that had paperwork stacked a foot high. I knocked on the doorframe, smiled, and asked, "Mandy Sue?"

She looked up at me with a confused look and asked, "Do I know you?"

I almost laughed at the question, but said, "Probably not. My name is Annette Dupart. I'm here with LeDuc and Johnson. Bucky Chalmers asked that we come in to offer him advice about his dealership. Are you busy now, because I think you and I have a few things we need to talk about?"

Mandy seemed totally surprised. She said, "Talk about? I don't understand. Why are you here again?"

"I'm sorry, I thought Mr. Chalmers might have told you about my visit. He spoke to Wolf LeDuc, and he hired our company to come to Columbus and offer business suggestions on how he can make more money and cut expenses. He also asked for help with a serious warranty audit the car company will be conducting in a few weeks. Are you aware of this audit?"

"That's the service department. I heard something was going on out there, but I really don't know, or care, whatever it is."

I thought, *"Oh, boy!"* I said, "I have a copy of your last month's financial statement. Mr. Chalmers has given me the authority to review the postings that make up the numbers on that statement. In order to do so, I would like to have your cooperation."

"You said Bucky gave you permission? I'll need to talk with him before I can let you see anything in our files. We have personnel records that are secret. No one can see them."

"Yes, I am aware of employee confidential protections. I need to see your accounting schedules from last month and where to find the source documents." I smiled and waited.

"Excuse me? I have no idea what you're talking about."

I nodded and said, "Okay. How do you keep track of accounts payable for parts shipments, accounts receivable for people who owe you money, warranty claims submitted, cash deposits, inventory reports, and car transactions. Just to name a few."

"Oh, Blanche reports, you know. As far as money coming in and money going out, see those two stacks? I put all the bills in one stack and all the checks that come in on the other one. Once a month, I put them into the computer, like Blanche showed me."

"Uh, Blanche?"

"Yep! That's her out there next to that filing cabinet."

I looked around to see where Mandy Sue pointed. I saw a woman passed her prime, slouched in an office chair, legs apart, eyes closed, head leaning against the file cabinet and her mouth wide open. I think I heard her snore. "That's Blanche?"

"Yep!"

"Who is she, a data entry clerk?"

"Oh, no. Blanche worked for Bucky's father, Dean, before he was sent up. She was the office manager till I took over. She showed me how to put things into the computer."

My head was reeling. I had so many questions. "I don't understand. She worked for Bucky's father, the prior dealer?"

"Yep! She was his girl Friday. They did everything together. She ran the office, went to meetings with him and she ran the place whenever old Mr. Dean was out of town."

"You said, 'sent up'. What exactly does that mean?"

"You know, prison. You see, one day Blanche's husband burst into the building with an old shotgun. He said he wanted his wife back. Mr. Dean just walked out with his gun and shot him, right out there on the showroom floor. He was convicted of manslaughter and sent to prison."

"Surely, it was self-defense." I said.

"Not really. Blanche's husband didn't have any shotgun shells; he just wanted his wife back. Everyone said Mr. Chalmers was waiting in his office with a loaded gun and he casually went out to the showroom to make a problem go away. That got him 20 years."

"Oh, so that was when Bucky became the dealer?"

"Yep, and Blanche ran the business while Bucky sat in his office until I took over. If I need to know something, I ask Blanche."

"Tell me, Mandy Sue, how much training *have* you had before becoming the office manager?"

Mandy bridled and said, "I went to school!"

"Yes, but where?"

"Columbus High School. My grades weren't all that good, but I graduated."

"Have you ever taken an accounting course?"

"You mean like going to classes someplace? No. Blanche showed me what I needed to do. I think I got most of it down. Blanche said, 'Just keep everything in the right books'. She showed me how to print checks and how to print the end of the month financial statement." Mandy Sue cleared her throat and continued. "Payroll is still pretty tough, that's why we hired Jill Boyd."

I listened intently while she continued. "Bobbi Jo over there, she does the title work. And she's pretty good. Lance, my boyfriend, said she can wash and clean any title that's put in front of her. She has a cousin in Kentucky and the two of them send titles back and forth until there is no prior record of any accidents, theft, or mileage disputes. Like I said, she's pretty good." That was the first smile Mandy awarded me with.

I rolled my eyes and was ready to run for the door. Then, I saw a man leaning in the doorway. He had blond combed over hair, a ruddy face, wide grin and wore a wrinkled white summer suit. Underneath, he wore a pink shirt with white tie. He said, "Why you must be Mr. LeDuc's cousin, Annette, isn't it? He said you were the best with accounting. Now, Mandy Sue, you listen to what this young lady has to say. She's right smart about these things and she can help you learn your job here in the office." Bucky said, smiling.

Mandy Sue sat open mouthed, and said, "Yeah, I'll do that."

A lot of things were going through my head at that moment. *"I cannot teach double entry bookkeeping and dealership accounting to a girl who is barely out of high school and thinks car title fraud is a good thing."*

I said, "Yes, Mr. Chalmers, I am a CPA, and I work for my cousin, Wolf LeDuc. His partner, Ezra Johnson, is in the shop working on your warranty claim submissions. I need to know if it is okay for me to review your, er, accounting reports and search for the paperwork that makes up those reports?"

"Oh, absolutely! Anything you need, Miss Annette. I gotta say, you are one fine looking young lady. Anyone ever tell you that?"

"Yes, a person or two. Thank you. I'll need security clearance to get into your computer and a place to work."

"Mandy, go wake up Blanche and have her set Miss Dupart up with whatever she needs. I'll be in my office, if you need anything, Annette." He winked at me, turned, and left.

I looked at Mandy Sue and waited. She honestly didn't know what to say or do. I presented my best winning smile and said, "I'm looking forward to working with you Mandy Sue. If you don't mind, that place to work? I could use a spare desk where I can set up my laptop and stack files?" I gave her my best Louisiana grin. Mandy Sue gave me a blank open mouth, deer in the headlight, expression in return.

I began looking for the exits in case I needed to make a hasty retreat.

Chapter: 8

It took Blanche two cups of coffee and a few moments to realize what universe she was in before she acknowledged me. As the dealership systems administrator, she followed Bucky's instructions and gave me an administrators' security clearance to access anything in the computer system. She showed me where the back up tapes were stored, sitting next to a half-empty bottle of Southern Comfort.

Blanche tried to smile but failed. She said, "Mandy Sue is a good girl. She's young but trying her best. She just needs a little training, you know. She needs to stay away from that rascal, Lance Butterfield. He's up to no good." She nodded and gave me a look like I should know this to be true.

I thanked her and carefully asked, "Do you know what accounting schedules are?"

"Of course I do. I ain't no idiot, you know. I suppose you want to look those over, too?"

"Yes, I do. I want to start with the warranty claims submissions that Mr. Johnson is working on in the shop. I also want to look at the cash deposits schedule, then the accounts receivable and accounts payable schedules, if you don't mind."

She gave me a grumpy "Humph!" nodded then she led the way to the sacred file cabinets where secret employee records are kept.

I was now armed with paper copies of schedules, last month's financial statement and access to the computer to see just how postings are being made. This work kept me very busy until lunch time when Ezra came into the office and asked, "Can you spare the time for a lunch break?"

I gritted my teeth and said, "Can't wait."

On the way out of the accounting office, I noticed that Mandy Sue was not in her office and neither were a couple of accounting employees. Blanche was back asleep next to the filing cabinet. A half empty whiskey glass sat on a desk next to her. *"What is it with Southern Comfort?"* I thought.

Ezra and I walked through the showroom and Luke Butterfield, with a toothpick in his mouth grinned and waved at me. I waved back and wondered if he was any relation to the Lance Butterfield, Blanche had warned me about.

Ezra and I left in his car and went to his favorite sit-down restaurant where he said we could enjoy a good meal. I trusted his judgment.

Chapter: 9

The thought of Grace Dowd's suspicious death continued to haunt Sheriff Nathan Turnbull. He remembered the cute flirtatious brunette girl as she sauntered about town. He was Sheriff at the time, and the child came on to him in a way that nauseated his sense of propriety. She was a kid. Her behavior made him angry because she shouldn't be tempting men much older than her. He couldn't help but notice how she acted around other men in town and how they paid more attention to her than they should.

He remembered seeing her flirting with Judge Horne and watched as he invited her up to his porch and offered her soda a couple of times. Judge Horne sat there grinning at her like a cat that got the cream. He seemed to be enjoying himself while sipping his Southern Comfort neat. She was all laughs and giggles.

Nathan remembered that Grace was a very popular babysitter around town. He knew of at least three babysitting families. There were probably more. The dads were always eager to have her babysit for their kids in those days, while the mothers, oblivious of the girls flirtations, were simply relieved to have a night off without cooking and washing dishes or making the children eat what was on their plate before bedtime.

Nathan searched his memory to remember who those families were. One came to mind, Bob and Judy Carter. Grace sat for their son, Robby, and his baby sister when they were small. He remembered this family because it was not too long after Grace disappeared that Bob left Judy and was never heard from again.

There was some speculation Bob may have run off with Grace, and they found a life together someplace. Judy was crushed when he just walked out. She poured all of her attention into her son. It was no secret, around town, that Robby is a good piano player. A concert was being planned at the community center by Vivian Chalmers, Bucky's wife. Robby and many of the other Columbus children would be featured playing orchestra instruments.

Tired, Nathan Turnbull sat staring at the medical examiner's report of the other bodies found on the island. Skeletal remains of Fats Donahue had been confirmed. The other two bodies were thought to be brothers who mustered out of the military after the Korean War. They worked for Donahue. A shrapnel fragment in one and broken leg in the other, matched military records and that positively identified the two as members of the Butterfield family.

County title records showed Nathan that Fats and the brothers were murdered, on property then owned by Shane Law. Who was Shane Law, he wondered? There are Law's around town; one was working for him. He would have to go back 60 years to find out who the victims were and why they were found on land that Law owned. He would ask his deputy, John, what he knew.

Sheriff Turnbull decided to assign the investigation of the 60-year-old murder to Deputy Investigator, Mike Riley. He wrote a note and attached it to the file, *"Who owned the island after Shane Law? How was the property zoned by the county? Were there any persons of interest questioned about the disappearance of Fats Donahue? Is the property worth anything today?"*

Turnbull's thoughts returned to Grace. He studied the State report that came back for the empty bottle of Southern Comfort found near the shallow grave. It didn't take a math student to figure out the girl had been with someone on that island and they had been drinking from that bottle together.

He speculated that things got out of hand, and the girl wound up being assaulted and almost murdered when she was thrown into a shallow grave. Somehow, he thought, *"The poor girl must have regained consciousness, dug herself out and ran to her bloody and painful death in a bear trap."* He shivered thinking about it.

The Southern Comfort bottle's state liquor label date was five years ago, definitely dating Grace's death. DNA on the bottle proved she had drunk from the bottle. There was no known DNA match for the other drinker of whiskey. When that person is found, the DNA test would be damning evidence. Five years wasn't all that long ago, and Turnbull suspected the murderer was still walking the streets of Columbus. He swore he would find out who in his community enjoyed taking advantage of girls barely into their teens not yet old enough to drive a car.

Grace's murder was now a cold case. The bottle evidence was strong but not enough to identify a killer. Around these parts, Southern Comfort is popular for it's sweet, almost fruity aftertaste. The 100 proof whiskey is enough to knock the Karate-Gi off a Sumo wrestler. Nathan decided he needed to narrow down the field of who is fond of drinking Southern Comfort 100 today. It could provide a link to a heinous murderer from five years ago.

It's common knowledge that young men offer the drink to young women who like the sweet taste. They use it to render young women into a willing frame of mind. That only means his search could be a futile one, but he vowed to begin scouring the area for known drinkers of the brand. It was a long shot.

His first visit would be to Judge Terrance Horne.

Chapter: 10

Judge Horne agreed to meet Sheriff Turnbull on his front porch. The porch overlooked a street that was shaded by giant magnolia trees. Nate parked in front of the large colonial revival home built in the early 1920's.

The Judge sat in his rocker, patiently waiting and watching Nathan amble up the side walk. Nate took his hat off and greeted the judge with, "Thank you for seeing me, Judge Horne."

Horne offered no hello, special greeting, or a place to sit. He only said, "Is this about some matter before my court? You know, I cannot discuss current deliberations."

"No, Sir. I've known you for a great many years, Judge. You have my greatest respect. I come seeking background information concerning a cold case."

"Was this matter before my court?" The Judge asked while taking a sip from his whiskey glass, the bottle of Southern Comfort nearby.

"No, Sir. It never got that far."

"Then, I'm confused. What information could I possibly provide to you?"

Nathan sat in a chair anyway, even though he wasn't offered to sit down. "It's about a missing girl, Grace Dowd. I'm asking if you knew her and if you have any background information that might help my investigation."

The judge's eyes narrowed and he slowly sat his whiskey glass on a side table. He stared at Nathan Turnbull. "And what information might that be, Nate?"

"I believe you knew her family, the Dowd's. What was her family life like? What happened when she went missing? She was frequently seen around town. Can you think of anyone besides her boyfriend who she may have gotten close to? Like I said, I'm just trying to put pieces of the past together. I want to get a picture of what she was like before she was murdered." Turnbull sat back in his chair and waited.

Horne sighed and said, "That was over five years ago. I think just about everyone in town knew who Grace was. She was rather precocious and very forward, almost adult like. Of course, she was only a child. Her mother and father had, how should I put it, several family issues. They seemed to argue a lot. The father was often away on long trips while the mother, well, she often sought comfort and sympathy with anyone who would listen."

"Do you think the mother was promiscuous?"

"No. Not that I know of, in a public sort of way. There were rumors, however, about her and Reverand Brand at that tabernacle near the Alabama line. I think the husband can't remember his name, Duke, Dwayne, I don't know. I think he simply got tired of her religious convictions. He left when Grace was 13. Grace missed her father. The girl sought approval from wherever she could find it." Judge Horne said, taking another sip from his glass.

Turnbull cleared his throat and said, "She had a boyfriend, Josh, who was questioned at length when Grace vanished. He was the most obvious suspect. But Grace seemed to be seeking attention from a lot of men during that time. Investigators thought he became jealous, they had a row, and he killed her then disposed of the body. No weapon and no body, nothing could be proved. He had an alibi with friends, albeit weak. The 17-year-old was at a deer camp getting drunk during the time of her disappearance."

"I'm afraid I don't know much more." Horne said bending over and picking up his glass of Southern Comfort once more.

"She was seen on your front porch on more than one occasion, Judge. Did she ever say anything to you that could have led to her murder?"

"I'm not sure what you're driving at. Yes, she sat on my porch a time or two. I gave her a Coke. She was a sad little girl. She wanted me to look into where her father might have gone."

"Did she ever ask you for anything stronger than a Coke?"

"You mean give alcohol to a minor? No! She did ask, and I didn't give her any. Are we done here?" The Judge asked abruptly.

"Look Judge, I am looking for background on Grace and people she knew at the time. You have provided me with things I did not know. You knew her. She trusted you and that's good. Did she ever talk to you about any other people she knew?"

"She mentioned a name or two. I think she said someone she babysat for was real creepy."

"Creepy? Who, Judge? I need names."

"I don't rightly recall. Listen, I have a brief that I need to study, if we're done here?"

Turnbull sighed and said, "Thanks again, Judge. I know you would like to see some resolution, like I do, for the death of this child, who disappeared five years ago in a dreadful way. Please do not take offence to my questions. Understand, I need to ask them."

The Judge didn't look mollified. He simply nodded solemnly while watching Nathan Turnbull slowly stand up, put on his hat and step down from his porch. Nathan walked to his SUV. He didn't say goodbye to the Judge and the Judge didn't say goodbye to him.

Nathan had an uneasy feeling about the Judge but that would not detour him from his mission to find Grace's killer.

Chapter: 11

I was blown away by the lack of common accounting basics when I reviewed Magnolia's books. Where were all of the checks and balances of a double entry bookkeeping system? Accounting 101; receipts should equal deposits. There were no receipts. So, nothing balanced. Mandy Sue was just throwing numbers into the journals in order to generate a financial statement. It was all fiction. Besides finding poor accounting practices, nepotism was out of control. Employees were hired because they were related to someone in the Chalmers family not because of *what* they knew.

Both the new and used sales departments were run by an overweight semi-bearded man, Eddie Chalmers, Bucky's brother. All car contracts went through him. I saw car deals that made no sense at all. Cars and trucks were bought with trade-in's that had little or no value. I saw deals where customers were skinned alive and roasted over an open finance deal. Eddie signed off on every transaction with his signature scrawl.

When cars were sold, financing on those deals was out of control. Buyers used credit cards for down payments, or they borrowed from friends. Interest rates on many financed vehicles were pure unadulterated usury.

What loan companies could not finance because of poor credit; Magnolia Fine Cars carried on the books. On those deals, I saw where accessories like floor mats and bumper deer whistles were added on to just to inflate a loan.

When I looked at the payroll schedule, salaries in the dealership, for the most part, were low with a few noted exceptions. So, I figured that prospects for performance were low as well. There didn't seem to be accountability anywhere in the dealership.

I strolled through the dealership looking for Bucky. He was nowhere to be found. I wanted to corner him and ask him about what on earth he planned to do with this dealership, but he was MIA (missing in action).

Word got through the receptionist that I wanted to talk to him. Bucky sent me a text. *"Bring what you have to my house around 6:00 this evening. I do need your help. Watch out while coming in."*

I had a laundry list of things I needed answers to. I called Wolf and he agreed. "Yes, we needed to know what Bucky intends to do about the crazy, loose management of his dealership. Does he intended to stay in business?" On *my* list, I warned Bucky that the car company wouldn't just stop with warranty records, they would delve into his financial affairs to see if he had enough working capital to keep this party boat alive. They would shut him down and sue him for breach of his dealer contract.

Since I couldn't meet Bucky, I spoke to Ezra and asked if he wanted to have supper with me. "I can't. It's Lavon's birthday. I'm driving back tonight. I can talk now, but not in here." Ezra said.

We left the building and walked through the used car lot away from curious ears. "I wanted to talk to you before I left for Memphis. I am convinced this dealership is a sinking boat. You and I may need to abandon ship. I think it's a lost cause." Ezra said.

"Funny, I was going to tell you the same thing. Accounting is a nightmare. The sales department is out of control. Fraud seems to be a work ethic. There are no guardrails on the business. My question, if we stay, are we complicit with the crimes being committed here? Can we be held accountable in court?"

"That sounds like a question for our lawyer, Baxter Grey. I agree with you. Wolf signed a contract with Bucky. I think we need to point out every flaw we find in a formal document. That way, we're covered in case Baxter announces our contract is null and void, if those flaws are not corrected. Even that may not protect us."

"Oh, my! I do have a list of things that are not right that I want to cover with Bucky. He said he needed help and to deliver what I have to his house this evening at 6:00."

Ezra shook his head. "Not a good idea. I think you need to document everything you've come across so far. Then leave it on Bucky's desk and go back home."

"I'll do the same, but before I do, I need to pull more warranty records first. I've spoken to the warranty manager at the car company. He's a man I know in Detroit. I explained to him what I've found. He said, dig deeper."

"Are you coming back tomorrow?" I asked.

"I am and will wrap up my findings in a couple of days."

"Then, I'll stick around and leave when you leave. What time will you be back?"

"Around 10 or 11:00 tomorrow. If you stay, be very careful. This business is a family gravy boat. Everyone is dipping in their biscuits in the company gravy for a taste of free lunch. They might do about anything to keep getting that paycheck." Ezra said grinning.

"Hmm. Interesting. Anything I need to know about the shop?"

"Blane Sloan, the service manager, is basically a figurehead. He has no clue what goes on in the shop. He keeps his head down and stays out of the way. He admitted as much to me. Lance Butterfield, the shop foreman, is the man who runs the show. He's guarded and doesn't say much. You can't miss him if you see him. He looks like a skinny drowned rat with tattoos from head to foot. And no one in the shop questions anything he says."

"Work is assigned, and repairs are made through a dispatch system. There's a ton of carry-over repairs because they don't have the parts or certified technicians to do the work. The dealership does hire several Hispanic workers. They're hardworking and do most of the simple work. A couple are SAE certified but not factory certified to do warranty work, but they do it anyway. Here's the fraud, only two technician employee numbers appear on all warranty claims. When I observed, they didn't actually do the work."

"Yeah, that will come back to bite them. You know, I think Lance is Mandy Sue's boyfriend. She's the office manager. How old would you say he is?"

"I'm not a good judge of that generation but I would say he's well into his thirties. Like I said, skinny and not quite six foot. He keeps his hair cut and he wears a dealership uniform that covers the tats most of the time. He signs off on all warranty claims before they're submitted through a family member warranty clerk."

"I agree. It looks like the inmates are running the asylum. I'll go to Bucky's place and deliver my list tonight. I want to know if he is really that clueless, afraid of his family, or if he's the king of fraud."

"Where does he live?" Ezra asked.

"On a farm not far out of Columbus. I have directions."

"Be very careful, Annette."

Chapter: 12

I checked my watch and decided I would drive to Bucky's farm even if it was a little early. During my drive into the country, I passed several large houses tucked away among trees and cattle ponds. It looked like there were several people living in the area who had a lot of money.

I found the gated entrance to Bucky's farm. I took the gravel road. White vinyl horse fence surrounded both sides of the road which wound past acres of empty pasture. I wondered if Mrs. Chalmers is a horse woman and where are all of the horses?

I passed a tree covered gravel road, and noticed a half hidden blue 4-door Dodge Ram pickup sitting in the shade. I saw no one near the truck. When I approached the house, the gravel drive appeared to continue beyond the circular drive, to where I presumed the garage was located. I parked on the circular drive, in front of the house, and studied the large home. It was massive.

I grabbed my shoulder bag, got out of my Camaro then marched to the door. A paper note was attached to the double front door that read, "Come on inside, Annette. I'm outside, in the back."

I pushed the door open, and walked through a large foyer, down a hall, passed the dining room and through the kitchen. At the back I walked into a large sun room. Outside, I saw a swimming pool and a gazebo with a hot tub underneath that held two people. I muttered, "Oh well!" then stepped onto the concrete pool decking.

Since the people in the hot tub seemed to be the only people around, I walked in their direction. The motor was humming, and the water was bubbling. Bucky waved. I saw the blond hair of a woman whose face I could not see in the tub with him.

I got within 10 feet of the spa. Bucky said, "Glad you could make it. Y'all are welcome to join us." He said with a grin.

"Uh, no thanks. I thought we would be discussing business."

"Yeah, change of plans. But I'm glad you're here. We can make some time now. Let's do that over drinks. What'll you have?"

He started to get out of the hot tub, and I quickly realized this visit was clothing optional. I said, "That's okay! I don't drink alcohol, and I didn't bring a bathing suit. So, please stay put."

"It's okay. Marcy don't mind, do you?"

Marcy turned her head and said, "No. The more the merrier!" She purred.

"I can see this is not a good time. Why don't you and I do this tomorrow? Is 9:00 a good time for you?" I asked hopefully.

"Oh, I don't know. I have an auction. I'm expecting someone I don't really want to see this evening, but I do want you to find out who's stealing from me. Dig deep. Do what you must. Help me!"

"Honestly, my meeting tomorrow won't take long, you should probably hear what I have to say." I said with a weak smile.

"You ain't quitting are you?" Bucky asked with a whine.

"No, Mr. Chalmers. I just have some things you need to know and be aware of. Is Mrs. Chalmers around?" I asked looking around.

"Oh, heavens no. She's in West Point visiting friends tonight. Why? Do you need to see her or something?"

"Not really. Her name was on a few documents for a local concert coming up and I wanted to ask her about that."

Bucky said, "Anything you have to say to her, y'all can say to me. Okay then, I'll see you in the morning. The person coming tonight was unexpected. It sounded urgent and I'm meeting them here. I want those accounts fixed Miss Dupart. You have 'cart blanche'. I'm depending on you."

He turned to Marcy and said, "She appears to be in a hurry."

"Bye, bye, Annette! Hope to see you again, soon." She said.

My head was reeling on the drive back to the hotel.

Chapter: 13

I was awakened by the hotel phone ringing in my ears. I checked the clock, and it read 4:47 AM. Almost time to get out of bed anyway. I sleepily answered, "Yes, who is this?"

"This is the desk, Miss Dupart. Sheriff's deputies are here, and they asked me to call and wake you up."

"What do they want?" I asked rubbing my eyes.

"They would like for you to come to the front desk to talk with them."

"Okay. I'll be right there." I said and hung up the receiver.

I quickly pulled on some sweats and running shoes, ran my fingers through my hair, grabbed my room key and shoulder bag. I took the elevator and walked to the lobby. When I arrived, two Sheriff's deputies were standing next to the desk talking to the clerk.

They asked me to sit in the dining area with them. One of them actually asked if I wanted coffee. I smiled and said, "Absolutely, what's up?"

"Just to be certain, tell us your name and do you have ID?"

I was now on my guard about their visit and handed over my driver's license and said, "Annette Dupart. What is this all about?"

"Miss Dupart, where were you last evening?"

"I ate supper at a café down the street, then drove to the home of Bucky Chalmers out in the country. I got there a little before 6:00 and left about 6:20 or so and came back here to the hotel. Why?"

The Deputy had a name badge that said Mike Riley. He smiled and handed my driver's license back to me. He said, "What were you doing at Mr. Chalmers' house last night?"

I knew something was serious and I measured my comments carefully. "I am an automotive accounting specialist. I have been reviewing Mr. Chalmers' books at Magnolia Fine Cars for the past two days. I tried meeting with Mr. Chalmers, but he was never available. He sent a text asking me to meet him at his home last night around 6:00 PM. When I arrived, there was a note on the door telling me to come in and walk to the backyard."

"I did that and found Mr. Chalmers in a hot tub with some woman named Marcy. They were not clothed. He asked if I wanted to join them and I quickly declined."

"What happened next?" Mike asked.

"I felt uncomfortable and left about 6:20, then came back to the hotel and went to my room."

"Anyone see you?" Mike asked.

"You can check the hotel's electronic key records. I didn't leave that room until you asked to see me this morning." I said.

"Why did you want to talk to Mr. Chalmers?" Mike asked.

"Where do I begin? His dealership accounting system is a total mess. I discovered things that did not seem, well…legal. I wanted to ask him about those things to see if they were just anomalies or if he was even aware of them. I never got the chance. We are going to meet this morning so I can present my findings. I've told you everything. Now tell me why you're asking questions."

"I cannot provide you with any details, but I can say your answers match our findings. Just to confirm, you say you left Bucky Chalmers house around 6:20?"

"I didn't plan to stick around and see two naked people in a hot tub get drunk. I got in my car and left." I said indignantly.

"Do you think he intended for you to find him and that woman together?"

"You mean, to see what I would do? Maybe. He could have meant to embarrass me. But he seemed thankful I was there. He had an urgent call and was expecting to meet someone. He said he wasn't looking forward to that visit. So, I left."

Deputy Mike nodded while taking notes.

Frustrated, I said, "Now, if I am not under arrest, would you please tell me why you are here and asking all of these questions?"

"Miss Dupart, I can tell you this, Mr. Chalmers was found shot to death along with a woman who was with him. There is security video coverage of you arriving and leaving during the time you described. I need you to confirm, was Mr. Chalmers alive while you were at his house?"

"Yes! He and Marcy were very alive while I was there, and alive when I left. If you're asking me if I had anything to do with his death, you are fishing in the wrong pond. Am I under arrest?"

Mike laughed and said, "No, Miss Dupart, you are not under arrest, but we must ask that you not leave the county while we conduct our investigation. I need to ask; do you have any firearms?"

I bridled at this question. Then answered, "I have a license to carry. If you want to ask any further questions from me, you may contact my attorney, Baxter Grey, in Germantown, TN. If you want to see any firearms, please present a warrant to me for any weapons I may have. Are we done here?"

Mike exhaled and looked at the other Deputy. They stood up and he said, "Thank you, Miss Dupart. Like I said, do not leave the county. We'll let you know if we have any further questions."

Chapter: 14

Before he met with me this morning, Sheriff Nathan Turnbull woke up to the news that Bucky Chalmers was found naked in bed with a blond woman. Both of them were shot and again, execution style in the head.

Nathan knew Bucky had a reputation as a bounder and a skirt chaser. He never tried to hide his wanderings. Nathan confirmed that Bucky's wife of 30 years, Vivian, spent the night at a friends house in West Point, MS. Her alibi was confirmed and Bucky's two children live out of state. When notified, Mrs. Chalmers said she would let her children know about their father.

Nathan Turnbull needed to find out who killed Bucky. That question was on his mind when Deputy Riley knocked on his office door. "Yes, Mike, what do you know?"

"Tom and I interviewed that woman from Germantown. She admitted going to Bucky's house and was there from roughly 6:00 to 6:20. She told us Bucky was in a hot tub with a woman named Marcy. They were both naked. Embarrassed, Miss Dupart quickly left. Security video confirms her arrival, a brief conversation at the hot tub and her departure. No camera coverage inside the house."

"What time did the Medical Examiner say was the time of death?" Turnbull asked.

"He said it was impossible to know because both victims had been in the hot tub prior to death."

"Okay, were they killed in the hot tub and taken to the bedroom or were they killed in bed?"

"It appears both were killed in bed, while having sex. The coroner is still working on an autopsy. We confirmed that Marcy was the woman's name."

"So, it seems someone broke into the house without security cameras seeing them. Then the shooter left without being caught on video. Is that about right?" Turnbull asked.

"We're looking at all possible access points to enter the house. Deputy Robyn is reviewing all video images to see if we missed anything. The Dupart woman admitted to owning a gun and said we would need a warrant to look at it. I'm checking her out. The timeline for her visit doesn't fit for when we think he was murdered. Someone else, aware of cameras, they snuck onto the property to kill him. It was a person Bucky knew." Riley said.

"The Dupart woman said Bucky was meeting someone and the meeting was urgent. One odd thing, a half empty bottle of Southern Comfort 100 proof was found on the night stand next to where the bodies were found last night by the security guard."

"So, where was that guard when Bucky was killed?" Turnbull asked.

"He said Bucky dismissed him, telling him to come back after midnight to check on things. He did and things didn't look right. The doors were not locked. He knocked on Bucky's bedroom door and got no answer before he entered. He discovered the bodies and called 9-1-1."

"How are you doing with the old murders at the lake?"

"Ancient murders, you mean. Forensics proves those murders were committed over 60 years ago. I did some checking. County records show the property deed was passed from Shane Law to Homer Chalmers after the property was to be sold on the courthouse steps. Homer filed a 'Quit Claim Deed' and he secured the property. That property has been passed down through the Chalmers family ever since. We're still checking on what happened to Shane Law."

"Homer Chalmers? Any relation to Bucky?"

"Yes, Sir. His grandfather. We've been looking into Homer, and we don't know much, yet. Census records say he was a local farmer. His family were known moonshiners back in the 1930's. There's no proof Homer ever sold his shine but if he did, that would be a connection to Fats Donahue who was famous for distributing moonshine. Was Homer a supplier? Don't know, may never know." Mike said while shuffling through some papers.

"That also begs the question, was Shane Law killed by Homer? Where was Homer when Fats and the two body guards were killed, and buried on that land?" Nathan asked. "And where did Homer suddenly get money to buy that car dealership 60 years ago?"

"Good questions, Nate. You know, burying all of that evidence took some planning and serious follow-up after killing Fats. They had to have access to heavy equipment and a way to get it onto that swampy land. That takes serious resources."

"Agreed! We need to find out who in the county during the 1960's had access to either a skid steer or a crawler with a shovel and some way to transport that gear back then."

"Did they even have skid steer equipment in those days?" Mike asked.

"I know Bobcat was introduced in the mid 60's. I would like you to find out who had access to equipment like that back then."

"I wasn't alive then, where do I start?"

Nathan chuckled. "The only places I can think of, as a kid, might have been the Airforce or the National Guard base. The Vietnam war was in full swing at that time. People were coming and going on both bases. Anyone could have stolen that equipment."

"You aren't suggesting someone in the military killed Fats are you?"

"We're just talking here. I'm not saying the military but someone with access to military construction equipment. We should be looking at people who had a vested interest in the moonshine trade at that time. Dig deeper into Homer. Find out exactly what he did before his family became car dealers. One thing nags at me, who did Homer know back in the day? Did he get a loan, or did he sell something valuable to get money to buy a new car dealership?"

"Okay, Nathan. I'll dig deeper. In the meantime, we need to find Bucky's killer. Any idea for leads on that murder?"

"He had a large family working for him. We need to look at all of them. The Dupart woman is auditing the business. What does she know about employees who work at the car store? Then there's the possibility Bucky diddled the wrong woman, and someone killed him for it. And there's always the disgruntled car customer or former employee. The man was everywhere. I'm sure the list goes on. Get our deputies working on all of the angles."

"So, what you're saying is, the whole county is full of suspects."

"Fraid so." Nathan said laughing. "But my money's on members of that crazy Chalmers family. We need to look at them closer."

Chapter: 15

I was totally shocked to hear about Bucky's death last night after I left him in the hot tub. And even more shocked that I was considered a suspect. After my shower, I sat down and called Wolf. He was still home. I told him the whole story.

"Murdered? That's awful! After speaking to Ezra, I was worried about how we would get out of our contract. He said the Magnolia dealership is a nightmare. Are you coming home?"

"Can't. Because I went to Bucky's house, I am a person of interest for the Sheriff's department. I believe they are putting together a warrant to seize my guns."

"How many do you have with you?"

"Just the Nano and the Beretta 92M9. I don't want to lose my guns while they hang on to them for who knows how long? I need to ask Baxter what can be done when he gets in today."

"I'll text him. He may reply to me right away. Do you want me to come to Columbus and help?"

"Ezra is supposed to be coming back today. He's unaware of Bucky's death. You might let him know. As far as your coming over, let's see how things play out today. If they arrest me, you will be my phone call."

"Yes, please, keep me posted." Wolf said.

I thought about going in early to Magnolia to pull some prior year-end financial statements from backup tapes. I have to go back several years. For the life of me, I couldn't figure out how everything got so far out of control. I planned on searching for a period of time when things were stable. I needed to see whose names were signing off on business transactions before things got this bad.

I knew Mandy Sue was not an early riser and who knew if Blanche would be alert enough to answer any of my questions. I made up my mind, gathered my laptop and guns, and headed downstairs to grab a Danish and a cup of coffee.

I parked in the rear service lot at the dealership and walked into the building through the shop. Most of the Hispanic technicians were clocked in and working in the service bays. I don't know what they were told but not one of them made eye contact with me.

I was sure news about Bucky would spread like a flu virus. I didn't plan to address his passing to anyone at the dealership. They would find out, soon enough, on their own. I planned to do my digging and leave as quick as possible. I was surprised to find Mandy Sue wasn't in.

I sat at Mandy Sue's desk and logged into her computer. I was beginning my quest for historical financial data. I wanted paper copies, in case I needed to make a hasty retreat.

I printed all of the year-end statements and schedules for the past four years. I then delved into the business ownership records. I searched for a property deed and the car manufacturer's contract with Magnolia Fine Cars. I wanted to see what liens there were against the business. I printed a current warranty schedule for Ezra and a payroll schedule for me. I was going to get to the bottom of what happened to this business and when problems began to crop up.

I stacked the printed copies of my work and hauled everything out to my Camaro and put it into my trunk. I checked my watch. It was nearly 11:00. Mandy was still a no-show and so was Blanche. I went back to find out who in the Chalmers family worked at this dealership.

I ignored fraudulent Bobbi Jo the title clerk and asked Jill Boyd if she would like to go to lunch with me. She was genuinely surprised, then shrugged her shoulders and said, "Sure, why not?"

We took my car, and Jill directed me to a diner called Zachary's. We found a discrete table where I could ask her the questions I wanted answers for. We ordered and while sipping sweet tea, I asked, "So Jill, how long have you worked for Bucky Chalmers?"

"Good lord! I've known the family for most of my life. How long I've worked here or how long I've been doing payroll?"

I grinned and said, "Both."

"I began working for the Chalmers when I was about 18 and mostly did filing. Then, I did data entry, posting documents into the computer system. They've had me doing payroll now for six years or so. Why?"

"I need to know because I'm constructing a management timeline for the dealership. Who was your supervisor most of that time?"

"Blanche and another woman, Mrs. Baker. She quit about five years ago. She's still around town somewhere."

I nodded while taking notes on a small pad. I asked, "Was Bucky the dealer when you started with the company?"

"No, it was Bucky's father back then. Dean Chalmers ran the store. Bucky was around, you know, selling cars. He was a wild one in those days. He even tried coming after me, but I wanted no part of his party life. I'm a good Christian girl, you know. I married Charles Boyd, and we have two children together. They're grown now and they've moved on. Charlie's still working."

"I need to ask, who are you cutting checks for on payroll that you know doesn't work here?"

She seemed startled by the question. She opened her mouth then closed it. She said, "I don't know if I can tell you anything about our payroll, I could lose my job."

"I'm asking because the company who sells cars to the dealership will come in and do a thorough audit and if things are not right, they will file criminal charges against any co-conspirators."

Jill's face lost color. I let the threat of crime sink in. She said, "Mr. Chalmers, Bucky, said to not let anyone look at our payroll."

"I suppose now is a good time to let you know."

"Know what?" She asked.

"Mr. Bucky Chalmers was found dead this morning. He can no longer do anything to you. I expect this dealership to be changing ownership and management very soon. You're better off telling me everything you know so it can go into my CPA audit report for the business. In all likelihood, this will save your job and any possible criminal charges that could be brought against you."

Jill's hand immediately flew to her mouth when she heard what I said. I saw a tear slide out of the corner of her eye. She said, "Oh! Oh! Bucky's dead? How? What happened?"

"That will all come to light when the press gets hold of the story. That's probably why Mandy Sue and Blanche were not in the office this morning."

"Let's start at the beginning, Jill. Tell me everything you know. I want to know who is related to whom in the Chalmers family that works here. Tell me what positions they hold. I want to know who is receiving a paycheck that doesn't work here. Explain to me how paying the Hispanics in the shop works. Obviously, the dealership is not withholding social security and taxes for them, or are you? I need details."

Over the next hour and a half, Jill told me everything she could think of. I said, "I am going to prepare a document that will be part of my CPA audit. You'll need to sign that paper to protect yourself under the whistleblower laws. When we're done here, you should go home for the afternoon."

"Can't. I need to run the weekly payroll. Employees rely on that paycheck in order to pay rent and buy food. And the brown people, they need their cash payment envelopes."

"Okay. Print out the checks. Who signs them, Mandy? And where is the money for the pay envelopes?"

"The money is in Mandy's left desk drawer."

"Put the checks on her desk with a note to sign them. Say you had to leave for an emergency tomorrow. I'll help you count the cash for the pay envelopes. This shouldn't take too long."

She reluctantly agreed and we headed back to the dealership to make sure everyone got paid.

Chapter: 16

Nathan Turnbull put the Grace Dowd case on the back burner to focus on Bucky's murder. He drove to Bucky's farm to see the crime scene for himself. Using roadblocks, deputies secured the property refusing to let employees or family members near the farm.

He entered the house and went directly to the backyard to look at the hot tub. He confirmed there was no trace of blood anywhere near the Jacuzzi. Puddles of water were still next to the hot tub where Bucky and Marcy got out of the tub. He noticed two near empty whiskey glasses sitting on a table next to the spa with some brown liquid left inside. Using a gloved hand, he picked up a glass and smelled. He said, "Not Southern Comfort."

Then he said to himself, "Bucky shared a drink with someone but why take a bottle he didn't use upstairs and why leave glasses next to the pool?"

Nate signaled a crime scene technician over and said, "Collect those glasses and have them tested for DNA and fingerprints. And look around for cigarette butts or any other trace evidence, like fabric and footprints on carpet. I'm going upstairs."

"Yes, Sir."

Nathan walked inside to check out windows and doors on the first floor of the house for himself. He sent a technician outside to inspect the soil near the house for fresh footprints. He searched for any access points that would allow someone to enter the house without being recorded on the exterior security cameras.

When he entered Bucky's home office, he studied the windows and a patio door. Examining the locking mechanism, he saw scratch marks on the door lock. He opened the door, stepped outside, and saw there was no camera coverage. The technician was searching a flower bed. He said, "Tom, over here. Check around this patio for footprints. If you find any, take a cast then dust the glass on this door for fingerprints. I think we have our access point."

"Yes, Sir." Tom said.

Nathan walked up the staircase and saw activity in the hallway. He pulled on rubber gloves and slipped on foot coverings before entering the bedroom. He asked, "Is this the Master Bedroom?"

"No Sir, that's down the hall but I think it was Mr. Chalmers sleeping room though. The closet is full of his clothes. Gotta say, he was a flashy dresser."

"What have you found so far?"

"We're dusting the entire room for prints. The sheets will be removed and sent to the lab for DNA testing."

"What do you know about the victims?" Nate asked.

"The Medical Examiner said there was a gunpower tattoo on Mr. Chalmer's head and the head of the woman with him."

"So, those shots were point blank." Nathan said.

"Yes, Sir. But they occurred after the victims were already dead from shots to their bodies while in the bed."

"What have you got on the Southern Comfort bottle?"

"That's the odd thing. We found nothing. No fingerprints of any kind. The bottle appeared to be wiped clean."

"That *is* odd. So, it would seem Bucky and Marcy didn't bring the bottle up here to drink. Someone, possibly the killer or killers, left it for us to find. They wiped the bottle and set it next to the bed. Wonder what the significance of that is?"

"I don't know, above my pay grade." The tech said.

Nathan laughed and said, "Mine, too."

On the way back down the stairs, Nathan ruminated over what he discovered. He thought, *"I wonder what ballistics will tell us about the bullets used. And how does the Southern Comfort bottle work into this crime?"* He said, "This looks like a professional hit, but there are flaws no professional would ever leave."

Chapter: 17

I watched Jill print the weekly payroll and place the checks on Mandy Sue's desk for her signature. I counted out cash for each pay envelope using a numbered schedule Jill printed for me.

By 2:30 in the afternoon both Mandy Sue and Blanche had failed to show up. I believed they both were told about Bucky early this morning and decided to stay home. I felt that both women were capable of engineering several fraudulent schemes for someone in the dealership. I intend to find out who allowed the crimes to begin and encouraged other people to steal at the dealership. I kind of suspected Bucky's chunky brother, Eddie, the sales manager.

The culture of crime in the dealership may have gone back to Bucky's father before he was convicted of manslaughter. Bucky may have simply allowed everything to continue as before. I planned to return to the hotel, spread the paperwork out on the second queen bed, then start to piece together a timeline.

Later, at the hotel, I studied the mess on the bed to exhaustion and said, "This simply is not going to work. I have too many questions that need answers first. And I refuse to be held prisoner in Columbus."

My phone buzzed, it was a text from my lawyer. His message read, *"Surrender your guns to the Sheriff and present your FBI credential. If anything goes wrong, call me." Baxter*

Decision made. I would drive to the courthouse and confront the Sheriff's Deputy, Mike. I would hand over my firearms and demand they perform a ballistics test and ask that they remove any restriction on my movements.

I gathered my guns and my shoulder bag then stomped downstairs to my Camaro. I easily found the courthouse and the Sheriff's office. A female deputy, Robyn, was acting as a receptionist. I said, "My name is Annette Dupart." I presented Mike Riley's business card and asked to speak to him.

"I'm sorry, he's not in. Is there someone else?"

I stood erect and said, "The Sheriff, please!"

"Yeah, I think he's busy right now."

"Please tell him I'm here and would like to turn my guns over for a ballistics test."

That got deputy Robyn's attention. She said, "Just a minute."

I was scrolling my cellphone when I looked up. I saw a uniformed man in his early to mid-fifty's, staring at me. He had a full head of brown hair with premature gray creeping at the temples.

He smiled with the stern look of a man who was used to being in charge. He asked, "Miss Dupart?"

I said, "Yes."

"Nathan Turnbull. Please meet me at the door."

I walked to a door with a sign that said, "Law Enforcement Personnel." The door opened and the man said, "Miss Dupart, I'm glad you came. Please come in."

I stepped in and he said, "Follow me to my office. I'm surprised to see you. I have several questions for you."

I thought, *"I'm still a person of interest for Bucky's murder."*

In his office the Sheriff said, "Please sit down. May I get you a water or something?"

"No, thank you. I'm here to turn over my two hand guns for you to run a ballistics test. I want to make sure there is no confusion about my guns being involved with Mr. Chalmers death." I put both guns on the Sheriff's desk along with my conceal carry license.

Nathan's eyebrows shot up. He picked up the 92M9 Beretta first. The magazine was out and the chamber was open. He closely inspected the gun. Then he picked up the Nano, the magazine out and the chamber open. He smiled and said, "Thank you. You may have your guns back Miss Dupart."

"That's it? I thought you wanted to make sure the guns weren't used in Bucky's death. At least perform a ballistics test."

"Not necessary. Wrong caliber."

"Then I am no longer considered a person of interest?"

"I'm not sure what Mike told you, but I don't believe you ever were. He just wanted to check your guns to see what you had. Like I said, I'm glad you're here, I have a few questions to ask concerning your audit at the Magnolia car dealership."

"Like what?" I asked while putting my guns into my bag.

"Is the FBI conducting some investigation into Magnolia Fine Cars or any member of the Chalmers family?"

"The FBI? No, not that I'm aware of."

"We ran a background check and discovered that you are a contract employee for the FBI, and you report directly to the Deputy Director himself. That's why I asked."

I smiled, "Yes, when asked, I sometimes help the FBI with certain cases. This is not one. I am a CPA working for LeDuc and Johnson out of Germantown, TN. I'm here because Bucky called Wolf LeDuc, begging him to come because he was being audited and he knew people were stealing from him in the dealership.

"So, have you found fraud at this dealership?"

I considered the question. There was fraud on so many levels, and our contract had a confidentiality clause. Bucky was dead and I was uncertain what I could tell the Sheriff. I sighed and said, "Let me make a phone call first, then I'll answer your question."

Nathan looked surprised and said, "Do you want me to step out of my office?"

"No. You can hear my end of the conversation."

I dialed Baxter, he picked up and asked, "Are you in jail?"

"No, Baxter. I'm not in jail. I'm with Sheriff Turnbull and I am asking about the confidentiality clause in the LeDuc and Johnson contract. Now that Bucky's dead is that contract still valid?"

"Yours is a consultation contract. You agree to keep what you find only available to the person who signed the contract."

"So, can I tell the Sheriff what I found?"

"In this case, the signer of the contract is deceased. If you found illegal activity that represents a crime, you are bound to report your findings to law enforcement, otherwise, you might be deemed complicit in the crime."

"So, I should tell the Sheriff?"

"Yes, if you found something that can be considered criminal activity." The lawyer said.

"Thank you, Baxter." I hung up, turned to the Sheriff, and said, "Yes, I found fraud, accounting, and business misdeeds on several levels. There are a lot of crimes."

Nathan's eyes glittered with curiosity. He said, "Do tell."

Nathan called in Deputy Robyn. She set up a recording device, and I spilled the beans on Magnolia Fine Cars. I reluctantly told him about shop technicians who were probably undocumented. I said, "And that is just the beginning."

"Can you provide me with a list of employees and their possible relationship to Bucky?"

"I started that list today, it's not complete."

"Please finish that list and supply a copy of it to me if you will. Now, I have a couple of questions about your visit to Bucky Chalmer's home yesterday."

"Okay."

"While you were at Bucky's, did you see anyone else in the house or somewhere on the property?"

"Funny you ask. I drove passed a 4-door blue Dodge Ram, fairly recent model, on a dirt road on my way to his front door."

"Did you see anyone?"

"I did look and saw no one around the truck. I thought it was odd because of where it was parked. But while I was walking through the house, I'm sure I saw movement of a shadow between the dining room and an office. At the time, I thought it was Mrs. Chalmers but Bucky told me she wasn't home. I didn't think anything more about it. Like I said, I couldn't believe he lured me to his place just to embarrass me. I quickly got out of the house and went back to the hotel."

Thank you, Annette. You don't mind if I call you Annette, do you?" Sheriff Turnbull asked.

"Annette's fine. Am I free to come and go?"

"You are, but I can use your help. As an expert on car dealerships, and your proficiency with accounting, you may provide information that we can use. I'm looking for people who may have a motive to kill Bucky. Complete that family employee list. Find out if anyone had a disagreement with Mr. Chalmers."

"I'll run that by my boss at LeDuc and Johnson. I'm here on an expense report for a specific audit mission. It's up to him."

Nathan nodded acknowledgement. He said, "I'll call Mr. LeDuc and talk with him. Are you expected to go back to the dealership to finish your audit?"

"I planned to, yes. A CPA analyses' the books, for errors and flaws then make suggested remedies to correct the deficient areas."

"Okay, you've been very helpful. Look, I don't want anyone to give you any trouble while you're providing information to me. So, if you're willing, I want to deputize you while you're working at Magnolia Cars. If you have any problem, contact Deputy Riley or myself right away. Someone may see your digging in files as a threat. I especially want to know who Bucky's successor will be. The car company involved is welcome to contact me, too. We'll let you know what, if anything, we might need from them.

I stood up, took an oath to become a Lowndes County sheriff's deputy. Nathan said, "Regardless of your conceal carry license, you are now legally authorized by my department to carry your gun. I hope you never have to use it while under my umbrella."

I said, "Thank you. Me, too. Do I get a badge or anything?"

Nathan smiled and said, "No badge."

I gathered my things and was escorted to the door by the Sheriff. My work day was done.

I called Wolf to tell him what happened and to expect a call from Sheriff Turnbull. My head was spinning about being deputized.

Chapter: 18

Deputy Investigator, Mike Riley, went home tired. Before he left the courthouse Sheriff Turnbull briefed him about what I had to say and told him about deputizing me. Mike's day had been busy following leads on a 60-year-old triple murder. Now with Bucky's murder, he was overwhelmed by his workload. On top of everything, he was still leading an investigation for Grace Dowd case.

The high-profile murder of a leading county citizen made Mike's head spin. Every time he focused on one case, something always drew his focus to another case. To top everything off, his son came home with an F on a math quiz. He had a headache.

He opened a beer. His sister, Judy, called to remind him that her son, Robby, was performing at a public concert. Students from High School to the third grade in Columbus would be performing in the concert. She invited Mike and his family to attend.

Mike had never heard Robby play the piano. Judy said he was good, but Mike had been to children's recitals before. Even though the kids tried their best, they couldn't keep up the rhythm or hit the right note at the right time. It was ear bending torture, but he would go anyway to support his sister and his nephew.

Judy told Mike the new music teacher was really good, but he wasn't so sure. It didn't matter, tired, overworked or not, he would go to the concert and support his nephew, sour notes, and all.

"Robby." He thought. *"He found that damned finger bone which opened up a whole can of worms of work for him."* He had a fresh murder case with Bucky; he should be focusing on that. That's where the action is. That's what he should be doing with his time.

When he stepped in the kitchen, his wife, Suzane said, "Thank goodness your home. I was at the pediatricians and got a prescription for Dotty. I don't have dinner tonight. I need to go to the pharmacy. Can you watch the kids while I'm gone?" She begged.

"Sure. What were you thinking for dinner tonight?"

"I haven't had time to think about anything. I've been at the doctor all afternoon with Dotty. I'll think of something, maybe sloppy joe's. I don't know! I'll be back soon."

The door slammed shut and Mike quietly said, "Bye!"

"Okay kids, how does pizza sound tonight?" He asked.

"McDonalds! McDonalds!" They screamed at once.

He rolled his eyes and sighed. "Okay, McDonalds. I'll call Aunt Judy and ask her to pick up some Happy Meals and bring them over. Chicken nuggets, right?"

Chapter: 19

Sheriff Turnbull wanted to know who would succeed Bucky as the dealer of record, so did I. When I returned to my hotel room, I ordered Chinese delivery. I poked at my meal with chopsticks, while reviewing lists of Magnolia employees related to the Chalmers family. My task was mostly speculative, guessing who was related and might succeed Bucky. I needed help, someone to tell me who was actually related to Bucky. I needed to ask at the dealership.

After a couple of hours, my first list was complete. I recorded every employee with an annotation of their family connection, as I understood, to the Chalmers family. My list looked more like an Ancestry.com family tree instead of an employee list. At least a third of the 130 employees were family members and not all of them were full time employees. But I needed someone to look over the list.

I began to consider the most likely candidates from people I met at the dealership. With Bucky no longer in charge and Blanche in an alcohol stupor, who would rise to the task. None of them seemed like dealer candidates to me, but it wasn't my call.

Eddie Chalmers appeared as a bearded overweight bully, no one seemed to like. In my book, which made him candidate number one. And he was Bucky's brother. I would talk with him first.

The service manager, Blane Sloan, was a close nephew. He was incompetent and tried to stay out of the way. In fact, the service department was run by tattooed Lance Butterfield. He was not on my list as a family employee but his girlfriend, Mandy Sue, sure was. So, together they were on my list of potential successors.

Troy St. Clair, another cousin, ran the parts department like an independent business operation. He sold a lot of wholesale parts to repair shops and body shops in the county and beyond. Except for the warranty parts thing, Troy St. Clair was a competent, close blood relative who could possibly succeed.

An outlier on my list was Chip Chalmers, another first cousin. The Mississippi State Bank had a lien on the building and land. Chip was the banker and could call in the loan and take over the business any time. *"Hmmm, might have to meet him."* I thought.

I thought about other family members who held positions like, salesmen, advertising manager, body shop manager and even the receptionist. I gave up looking through the employee list. There were more Chalmers in this dealership than bedbugs in a cheap motel. I haven't met most of them and couldn't pick them out of a lineup. They all seemed to be happy sailing along on the good ship gravy boat. I didn't know if I could plug the holes in that sinking boat fast enough. Where would I go for answers next?

I went back to what I know, accounting. Follow the money. Money the dealership took in should be documented with a receipt. Then, the money should be deposited into a bank account. This is the first dealership I have ever been to that did not have an accurate accounting of receipts that matched the bank deposits. This is unheard of and a crimson red flag.

Bank cash withdrawals should be rare and used to fund things like cash drawers and a petty cash account. Bank statements showed weekly cash withdrawals in large sums. Withdrawal slips were not kept for accounting to note why the money was withdrawn. Then, it occurred to me, that was how they paid the Hispanic technicians, using pay envelopes.

Worse yet, was tracking pay for the salesmen. Thanks to Eddie, car sales records were unintelligible. Commissions for car sales didn't seem to have any relation to sales gross. The sale amount, minus the cost of sale. Eddie Chalmers subjectively chose what to pay each salesman. It looked like he chose numbers rewarding some salesmen, while punishing others.

Eddie's name was clearly on every car deal. That made accountability for answering my questions much easier. Tomorrow, I planned to corner him for answers on a list of car deals and how much was paid to each salesman. I wasn't sure if he would answer any of my questions, but it was worth a shot.

Chapter: 20

Eddie Chalmers was a frequent customer at "Y'all's Balls" a pool and billiard hall tavern near the railroad tracks. He was good enough to be declared a pool shark. He hauled his girth around the green felt using a pool crutch to make shots he couldn't reach. Local players avoided him for money challenges because the was known locally as the Willie Mosconi of Columbus, the great pool champion.

His children had grown into adulthood and moved out of the county. He had little interest in going home to a surly, overweight wife. When he met his bride, she was a hot well-proportioned redhead with a feisty personality. She was attracted to Eddie when he was discharged from the army after serving in Viet Nam. Coming home, he was handsome, tanned, and fit. She was working at the Magnolia dealership for his dad as a journal entry clerk. They hit it off instantly. Eddie went to work for his father selling cars. Over time, he did well with Dean's coaching and learned a lot of tricks, which helped to pad his paycheck. Over the years, he and his wife ate very well, and they both gained a lot of weight.

Eddie took up pool while he was in the service. Pool was a good way to earn a quick buck, and it now got him out of the house. He honed the sport and was now the town's pool hustler.

On this particular evening, he downed his usual five beers and ate a pastrami sandwich in between pool matches. He was a heavy smoker. The pool hall allowed this smoking behavior as long as he didn't rest cigarettes on the top rails and cushions. He was careful to use nearby ashtrays. People loved to watch him play. He would often put on trick play demonstrations that never failed to "Wow!" the crowd.

Tonight, he lit another cigarette using a cigarette, while walking to his new stretch Chevrolet Silverado. His brow creased when he saw someone he knew in the parking lot. Angry, he quickly flicked the cigarette in their direction and got into his truck to avoid talking to them. Ignoring those people, he slowly took the back roads to his small farm near Bucky's place.

After Eddie left the main Highway, he followed a road he had traveled on for most of his 58 years. He was almost to his farm when he quickly stomped on the brakes. His truck lights illuminated two people standing in the middle of the road. One raised an AR15 the other a handgun and they aimed at Eddie.

Eddie's eyes widened and he abruptly turned the wheel to avoid them. Panic stricken, he stepped on the gas to make a U-turn. The road was not wide enough for the turn and the truck hit a large hickory tree. His head came forward and he smashing his head on the steering wheel, knocking him unconscious before the airbag deployed which tossed his head back.

One of the people walked over, opened the driver's door. Dazed, Eddie looked up. The man grinned and used a buck knife to slice Eddie's fat throat. His attackers siphoned gas from Eddies truck into an empty Slurpy cup that was rolling on Eddies' truck floor. They took their time pouring gas around Eddie and beneath the truck. One of them, on their knees, punctured the truck's fuel cell causing a gas leak. A match was lit and tossed. They ran away.

Eddie's new truck burst into flames. Inside, Eddie was bleeding from a poor cut to his neck, but he was not dead. With the fire burning around him, the airbag deployed he couldn't get out of the truck. He screamed pounding at the airbag, trying to get out.

A passing car saw the fire and stopped. A man and his wife immediately lept out and ran to Eddie's truck door. They undid Eddie's seatbelt and burned their hands while pulling on Eddie's burning body to free him from the truck. They were barely able to power Eddie from the truck and away before it exploded into flames.

Exhausted, the man and the woman sat on the ground next to Eddie and nervously dialed 9-1-1. Eddie's rescuers were taken to the hospital and treated for burn injuries. Eddie, however, would sell no more cars, his burn wounds were severe, but he was pronounced dead at the scene, a victim of a sudden cardiac arrest.

Chapter: 21

I had been working in Columbus for four days. Today, Friday, I looked forward to going home. I was not sure if I would return. I pulled on sweats and ran a five-mile route through Columbus. I ate a good breakfast in the dining room, then retired to my room to shower, get dressed and pack my things.

I gathered my bags, went down stairs, and checked out of the hotel then stopped to gas up my Camaro. I drove to the Sheriff's office to hand him my list of Chalmers family in the business. I debated if I would go to the dealership. I could prepare my CPA report in Germantown. I had no idea who I would even submit my CPA audit report to. I needed to hand a LeDuc and Johnson invoice to Mandy Sue for payment. Maybe I would email it.

I walked into the courthouse and met Sheriff Turnbull. He invited me into his office, and I handed the employee list to him. It had my notes about family members, possible successors to the business and a summary of crimes I believe were committed.

He said, "Bad news. Bucky's brother Eddie was killed last night in an apparent auto accident. His truck hit a tree and caught fire. A passing couple tried to save him, but he died anyway."

"A truck accident? Was anyone else hurt?"

"No, it was a single vehicle collision."

"Was he drunk?" I asked

"He was a known beer drinker. An autopsy will determine the cause of death. The motorist pulled him out of the truck after it caught fire. Eddie was badly burned and died."

"How odd. He was top on my list as the only potential successor to the business. So, it was just an accident, then?"

"I'm not ruling out foul play. What's odd was the unopened bottle of Southern Comfort found near the truck. There are tire skid marks on the road, like he just made a sharp left turn to avoid something, or someone, then ran into a tree. I'm glad you came in this morning. Bodies are piling up in my county and I need help."

Nathan continued, "I called your cousin, Wolf. He agreed to let me use you with our investigation, if you agree, for a fee. It's entirely up to you. I got permission from the County Commissioners to hire you as a consulting investigator. We'll pay you at your going consultation rate, plus expenses. What do you say?"

"Uh, okay. I was planning to wrap up my work and return home today. I have laundry and need to catch up on my mail."

"We'll cover sending your things to the cleaners. Have you checked out of your hotel yet?"

"Yes, I did. I'm flattered. You caught me off guard. I'll do it, but I need a place to work and a place to stay."

"Got you covered. The county owns a historic house in town. We use it as a B&B for visiting dignitaries and county business meetings. You'll have a large bedroom, a library to work in and they serve breakfast. The B&B will handle your laundry for you. Check in this morning. We want you to go back to the car dealership and nose around. Keep your eyes open and continue to probe through the accounting system for fraud. I believe Bucky's killer works there."

"Wow! Okay. I'll go back and see if Mandy has sent out the payroll yet. I sent the payroll clerk, Jill, home for her own safety because of what she told me. Should I bring her back in?"

"No one knows what she told you and no one knows what you gave to me. I think you're both good. Go in and continue as if nothing happened. Bucky was a randy rascal, he crossed a lot of lines, he has a line of enemies as long as a list of prime numbers. I'm focusing on who, in that car dealership, is capable of murder. You've discovered a lot of crime. It would be good to know when it all began. Victims are piling up and I see a lot of lazy, greedy family members working in that car store. Someone there is capable of murder, and I want to find the weasel in the woodpile."

"I'll do my best. I do plan to remain armed while probing files at the dealership if you don't mind. And yes, I can dig deeper to identify specific crimes and who committed them."

"You should know, Columbus is proud to feature its young musicians tonight at a youth concert. I think you'll enjoy yourself if you come as my guest. The concert will be held at 7:00 tonight, in the community center, just down the street. I know Deputy Mike Riley and I would be honored if you came to watch our young performers tonight. It's not far from your B&B. We'll have a ticket waiting for you. Will you come?"

I was surprised by the request and didn't know how to refuse. I said, "Sure, what do I wear?"

Nathan laughed and said, "Miss Annette, we're in Columbus! We come as we are. Mike will bring his wife and I'll bring a guest. We both would be happy if you joined us at my house for drinks after the concert."

"I don't drink alcohol, but I would be delighted to come and listen to the children play. What kind of music?"

"Classical, I think. The kids are supposed to be good. Robby Carter, I'm told, is one heck of a piano player."

"Sold! Sounds like a good time. I'll be there."

"Good!"

Chapter: 22

I drove to the address Sheriff Turnbull provided and checked in with a pleasant woman at the B&B. The place was a large colonial revival home built in the 1930's with plenty of parking for my Camaro behind the place. It's located in what is probably considered the better part of town. The Sheriff was right; the bedroom was huge with a spacious ensuite. I sorted and placed my soiled things in a laundry bag and gave them to the B&B manager.

I didn't have anything special to wear at a concert tonight, so I decided there's plenty of time. I'll go shopping before I go to the dealership. Yea! One of my favorite pastimes.

There were several wonderful boutiques in the downtown shopping area. I had fun going from store to store to choose my clothing. I took my time making my buying experience joyful and fun. Shopping always makes me happy. I was in a good mood by the time I parked in the Magnolia Cars service parking lot. By now, employees were beginning to recognize me, and I got several nods and hello's as I walked through the building.

My mission today was to meet key family members. I would start with the parts manager. But first, I intended to present the LeDuc and Johnson invoice for payment to Mandy Sue.

Mandy Sue was back at her desk. She had a sour look on her face when I walked in and sat down at my assigned desk. Jill Boyd had not come in, and Bobbi Jo was busy chatting on the phone. I suspected she was talking to her cousin in Kentucky.

I opened my computer and was focused on adding details to my CPA audit report. I sensed someone standing near me, looked up and Mandy Sue was leering at me. I put on my best smile and said, "Mandy, you look nice. How are you doing today?"

She didn't smile back. She bluntly asked, "Are you about done yet?"

I tilted my head to one side and said, "I'm not sure what you mean. I am working on my audit report. I have several things to add and still have source documents to look up. Why? Do you need this desk for something?"

That angered the young woman. She said, "I do not need the desk for anything, and I think you've outstayed your welcome."

I said, "Audit work is thorough and detailed. I am bound by law and ethics to be as complete as possible. Where is Blanche by the way?" I said looking around.

Mandy looked around and shook her head. "That has nothing to do with you. I think you need to leave."

"I understand your frustration, I really do. But I'm bound by a contract to stay and complete my job. I could lose my license if I leave." This wasn't true of course, but I was pretty sure Mandy didn't know the difference.

"Look, Uncle Bucky is dead. I found out this morning that his brother, Uncle Eddie, is now dead, too. I don't think you have a contract with anyone to continue working on an audit." She said.

"Oh, but I do." I pulled up the LeDuc and Johnson contract on my computer, turned my laptop around so she could see and said, "See? It's signed by the dealer."

"He's dead! And what will happen to your audit report when you're done? Who will you give it to?" Mandy asked in frustration.

"Why it becomes the property of Magnolia Fine Cars, of course."

"Magnolia Fine Cars? That's me! What's in that report?" Mandy demanded.

"I'm not quite through yet, but an audit report lists deficiencies and possible accounting errors in procedures that need to be corrected. Please understand, I'm not your enemy here." I lied. "Things that I find will only help you to become a better bookkeeper. I can even coach you on how to use your accounting software better. I'll show you ways to improve profitability." I smiled pleasantly. I don't think she bought it.

Inexperienced and defeated, Mandy turned to storm off, before she did, I said, "Oh, Mandy." She turned and glared at me. I handed her the LeDuc and Johnson invoice and said, "If you don't mind, would you see to it that a check is cut today for our service through this week?" I batted my eyelashes and presented a smile.

She surprised me when she abruptly snatched the document out of my hand, turned and stalked off to her office. I thought to myself, *"We'll see if she cuts that check or not."*

I noticed the stack of payroll checks was missing from Mandy's desk. At least she was functioning on some level. Murdered dealer and sales manager or not, everyone in the dealership was getting a payday. At least, because of Jill and me, all the Hispanic technicians got paid.

I planned to meet with Troy St. Clair but something in me just wanted to annoy Mandy Sue. So, I took my time adding details to my audit report.

Mandy was not high on my list of successors to the business. There were several family members still alive to talk with. I looked up while typing on my report. Mandy Sue continued glaring at me through the glass of her office. She didn't seem to be working, just staring daggers at me. I had the feeling she was plotting some devious ways to put me out of her misery.

Chapter: 23

I spent an hour and a half making copies of documents on which I found egregious mistakes, or were they were simply acts of fraud? I checked my watch then closed my laptop and slipped it into my backpack. I didn't trust anyone in the accounting department, so I stuffed the photocopies into my backpack next to my computer and threw it over my shoulder. As I stood up, I heard a sing-song voice ask, "So, are you leaving, for good?"

"No, Mandy. Just going to lunch. See you in a bit. May I bring you something?" She didn't answer. Out of the corner of my eye, I actually saw her bite the pencil in her mouth in half. Boy, she had a lot of pent up anger.

Instead of going directly to my car, I walked into the parts department and knocked on Troy St. Clair's door. He was studying something on his desk then his head slowly rose, and he gave me a sad, red-eyed look. The man was in his forty's, not as old as Bucky, but he had the same blondish hair. He sat leaning over his desk, emotionless. He stared at me, not saying a word.

I knew him from the payroll records, he was Bucky's cousin. He waited for me to say something. I finally said, "Troy, my name is Annette Dupart, I have…"

"I know who you are. You're that woman causing all of our problems."

That was the weirdest introduction I've ever had. I said, "How so?"

"Some of the family had a meeting last night after we heard about Eddie. It seems family members are all of a sudden dying around here. Why is that? Everything was fine until you came here. You've been sticking your nose where it doesn't belong. Some of us don't like that. We know how to do our jobs. We don't need you."

I understood his grief by losing a family member and nodded. "I'm an accounting auditor hired by Bucky to help him save his failing dealership. He knew the end was coming fast and he desperately wanted to know why. My mission is to look for solutions to turn the business around, so everyone here has a place to work."

Troy suddenly burst into laughter. He said, "Desperate? Hell Bucky wouldn't know the meaning of the word. We think you wormed your way in here with that black fellah to take the business away from our family. This dealership has been in our family for three generations. You're just one of many who've tried to steal our gold mine."

"I'm sorry? Gold mine? This is a car business. You and your family work here to generate profit so you can make a good living. My job is to make sure you continue to do that. No more, no less."

My voice had risen and I pledged to get myself under control. I let what I said sink in. In a softer voice I said, "Your parts department makes a good amount of money for the dealership. You are an aggressive wholesale parts dealer in this corner of Mississippi. I have no power to take anything from anyone. I point out things that could get Magnolia Cars in trouble with the tax laws. But it's up to management, like you, to correct those things, not me."

"That's not what we agreed on last night. We think you're a spy for the government and we don't like it. You and that black fella had better pack up and leave if you know what's good for you."

I had heard enough. I said, "Really? What government? Is that a threat? Because if it is, that will go into my audit report along with all of the fraudulent business practices your family has cheated out of this dealership. I am not going anywhere, Troy, until my work is done. Like I said, I can't close anything down."

"That's not what we heard. We think that you're a female sharpshooter sent in to destroy our dealership. You even carry a gun. Heck, you probably killed Bucky and Eddie yourself."

I thought, *"I'm a sharpshooter alright but not the kind your thinking of."* I said, "That is simply untrue."

"Lance said, y'all are closing down the shop and will put people out of work. Look around. The Mexicans have already left and so have some of our family members. There won't be anyone left to work in the store."

"I won't put you out of business, but people from the factory can and they will, when they show up with their team of auditors because of warranty fraud. I looked at some of those claims. Your parts were used on claims completely unrelated to the repair. Submitting warranty claims like that will get the dealership closed."

I continued, "Packing parts onto warranty claims, makes you a co-conspirator of fraud, facing jail time. Ezra is here to help clean up and resubmit those claims to get you and the business out of trouble. I'm here to provide an examination of accounting practices and make a report. What I've found is not good."

"You look like a smart man, Troy. Instead of threatening me, I think your time would be better spent correcting your mistakes and listening to common sense instead of Lance. He'll only get you into trouble. Either work with me, Troy, or start looking for a good lawyer."

I pivoted and walked out of his office before Troy could respond. I was now officially working in a hostile environment, and I would report Troy's threat to Sheriff Turnbull while being extra careful about where I went and what I did while I was in Columbus.

Chapter: 24

I took a deep breath and decided to check on Jill Boyd. I didn't have her phone number, but I had her address. I was concerned about her wellbeing especially after the ill-informed parts manager threatened me.

I knocked on her door and saw a shadow on the other side of the glass. I said, "Jill? It's me, Annette. May I come inside. We need to talk."

Through the door Jill said, "I can't be seen with you. I'm not safe. My sister told me the Chalmer's family is on the war path now that Bucky and Eddie are both dead. They are looking for revenge against anyone who they think is against them."

I looked down the street and didn't see anyone watching me, but in a town this size, they knew everything about their neighbors. I said, "Alright, May I have the Sheriff look in on you?"

"No! I don't want help from anyone. Now go away. I'm sorry I ever talked to you."

I was deeply concerned about Jill's safety. She was right, I was not helping her stay safe. I slipped my card into the screen door and said, "Come back to work. No one knows we spoke."

Now concerned that I was being followed I checked carefully up and down the street and didn't see any cars or trucks.

I went a local diner and sat in a remote corner booth where I could watch the door, the waitress took my order for a burger and fries. I checked my cell phone and sent a text to Wolf. Munching on fries, I sat back in my booth and considered my circumstances.

Maybe Troy was right. My audit could have tipped over the apple cart, and someone is taking it out on members of the Chalmers family. Mandy Sue was upset, and Troy St. Clair was just downright rude. Bucky was murdered and so was his brother, Eddie. How many more Chalmers would die as a result of my probing? I wondered.

While digging through Magnolia's financial records it seemed that anyone with the name of Chalmers was up to their necks with larceny and fraud. But now, they're the ones paying for their crimes. Who the heck is killing people and why?"

I only had a couple of hours left for work. So, I didn't return to the dealership. Instead, I decided to quit for the day and go to the B&B. I would take my time preparing for the children's concert tonight. Before getting ready, I summarized my findings and sent them to Wolf and Ezra before going to the concert.

Chapter: 25

In spite of all of the murders on his plate to solve, Grace Dowd's murder haunted Sheriff Turnbull the most. Her miserable and painful death kept going through his mind. He never knew the girl, only met her once, but he knew people around town who did. He wanted to know what they knew. Grace's boyfriend, Josh, was now a senior in college taking finals. He could wait.

Nathan's plan was to talk to neighbors of the Dowds who were around five years ago. He wanted a comprehensive list of everyone Grace babysat for. He wanted to know how her parents got along and why Drew left. It was a longshot, but he needed a lead.

He also planned to visit liquor stores and local bars to discover who were regular drinkers of Southern Comfort whiskey. He was as determined as a bloodhound looking for a wounded deer.

County courthouse records provided him with a list of the addresses and residents by date. Nathan searched for names and addresses around the Dowd house during the time Grace was reported missing. He recognized a few names, and they still lived on that block. He made notes and decided to make a few personal calls by knocking on doors. This was old school detective work, and it suited him, just fine.

Nathan knocked on the door of Margaret Cook, a 68 year old county retiree. She opened her door and said, "Nathan, what a surprise. How's the family?"

Nate didn't mention his wife's death a year ago. "Thanks for asking. Sorry to bother you. I have a couple of questions about one of your neighbors, Drew, and Sharon Dowd They lived down the street a few years ago. Did you know them very well?"

"I knew of them, but I didn't know them. I think Drew high-tailed it a couple of years before Grace went missing. Sharon, well, I don't like to speak ill of people but let's say she may not have been the best role model for Grace."

"How so?" Nathan asked, taking notes.

"She seemed to make a lot of male friends who came at all hours to the house. If you know what I mean."

"Was she doing that while Grace was alive?"

"Yes. I was concerned for the girl. Sharon didn't seem to care. You might check with that reverend at the tabernacle out near the Alabama border. I've heard stories about him."

"Judy Carter lives on this block, too, with her son, Robby, and her daughter, Dotty. Roxanne and I plan to go to the concert tonight with them. Will you be going?" Nathan asked." Oh, and did you know Bob Carter before he left five years ago?"

"Yes, I'll be there tonight. You know, that was another dad who just up and left. No, I don't know much about Bob. What is it with those young fellas, anyway?" Margaret asked.

"I'm not sure but I want you to think back five years ago about the time Grace went missing."

"Well, I know Sharon and her husband seemed to be arguing all the time. He just packed up and left."

"Do you know where Drew went?"

"No. I don't think anybody knows. Sharon sure didn't. She filed for child support, but the county had no place to serve papers."

Nathan said. "What about Grace, what can you tell me about her? What she was doing? What was she like? Who did she know? Anything you can remember."

"Grace babysat for several families back then. Let me see, she sat for the St. Clair's, the Bakers, a Chalmer or two, and Robby's mom, Judy. There were others, I can't remember. Grace was an only child. I saw her smoking and hanging out with those other two, Mandy and Bobbi. I think they were up to no good."

"Thanks, Margaret, that's very helpful. See you tonight?"

Margaret brightened. "Yes, Robby's quite good, you know."

Chapter: 26

While clothes shopping, I found a black dress and purse with matching shoes that seemed like the perfect choice. I wanted something to look nice but not too flashy and something that would be appropriate for a concert tonight. I also added a light gray shawl.

I walked to the Columbus Community Center instead of driving the short distance. I was surprised by the line of people at the door. I went to the ticket counter and gave my name. My ticket was handed to me with a smile.

I was impressed by the size of the auditorium which was larger than I expected. I wanted to see the performance, but not too close. I was sure parents would be standing up to take photographs of their little musical geniuses, and I didn't want to be in the way.

My decision was made for me when Mike Riley and his wife walked over and greeted me. He said, "This is my wife, Suzane. Please come and sit with us and next to Robby's mother, Judy."

Judy was an animated talker. Her daughter, Dotty, was with a sitter and she had nothing but wonderful things to say about her son, Robby. I remember he was the boy who found the finger joint, launching a massive search looking for bodies.

I studied the musical program and was amazed that Robby would be playing several pieces from Chopin in the middle of the program. I looked up when Nathan Turnbull and a lovely redheaded woman sat in the two empty seats next to me. He said, "Miss Annette, I would like you to meet my date Roxanne. Roxanne, Annette." Turnbull smiled with pleasure.

I said, "Hello Roxanne." *"Date, not wife."* I mentally noted.

"Yes, Annette. Nathan has told me so much about you and your work at Magnolia. You know, I can't talk about it in public, but he thinks *you* are a good investigator." Roxanne said with a smile.

That caught me off guard. I said, "Uh, I'm just a CPA actually. I'm looking forward to seeing both you and Mrs. Riley after the concert." I said smiling.

Roxanne said, "Me, too. I understand you're staying at our wonderful county B&B. They've done such a good job, fixing it up."

I grinned and mischievously said, "Better there than the B&B in the courthouse."

Roxanne laughed and just at that moment the orchestra conductor walked on stage and the audience began to applaud. He smiled while waving at people he knew in the crowd with his baton, including Jill Carter. The audience stood up and continued to applaud. The conductor looked embarrassed, but he smiled. He raised his baton and the room went quiet.

The applause ceased and he said with a slight accent, "Columbus, Mississippi has a treasure house of talent. I am so honored to be the teaching inspiration for this wonderful assembly of young people." He shrugged his shoulders and said, "The ages of our young musicians tonight range from 6 to 19. That's right, and they all play wonderfully. I see in the audience, nearly 200 or more Columbus citizens. I guarantee, you will be proud of their performance tonight."

He bowed to the audience, pivoted and stepped up to begin the first piece; it was the theme from Frozen. He tapped the music stand raised the baton and the music began slowly, building up. I was shocked and surprised by the orchestral effect, no missed notes.

After the first set, the crowd went wild applauding. The conductor smiled and addressed the audience one more time to introduce Robby Carter. "I think you will enjoy this young man. He has worked very hard on a series of Chopin waltzes. They are difficult pieces of moderate length for piano solo. Composed between 1824 and 1849, all are in waltz triple meter. Enjoy."

Robby walked out dressed in black trousers and a white shirt. He bowed to the audience and took his time sitting on the bench of the grand piano. He adjusted his glasses and began slowly tapping away, one piano key at a time. Then the piece came together with extraordinary skill. I looked around and saw men, women and children mouths open, mesmerized by the boy's focus on the piano.

I ventured a look at Robby's mom. She was crying into a tissue. The citizens of Columbus had just discovered a new community treasure.

When he finished his last piece, he sat quietly in front of the piano not moving. Suddenly the whole room erupted into applause. Everyone stood up, including the youthful members of the orchestra. The applause lasted for nearly ten minutes. Robby didn't move for the longest time. He finally turned, stood up, smiled, and bowed. The audience applauded even louder. The town had a new hero. He was no longer the kid who found a finger bone near an oxbow lake. He was Robby the piano player.

Robby sat back down to the piano and the conductor walked out and tapped his baton again. The youthful orchestra began playing the French composer, Gabriel Faure's Pavane, Op 50. The director used an arrangement that included Robby on the piano. It was fantastic. When it was over, the audience couldn't stop applauding.

Two more pieces were played and when the concert concluded, proud parents of orchestra musicians, friends, and community leaders were effusive with their praise and photographs. Nathan said, "I am not a classical music guy, but this was good."

"Nothing like this has ever happened before until that musical director showed up and began working with the children. He's from Lithuania and came to the US to study music when he was only 15. We're lucky to have him here in Columbus." Nathan said wiping a tear away from the corner of his eye.

I confessed, "It was the most beautiful thing I've ever heard. Those kids are wonderful. The violins were fantastic!"

The orchestra was photographed over and over. Robby was featured both sitting at the piano and standing next to it. Judy Carter was beside herself with tears of joy. I hugged her and she said, "The orchestra has been invited to play in Jackson for the Governor at a State dinner. Robby will be the featured pianist."

After all of the photos were taken, the children packed up their instruments, parents collected their musical geniuses and left for home. Robby, his mother, Mike, his wife Suzane, Nathan and Roxanne and I drove to Nathan's house to celebrate Robby's musical success. I hitched a ride with Nathan and Roxanne.

As we pulled up to the Turnbull home, two men sat watching from a blue 4-door pickup. One man said, "That Dupart woman is with Sheriff Nate. What do you think is going on with that?"

"Not sure. Friends maybe? But how? We told the others that she was the problem at the dealership. We promised that if we had to, we would get our guys and get rid of her, one way or another. I'm thinking with the Sheriff, we might have to be more careful how we go about it."

"Yeah, I don't trust that Sheriff or his chief deputy, Riley. They ain't family and they ain't no part of our gun club."

Chapter: 27

I enjoyed my time chatting with Sheriff Nathan, Deputy Mike and all of the family members who joined us at Nathan's home. I was talking with Roxanne; she told me about Nathan's wife dying from cancer a little over a year ago.

I noticed that when Robby was with family, he was just like any other lively 9 year old. He was playing a video game, ignoring his sister and cousins while listening to music. I asked Judy, "What kind of piano does he practice on at home?"

Judy said faintly, "Just a standard upright. I can't afford the kind of grand piano he needs for concert practice. He does that at his piano teacher's home and at Miss Vivian's. Besides, we have no room in our house for something that big."

I pulled a handful of my hair in front of me and said, "You know, I could do with a visit to the beauty shop. When do you think you can get me in?"

Surprised, she smiled and said, "Tuesday mornings are generally the best. Wednesday's I work on mostly older women at the senior living home. They can't get out, so I go there. They're grateful for my visits and they tip well."

She admitted, "I'm still hoping I can track down Bob to get him to pay up on Robby's child support. That would help a lot."

"Oh, do you know where he's at?"

"That's the thing. He just disappeared. I can't afford a private detective to find him, or I would. It's odd. He worked from home and was a good father. We had our ups and downs. He didn't make much money. One day, he just took his truck, clothes, some guns and left without saying goodbye."

"Look, I know someone. If you give me everything you can about him like name, birth records, vehicle records, whatever you can think of, my friend might be able to track him down."

"I can't afford that."

"Consider it something from a grateful music fan. Robby needs to have that extra push to take him to the next level. If we can get the dad to help, that might take some of the burden off."

Saturday morning, I sent a detailed email to Chick Farrell at Reliant Security to see what he could do to find Bob Carter. I gave him everything Judy supplied to me. I hoped that Bob could be found, and willing to contribute to Robby and his 6-year-old sister's child support. I am a firm believer that deadbeat dads need to be made accountable and I was glad to pay for this service. Besides, Chick gives me a family and friends discount.

After a good breakfast Saturday morning, I decided to go Magnolia and continue searching through files for people who owed the dealership money. I identified a handful of accounts with especially large balances due to the dealership. Upon checking the payment records, two of them stood out for non-payment.

Mandy Sue apparently was not a Saturday worker, but I was not alone in the accounting office. Bobbi Jo was busy doing her brand of title work. A part time data entry clerk, Sandy, was busy posting documents into the books. This allowed me the freedom to search file cabinets to find out what people bought that amounted to so much debt in the receivables schedule. Cars maybe?

On the payables schedule, I saw a name that confused me, Marion St. Clair. *"Any relation to Troy, the parts manager?"* I wondered. Another other large balance was sent to Doris Butterfield. Once again, I wondered what relation to Lance this person was.

Why was Bucky floating money to people using business funds? The amounts were large. I needed to check invoices to see why the money was given to these women. Of course, Bucky was not going to answer any of my questions.

I left a text message for Sheriff Turnbull that I wanted to give him an update because I planned to drive back to Germantown this afternoon and spend the night. Then I would come back late on Sunday. My own bills were due and they would not wait.

Chapter: 28

While I was busy at Magnolia, Deputy Riley met with Sheriff Turnbull. Nathan said, "Tell me Mike, what have you got on the old murders, so far. Then I'll bring you up to date with what I've found."

"Fair enough. County deeds show Shane Law was the owner of that swamp land before the Tennessee-Tombigbee waterway was constructed. No one knows for sure who owned it before him, because the court house burned down in 1862 and again in 1896. It's believed that land had been in the Law family for generations. A half Choctaw man named Jonas Law was an early settler in Lowndes County. He made a living by trapping, skinning, and preparing beaver and otter for fur. He tanned leather for sale in New Orleans. That is information found in the Columbus historical records."

"That was well before Fats Donahue was alive." Nathan said.

"That's right. Shane Law's occupation in the 1940 census was listed as farmer and the same on the 1960 census. What he farmed was not mentioned. There are not many members of the Law family around any longer, with the exception of our deputy, John."

"So, Law owned the land and Fats was killed on that land. What happened to Law?" Nathan asked.

"Don't know. I couldn't find anything further about Law. He must have skipped because he didn't pay property taxes. Ownership was transferred to Homer Chalmers with a quit claim deed in 1964. The land was basically worthless then. The Tennessee-Tombigbee channel was carved along his western property line. No roads went into that swamp or his land at the oxbow lake. The land around it was declared a nature preserve in the 1970's. I can't see any reason for Homer to own that land back then." Mike said.

"Unless it was to cover up a murder. Did you find out anything about how heavy equipment got onto the island?"

"I checked both military bases around Columbus, and they didn't have any records of equipment being used at that time. They did show me a couple of old photographs and that wasn't any help."

"Okay, but what did you find?" Nathan probed.

"It was the US Army Corp of Engineers who were creating the Tennessee-Tombigbee channel at that time. They had all kinds of heavy equipment. The channel goes right by that property. Calling the place an island where the bodies were found is a mistake. You see, the oxbow lake almost goes around the property on more than three sides, but its drainage from the Luxapallia creek that makes the place an island. Equipment was probably secretly borrowed or stolen from the channel project, then brought in from the levee side. They dug a big hole, buried the car and the men, then took the equipment back to where it was found."

"Very good! That explains the mystery of how the car got buried. I'm guessing they got rid of the car to hide evidence. Now, what was everyone doing on that property when those men got killed? Why did Homer claim ownership of worthless land? That wooden building was solidly built. What was it used for? And who deployed all of those animal traps on the land, and why?"

"All good questions Nathan. That evidence trail is cold. I think the answers to those questions resides within the Chalmers family. They know something. Where did they suddenly get a lot of money back in the 60's to buy a car dealership?" Mike asked.

"You know Dean is still at the State Penitentiary. I might go over there and ask him a few of those questions. I doubt I'll get anything out of him but two of his sons are dead and he might be in a mood to talk." Nathan said.

"Good luck. Tell me what you've found about Grace."

"I questioned neighbors of the Dowd's and got some pretty interesting answers. Drew Dowd was apparently cuckold by the Reverand Samuel Brand. The rascal still preaches at that evangelical tabernacle near the Alabama border. Drew's wife, Sharon, was a devoted follower and involved with the preacher. I believe Drew was ashamed and had nothing to keep him in the area. I'll follow up on that theory. Sharon eventually left the Reverand and moved to Mobile. I've tried contacting both parents to let them know Grace has been discovered. So far, I can't find either one of them."

"Are you thinking the dad killed Grace?" Mike asked.

"Not really. He left two years before Grace disappeared. I think the reason for leaving was the wife. No, our killer was someone else and that person may still be in Columbus."

"Who did Grace know back then?" Mike asked.

"I tracked down a few of her former classmates. They are all about 20 or so by now. Those I spoke to remembered Grace. A couple of them said she was having a lot of problems at home. Her parents were constantly arguing, her father left. She felt abandoned."

"One classmate, I've not talked to, is Mandy Sue. She's a Chalmer's and she works at the car dealership. I understand the girls were close when they were in school." Nathan said.

"What was Grace doing then?"

"Babysitting. Oddly enough, she sat for three of the boys who discovered her severed finger. Pete Baker, Billy St. Clair and our piano genius, Robby Carter." Nathan said.

"I think she or Bobbi Jo may have sat for us back then."

"I'm trained to not believe in coincidences, but this one is beyond belief. Grace was a girl trapped between bickering parents and one of them left. She was struggling for approval. She frequently met with Judge Horne. He told me she wanted him to find her father. I don't think he ever tried."

"Just thinking, Joe Baker is Pete's dad, Troy St. Clair is Billy's dad, and Bob Carter is Robby's Dad. Both Bob and Drew took off about the time that Grace went missing. These adults hired Grace to watch their kids. It's not unheard of, you know, for men to become attracted to a babysitter." Mike speculated.

"I've considered that and yes, I think all of them are suspects for Grace's murder." Nathan said.

"So, who do we have, so far?"

"Joe Baker, Troy St. Clair, Bob Carter, The Reverand Brand, and Drew Dowd are on my list And Judge Horne as a maybe. I still need to question Mandy Sue Chalmers and Bobbi Jo. Did Grace go willingly to that oxbow property or was she taken by force against her will? Did another girl go with her?" Nathan asked.

"It will be interesting to see what Annette digs up at the dealership. I understand Mandy Sue and Troy St. Clair have both been uncooperative. And I think we should note that Joe Baker has been making unwanted advances toward Judy Carter."

"Annette is leaving and will return Sunday evening. I think you and I will finish up here and enjoy a nice weekend. I plan to do a little fishing. I believe that's our girl, Annette, now."

"Well, Mark likes to help with that old project pickup truck were working on. I just want to forget about murder for a while."

Chapter: 29

I walked to my Camaro parked in the service lot with the intention of going to the courthouse before driving to Germantown. Something caught my eye. I don't know how long they had been waiting for me, but they were easy to spot. I saw two fairly heavy looking, older men, both wearing stocking caps to cover their hair and N95 Covid masks to cover their faces and beards. They were crouched behind my Camaro.

They popped up like meerkats, and both were armed. I reached to my belt holster and withdrew my Beretta 92M9 and pointed it first at one man then the other.

One of the men shouted, "Damn, she's got a gun!"

I said, "Drop your weapons, Now! Do so or I will shoot and kill both of you." My body was turned sidewise to the men, making me a difficult target. I said, "Don't make me wait. One, Two…"

"Okay, okay!" The man nearest to me threw down his gun and they both took off and quickly ran away, clumsily ducking around and between parked cars. I thought, *"They move pretty fast for old fat men."*

I sighed, put my gun back into my holster, then unlocked my car. For good measure, I used a tissue to pick up the handgun behind my car then looked around to make sure no one else was lurking. I got into my Camaro and drove to the Sheriff's office.

When I arrived, I told the Sheriff about my encounter at the Magnolia parking lot. I presented the handgun to him, holding it with the tissue I used before. He said, "You stared down two men with guns? Then you threatened to kill them and they ran away?" He began to chuckle.

"Two white males about five-six and both were well over 200 pounds. I've got to say, they moved pretty fast for pork on the hoof. They wore stocking caps and N95 masks over their nose and mouth. I could identify both in a line-up. They wore dirty jeans and plaid shirts. The one nearest to me had new Skecher athletic shoes. Oh, and he had a tattoo of a catfish on his gun arm."

I saw Mike roll his eyes and he said, "Sawyer!"

Nathan asked, "What do you think they wanted? Did they want to rob you, take your car, kill you or scare you off?"

"They didn't have a chance to tell me. My guess is they were not killers, or they would have just shot me. They were probably doing what someone from the dealership asked them to do. They want me out of the business and I'm refusing to leave."

Nathan laughed, "You are one determined young woman."

"They'll get their wish, at least for tonight. I'm going to Germantown and will be back tomorrow evening or Monday morning. Here's my summary of things I found while poking through the accounts payable and receivable files. There are a lot of buried bodies in that accounting system. With Bucky and his brother dead, I'm thinking you should have someone watch the business in case they decide to burn the place down to cover their crimes."

Mike said, "Woah! You think they might go that far?"

"Someone committed murder twice that I know of, and they threatened me. Yes, I think they might do just that."

Nathan turned and asked his top Deputy, "What do you think Mike? Who do we have to cover that building?"

"I'll call the Fire Chief to see if his people can keep an eye on the place during their weekend shifts."

"I'm leaving as soon as we're done here," I said.

"Drive careful. Please let the desk know when you get back to the B&B.

"I will, thank you."

Chapter: 30

Sunday morning, I was slow to get out of bed. My trip to Columbus had completely worn me out. I padded to the kitchen deciding coffee was the better part of morning valor before I took my early morning run.

The aroma and flavor of the coffee helped to awaken my brain cells to the point where it was time to pull on my running clothes for my 5-mile run. I installed my iPods and wore my best running shoes. The run around Germantown was familiar with people walking their dogs. They waved or said, "Hi Annette!" as I trotted the streets and parks before arriving back to my apartment.

I sent an email to Wolf and Ezra last night before going to bed. In bullet point, I outlined what I discovered at the dealership. I also made them aware I was home.

I have to admit sleeping in my own bed last night was like sleeping on a cloud in heaven. I was not looking forward to driving back to Columbus, but I knew the Sheriff was depending on me to be their inside person to help find potential suspects for both Bucky and Eddie's murders. Besides, LeDuc and Johnson was getting paid my consulting fee from them, so I was on the clock.

I was doing laundry when Wolf called my cell. "Annette, I'm glad you're back."

"Two people have been murdered since I arrived in Columbus. Sheriff Turnbull thinks it's because of things I discovered during my audit. He wants me to stay and dig further into files and report what I find to him."

"So, where does our audit now stand?" Wolf asked.

"Right now, it's unknown who will take over the business. The dealership is barely running. If anyone is in charge, it's the office manager, Mandy Sue. She and her assistants cut the payroll and titled the car sales. She's the fox in charge of the henhouse."

"Your email said, you and she are at odds. She's not cooperating?" Wolf asked.

"Not cooperating. But I'm there with the reason our contract is still valid. She has no answer for that. I'm thinking the two armed dufuses in the parking lot were sent by Mandy or her boyfriend, to scare me away."

"Do you think she and this Lance murdered Bucky?"

"Anything is possible. She's a second or third niece. Families have been known to knock each other off, you know. That's for the Sheriff. Bucky's and Eddie's deaths were well planned. I believe someone out there plans to either destroy the dealership or take it over. They've milked a lot of cash out of the business."

"If you go back, what will you do there?"

"Oh, I'm going back. For one thing, Mandy needs to cut a check to LeDuc and Johnson, for our services and expenses. I also would like to find out what happened to Jill, the payroll clerk. She avoided me when I tried to check on her. I think she's in fear for her life. And I want Judy to do my hair. I'll see this thing through."

"I'll ask again, should I come over and help?" Wolf asked.

"To keep me safe?"

"No! Four eyes are better than two. I could work in the sales department while looking over your shoulder."

"No offence, but I would rather have Chick Farrell and Clarence looking over my shoulder. By the way, Chick was looking into two missing dads for me."

"Missing dads?"

"Robby Carter's father, Bob, who left five years ago, about the same time the dead girl went missing. Is there a connection? Unknown. But if I can find him, his wife Judy may be able to collect child support for her two children. The son, Robby, is a really great piano player who needs financial support to follow his talent. He's that good. The other dad's been gone seven years."

"So, you're going back to protect a payroll clerk and to help find the father of a child prodigy piano player. Is that about right?"

"Yeah, and to find Grace's dad, Drew, too. But I really want to know who killed Bucky and Eddie after I was hired."

Two people killed and more who may have died in the past. Do you think this is all connected, somehow?" Wolf asked.

"The number of deaths makes this look like the fall of the House of Usher. Instead, it's the fall of the house of Magnolia Fine Cars."

"Interesting comparison. I take it, you don't want my help. I'll contact Baxter today. He and I discussed a plan that might help you in Columbus. I might yet come over. Let me know if anything changes. Be careful, I don't want to tell our Aunt Eulalie what happened to you."

I smiled and said, "Our Aunt will never hear about any of this, and neither will my mother, understand?"

Wolf and I disconnected. Confident that Wolf's call to Baxter would work, I went to the grocery store to restock my refrigerator before I left town. With my laundry folded, my carpet vacuumed, my dishes cleaned and the fridge restocked for when I came back. I was now ready to return to central Mississippi in the morning and complete my self-imposed mission to root out whoever is murdering people involved with Magnolia Fine Cars.

Chapter: 31

Thankfully, my drive back to the B&B was uneventful. This time, I brought a couple of dresses along, just in case. I planned to have Jill do my hair while I was here this week. Perhaps I would cut my hair to shoulder length, and have it feathered like I did this last year. I thought the effect was nice and easy to take care of.

Not knowing what I would face today, I chose to wear a tan skort with a blue loose top and sweater, so I would have access to my thigh holster and Nano. I also carried my 92M9 Beretta in my purse. I didn't want to look like GI Jane but would not leave anything to chance. People are playing for keeps and I did not intend to become a victim.

I sent a text to Sheriff Turnbull to let him know that I would be in the accounting office at Magnolia, should he need me.

He quickly responded with a phone call. "You were right. Fire was attempted and stopped. No serious damage behind the building. A deputy is on duty at the dealership today, along with a local police officer. They're waiting for you to come in."

"A fire? Wow! What did they hope to accomplish? Are they trying to destroy the business or create havoc?"

"That, I hope you can provide an answer to while you are there. Your lawyer, Baxter Grey, sent his suggestion to Judge Horne and he is moving forward with that brief this morning. You'll get notice. Go in, a deputy will be with you. And keep me informed."

"Yes, Sir." I said and hung up.

Mandy Sue was in her office working. She looked up when I walked into the accounting office. Jill was busy working at her desk and so was everyone else, including a surprisingly alert Blanche. I sat down and logged into the dealership's computer.

Mandy Sue stood up straightened her dress and walked out to where I was sitting. I looked up and she said, "You! I thought you were gone. I know you signed a contract with Bucky when he was alive to help him out of 'Warranty Jail', but as I stated last week, your services are no longer needed. Pick up your things and leave."

I nodded pleasantly and said, "Yes he did and he asked that we look for ways to improve cash flow and profitability. That's what I have been doing and I'm still doing. What I need to know now, what is *your* role in the dealership by asking me to leave?"

Mandy gave me a death stare. Then she said, "Why, I'm the office manager. Blanche will agree to that. I am making the financial decisions for the business right now." She gave me an aloof pose.

"Okay. I can see why you're saying that. But by what authority? Is there a successor to Bucky, we should be talking to?"

"I'm a Chalmers family member and so is Troy and a dozen other employees. All of us think you should go, now!"

"Well, in that case…but do you hold any stock in the company? In other words, do you have any real authority to void my contract? I work for your corporation. You've paid us nothing so far. I need to finalize my audit report for the shareholders."

Mandy looked surprised. "Report, for what?"

"For the courts, of course. Bucky's will has yet to be read. If he names a successor, the car manufacturer will require an accounting audit for succession of the franchise to go into effect. My document will help them with that. Also, if the dealership is accused of warranty fraud, Ezra's and my documents will be used in court for any criminal charges that will be made. Do you have a good attorney, Mandy Sue?"

Her mouth fell open, and no words tumbled out.

I continued, "Two people have been murdered, and I was held at gunpoint in your service parking lot Saturday. Authorities are interested in finding out why. I'm thinking you and maybe a couple of family members think you can just take over the dealership to steal money."

Mandy's eyes narrowed. She said, "What do you know?"

"I know you'll need a lot of legal help if your plan is to succeed. In the meantime. I am here, and as we speak, I'm being appointed as a 'Friend of the Court.' I am appointed as the official care-taker manager of this business. My role will be to offer expert advice with options and audit data to help the court make an intelligent decisions about how to proceed civilly and criminally.

"Proceed?"

"Yes. With regard to the disposition of the business assets and with any criminal charges that may be forthcoming. Once again, I ask, do you, Lance and Uncle Troy have good attorneys?"

"Lance? Why are you talking about Lance?"

"It's pretty obvious, don't you think. You and he are as close as bread and butter. Whatever one of you is into so is the other."

Mandy stammered when she said, "Y-You can't just come in here and take this dealership away! It's mine! I run this business. I'm calling Lance now to get you out of here."

"I'm afraid I can come in here. It's not me, it's the law until Bucky's estate is settled and the car factory decides what to do with the franchise."

Blanche stood up and marched to where I was sitting. She yelled, "You witch. How dare you. If Dean were here, he would poop his pants and toss you into the street."

I laughed. "Colorful image. Mr. Dean is in prison and two of his sons are dead. Members of the Chalmers family are the ones in deep do-do, not me. Your problems began when you decided to just take money whenever you wanted. That's called larceny and fraud."

I looked over at Bobbi Jo and said, "I have no evidence of your title washing, only hearsay. If you wish to avoid prosecution, you should pick up your toys and leave as soon as possible."

"You can't do that!" She shouted.

"I can and I am doing so, right now." I picked up my cellphone, and speed-dialed a number then said, "Now, Deputy!"

Deputy Tom was standing outside the door. He stepped through and said, "All files and records of Magnolia Fine Cars are now under the protection of the Lowndes County Court. Miss Bobbi, I am escorting you from the building, leave everything on your desk. Mandy Sue, the same goes for you. Blanche, you, and the other ladies may remain, but I warn you, do not to destroy any files or documents under threat of prosecution and time in prison."

"Thank you, Deputy Tom." I said.

Blanche looked at me slack jawed and asked, "Just who the hell are you lady?"

"Thanks for calling me a lady. I'm the one whose putting an end to this circus of fraud and death. Now, you can either help me, or you can leave right now." I said staring her down.

I turned and addressed the women in the room. "Beginning now, we are going to find out who's murdering people at Magnolia Cars and attempting to destroy this dealership. I have documented fraud, graft and corruption that is taking place in this business. You either help me find out who's behind these crimes or you may leave. Each of you know something, it's time you told me what you know."

The office staff looked at one another, stunned by my bold announcement. As Mandy and Bobbi were escorted out, I marched into her office, sat down, and opened the accounts payable schedule on her computer. I cut a check to LeDuc and Johnson for the invoice I submitted last week. My immediate plan was to keep the wheels on the car dealership rolling until Bucky's will was read. Then it was up to the shareholders to decide what to do.

The women in the office were unusually quiet at their desks. I wondered if any of them would bolt and run. Surprisingly, they all remained seated and went back to work chatting away with one another. I heard the occasional loud chuckle.

I focused on the accounts payables books, and questions immediately came to mind. I would be digging deeper until I understood where all of the dealership's money was going.

I thought I knew who the new majority stockholder was. I intended to meet with that person at my first opportunity. The day was young and all I wanted to do now was not fall off the skateboard I had just gotten onto.

Chapter: 32

"Any word from Miss Annette about who may have killed Bucky or Eddie?" Mike Riley asked.

"No, but she and her attorney have given us a gift. They have conspired with Judge Horne to take control of the dealership to protect records and secure proof of the unfettered abuse of business assets to commit theft and fraud. She believes a number of family members are involved with these schemes." Nathan Turnbull said.

"Take control, how?" Mike asked surprised.

"Today, she was named 'A Friend of the Court."

"I'm not sure what that means." Mike said.

"It means she will seize control of Magnolia Fine Cars to protect records for the Lowndes County Court. County prosecutors, probate judges and possibly a grand jury will review what she has found and make decisions about civil and criminal matters she is bringing to light."

"Wow! I guess your convincing her to stay makes you a genius. Well done, Nathan."

"I would like to take credit, but this last move was done entirely without me."

"But it's a good thing, right? I'm hoping there is enough proof in those accounting records that hold up. We still don't have any leads for who killed Bucky or his brother." Mike said.

"No, but she provided me with a lead on one of the missing fathers, Bob Carter." Nathan said raising his eyebrows.

"So quick? On Robby's dad? Where is he?" Mike asked.

"Australia. He's working for a computer tech company in Melbourne. He's trying to become an Australian citizen, and he has another family."

"So, my former brother-in-law has another family? When Judy filed for divorce a couple of years ago she didn't know where to send the papers. I wonder how long he's lived there?"

"Long enough to get married and father two children."

"Uh-oh! Bigamy! This could turn out to be a mess in family court. He owes five years of child support and now he'll have to face charges of bigamy. Has anyone contacted him yet?" Mike asked.

"Not that I'm aware of. Annette said the company she uses, Reliant Security, dig up a whole file on Bob. How he's contacted will depend on Judy. I think you should suggest a good lawyer to handle the matter for your sister," Nathan said.

"I don't think there's one around here that handle's international law. She'll need some expensive lawyer from New Orleans or Chicago to go after Bob. She may even need a lawyer in Australia to handle the matter which could require her going there."

"Tell her to call Delta Figg. Right now, Bob Carter is a suspect along with several others for Grace Dowds' murder. How he's contacted needs to be handled with kid gloves." Nathan said.

"Should I tell Judy?"

"Absolutely. I think you should. She should file papers for child support and should do so right away. She may scare Bob enough for him to reply. Bob left five years ago; Robby and his younger sister need to know their father is still alive and living with kangaroos." Nathan said.

"Today is her day off. She works at Olson's Grocery as a part time checker. I'll go over there to deliver the news. Thanks, Nathan.

"I plan to continue visiting people around town to find out who's fond of Southern Comfort. I believe the killer is leaving a trail of Southern Comfort to tease us, and I think they like that liquor."

"Can't stand the stuff myself, sweet and fruity. Not my thing." Mike said.

"Me either." Nathan agreed.

Chapter: 33

It was the following Monday when they arrived. They showed up in force. A team of twelve car company employees in three full sized Chevy Suburbans arrived. They marched into the dealership and slapped down paperwork at the receptionist desk claiming ownership of all new automobiles and the parts inventory.

Of course, Bucky's receptionist niece had no idea of what she was looking at or even who to send the factory people to, since no one was in charge. Several days ago, Mandy Sue and her title clerk were escorted from the building by Sheriff's deputies.

"We demand to see the Dealer, Bucky Chalmers, or your General Manager. I'm Terri Foster, field warranty manager for the factory that supplies all of the new cars on your lot and the parts in this dealership. I'm here to assume control of this business and all of its assets," she said with flair.

"Uh, my Uncle Bucky, died a couple of weeks ago. Eddie, the Sales Manager is also dead, and our office manager, well, she left a few days ago." She threw up her hands indicating that what they wanted was out of her control.

Terri looked totally confused. She was used to storming in and reclaiming inventory by presenting UCC lien paperwork to frightened employees and demonstrating her right of ownership for property on behalf of her company. She had done so six times and always got what she wanted using this intimidation tactic."

"Well then, who's in charge?" Terri demanded.

"Don't know for sure. Miss Annette is in the accounting office. She took over the business. You might ask her."

"What?" Terri shouted. "Another lien holder? We'll see about that. I have first dibs on all property. Where's this office?"

The receptionist pointed the way. Terri and her entourage thundered down the hallway ready to storm the Bastille. Deputy Tom stood his ground and barred their way. Terri raised her voice and shouted, "Out of my way Deputy Dog, I have a legal right to be here, and I demand to see who's in charge."

"Sorry, ma'am. I cannot allow you to do that."

Terri tried to push Deputy Tom aside and he calmly said, "Do not touch me. If you do so again, you will be arrested. I've called for backup and they should be here any minute."

"I am with the car manufacturer. We believe the dealer is out of trust. We're here to recover assets owned by my company. You cannot stand in my way. Do you understand?"

The Deputy patiently said, "The Sheriff will be here shortly. Take your people to the customer waiting area. He will sort this out. I am here by an order from the Lowndes County Court to protect the building and its contents. Now, please, do as I say. Wait quietly and I'm sure you'll get answers to all of your questions, very soon."

Terri had never come up against this problem. She was always able to bully her way into a dealership and seize cars, trucks, and parts inventory at will. She pivoted on her heel and said, "Come on. We'll sit in the Suburbans and wait while I call legal in Detroit."

I was sitting at Mandy Sue's desk reviewing technician pay when I heard the disturbance. Deputy Tom entered the accounting office. I asked what was going on. He said, "There's some people from the factory. I think they want to shut the store down."

I exhaled and said, "Are they outside?"

"Not yet."

"Tell them to stay put. Do not to let anyone have access to the accounting office until the Sheriff arrives. Then, the county prosecutor, the Sheriff and I will meet them in the conference room. I'll call Nathan and Emanual now."

"Yes, Ma'am."

Chapter: 34

An hour and a half after the car company people arrived, legal minds bickered with one another on the phone. Lawyers in Detroit and lawyers in the county prosecutor's office worked out all of the details. It was decided that my role as a 'Friend of the Court' took precedence over a warranty fraud raid by the car company.

The county was investigating two capital murders and several felonious crimes and was searching for evidence to be presented to the court. It was agreed that the UCC filings would be honored in due course, but the county court demanded detailed proof of all claims of fraud and theft before UCC filings could be honored.

By the time I met with Terri and her army of eager employees in the conference room, she was totally steamed. I offered to shake hands and she refused. Instead, we sat down at the conference table to begin our meeting.

Terri stood up and began a rant about her authority to claim property belonging to the car company. The Prosecutor cut her off and said, "Please, sit down Miss Foster. This was all covered by our phone call with Detroit. You will have time to present your case, but first, we will explain our position to you."

The Lowndes County Prosecutor is a handsome young black man by the name of Emanual Jackson. He was not much older than me. He was impeccably dressed, very confident and well spoken. I'm betting he was dynamic in front of a jury. He laid out the argument he presented to the Detroit lawyers. He wrapped up by saying, "No one denies your right to claim inventory based on any evidence you have that proves fraud against your company. Timing is the issue here."

He checked his watch and said, "4:00, our Sheriff has locked down the dealership and sent the employees home. This property is now secured by the Lowndes County Sheriff's department. No one will touch any document or item of inventory. I am now presenting you with a 48 hour cease and desist order. I trust you and your people have adequate lodging for the evening?"

Terri was in a state of shock. She said, "You do not understand. It's not just me and my staff, we have three car carrier trucks, two semi-trucks and trailers parked out there to gather up the cars and parts. They're on the clock. What am I to do with them?"

The Prosecutor gave her a stern look and said, "48 Hours Miss Foster."

The Prosecutor called the meeting to an end for the evening. I stood up and Terri pushed her way past a Deputy and she asked me, "Who the hell *are* you, and what is a Friend of the Court?"

I smiled and said, "I can see you are new to diplomatic negotiation. Let me help you. You are here, because Ezra Johnson of LeDuc and Johnson made a phone call to your boss in Detroit. He told him about corrections being made on disputed warranty claims. You were scheduled to come in next week to do an audit. Instead, you showed up to close down the business. To answer your question, I am Annette Dupart, a CPA and auditor for LeDuc and Johnson out of Germantown, TN."

"What gives you special consideration here, Miss CPA?"

"If you cool off and think, you will realize that I am not your enemy. I have documented many concerns with business practices at this dealership. I have been appointed by the court because I am collecting evidence that will ultimately point to one or more people responsible for the murder of both Mr. Chalmers. Now, we can do this together or you can take your attitude and go back to Atlanta."

Terri was unused to people talking to her in this manner. She said, "You know, I can get you fired."

"I doubt that, but I would rather work toward a cooperative solution than take an adversarial position. Wouldn't you, Terri? Our goals are similar but mine are on a broader scale than shutting down a local business that hires over 130 people in Columbus."

Terri looked unconvinced and I said, "Where are you staying? Why don't you and I have dinner tonight? We can talk this over where there aren't so many people," I suggested.

Terri said, "First, I need to figure out what to do with all of those truckers and hired help." She said pointing. "Okay, I'll send some of my staff back to Atlanta in the morning. The truckers will have to leave then come back when we have access. I'm staying at the Marriott. How about you, are you a local?"

"No. Germantown is not local. I can meet you at The Old Hickory House Steak restaurant. They have excellent food."

"Okay, allow me time to handle the truckers and my people. Is 7:30 okay?"

"7:30 is fine. I'm looking forward to our meeting." I said.

Terri, a woman in her mid-to-late-30's, stomped off in high heel boots. I said to Nathan, "That went well, don't you think?"

He laughed and said, "She's a pushy type. You going to be alright? I can have a Deputy accompany you if you like."

"Nah! That's okay, thanks. I don't think she's as tough as she thinks she is. Thanks for your department's help today. I think we averted a disaster."

"I just want all of the proof to go to the grand jury when they convene, then we can nail whoever killed Bucky and Eddie."

"I hope so, too." I said.

Chapter: 35

Last night, the more Chablis Terri Foster drank, the more she mellowed and became quite giggly. She confessed to being under a lot of pressure from her boss to meet a performance objectives to save the company money. Magnolia Fine Cars seemed like the perfect target. It was her decision to go to Columbus and shut down the car dealer, thereby claiming a substantial victory.

Her plan would have worked if it hadn't been for me. At dinner I said, "Ezra Johnson discovered some parts on warranty claims were never installed. The signature on all warranty claims is Blane Sloan, the service manager. I've met him, he had no idea what he was signing. This was all the work of a couple of employees who are now being investigated by the Sheriff."

"Are they related to the Chalmers family?" Terri asked.

"Yes, Blane Sloan and Mandy Sue are Chalmers. Lance Butterfield, the shop foreman, and Mandy Sue are a couple. He has total control over the shop, including warranty repairs and claims. Not sure I understand how Lance intimidated Blane to do this."

"This Lance, how come he's not the service manager?"

"Not family. Also, Lance has recruited several Hispanics who work in the shop for minimum wage without benefits. They do repair work, including warranty work. Lance signs off on it."

"Undocumented workers? That's illegal, isn't it? How do those technicians get paid for that work?"

"I do not know if they *are* undocumented. They pay them in cash at the end of every week, but I believe they're not certified."

"Okay, tell me why you think I shouldn't close this dealership down and pull the franchise?" Terry slurred.

"The car dealership hires about 130 people from Columbus and the surrounding area. That would have a devastating impact on the economy of the city and county if all of these people suddenly lost their jobs. I'm thinking a more gradual transition of ownership is a more logical solution."

"Gradual? How so?" She asked with crossed eyes. I could tell she was getting woozy.

"One thing my firm does is to find well financed buyers for car dealerships. We keep the business running and the employees keep their jobs until a new owner takes over. The bad eggs, like Ezra and I discovered, are taken out of the mix to correct fraud."

"So, are you saying, I should not do my warranty audit? I don't think you can do that."

"No, no! You perform your warranty audit. Find the deficiencies, charge the business back with penalties. That's your right and good business practice. Sloan needs to attend Service Manager training if he wants a job. If he refuses, he'll be replaced."

"So, are you going to fire people?"

"Not within my authority. But I did send home Mandy Sue who set up a lot of the fraud schemes and the title clerk, Bobbi Jo, who was performing illegal title washing. Mandy's boyfriend, Lance, needs to go but Sloan doesn't seem willing to take charge of the shop. I have no one else to handle the work."

"You seem to have a lot of ideas. When and how will you do all of these things?"

"As a caretaker manager, I'm calling all of the employees back to work tomorrow morning. I'm asking the prosecutor to file fraud charges against Mandy Sue, and Lance Butterfield I expect them to be arrested by noon if they show up."

"Where does that leave me and my company?" Terri asked.

"With Mandy gone, Bucky and Eddie residing at the car lot resort in the sky, we have an opportunity to clean up the dealership. The business will go back to using factory financing and after-warranty policies. I know Magnolia failed to order vehicles from your sales rep. That changes immediately. Your rep needs to come here and take an order for new vehicles this week."

"Not in my wheelhouse." Terri said slurping her wine.

"Like I said, I'm just a caretaker manager working for the county. It will not take long for a potential buyer to make an offer."

"Offer? Bucky's dead and so is his brother, who then?"

"The corporation's majority stockholder, Bucky's wife, Vivian Chalmers. I plan to visit her. It'll be interesting to see where she stands with nepotism that has been the sticky glue holding this business together."

"Okay. I admit, I had you all wrong. I'll call Atlanta and tell them what's going on and why we should keep this dealership market area open. If you talk to Mr. Ezra, tell him that our department is grateful for his report. I'm a little tipsy now. It would be helpful if you could outline what you told me in an email. I'll use your thoughts for *my* plan to save the sales point." She handed her card to me. I thought, *"This must be her idea of collaboration."*

"Good. Be careful, people are getting killed around here."

Terri looked horrified. She said, "Killed, are you sure?"

What I didn't see on my way back to the B&B were two men in a blue 4-door pickup truck. One of them asked, "Who was that other woman?"

"She's from the factory. They're here to close the store."

Chapter: 36

School was officially out for summer, when the boys called their first meeting of the Finger Bone Club. They met beside the 400 year old oak tree in the city park. All of them had been with Robby when he discovered the finger of Grace Dowd. They discussed the impact of the finger's discovery, and they were thrilled with their short brush with fame and the reason for naming their club.

A couple of weeks later, Billy St. Clair, called for another meeting of the Finger Bone Club and asked them to meet behind the large Gateway Film Center movie theater building.

The boys arrived and parked their bikes. Their purpose was to discuss Grace Dowd and ask how things were going in their homes. Some parents were home, not working. Others just chose not to go into Magnolia for work. Parents were unhappy.

"Yeah, I remember Grace," Mark said.

"Me, too," Robby said. "She was alright, I guess."

Billy said, "She sat for almost all of us, along with the other two, Mandy Sue and Bobbi Jo."

"I remember Bobbi Jo. She never paid much attention to us."
Pete said kicking a pebble. "I remember Grace, too."

Oron asked, "Okay why are we here? What's so important? I
have a pick-up baseball game I'm missing."

Robby added, "And I have a piano lesson."

"Okay, okay, we all have things to do. I just wanted to find
out how things were at your houses. My dad came home early, and
was in a bad mood, still in a bad mood. He kept saying over and
over, 'she could be right'." Billy said.

Lawrence said, "Yeah, Uncle Lance ain't happy either. He
was yelling and throwing things around his house, mad as hell. He
put a dent in Mandy's car. She's not happy either. She was sent
home. Both are saying bad things. Mom threatened to leave."

Oron and DeShawn began to talk at once and Pete said, "My
dad says it's all that woman's fault. The one with the black hair. She
came to the car store, then everything went bad."

"Mine too," a couple of the boys chimed in.

"What did she do?" Mark asked.

"How could she just send everyone home?" Robby wanted to
know.

"My dad says they need to do something about her," Pete
said. Everyone stopped talking and stared at Pete.

"Like what?" Billy asked.

Pete put a finger to his throat and drew it across to mimic cutting Annette's throat.

"No! He didn't say that?" Mark asked.

"Well, my Dad is sure mad as hell." Oron said.

"Maybe *we* could do something." Pete suggested.

"Yeah! Maybe we can grab her, tie her up, and throw her into the Tennessee-Tombigbee channel," Billy suggested.

Both Robby and Mark were quiet. Mark couldn't believe his ears. The boys were wanting to attack the woman and hurt her. His dad told him she was a good woman and was working with him and Sheriff Turnbull. Robby met Annette. She seemed okay to him, but he didn't know what to think. Violence was not in his nature.

The boys went on arguing, trying to outdo one another by dreaming up devious ways to punish Annette.

Oron said, "I heard she was at my uncle's place when he was shot and killed. Maybe she's the one who killed Grandpa Bucky."

"We need a gun," Lawrence blurted out.

"Everyone around here has a gun. That's no big deal," Pete said. "And what would you do, kill her?" Pete said taunting.

"No. I mean I'll get the gun, and we can use it to shoot that woman." Lawrence said with a serious look.

It was Billy who said, "I don't think we need to kill anyone. I mean, we would all go to jail."

"Nah," DeShawn said. "We're just kids, they wouldn't put us in jail, would they, Mark?"

Mark was cornered. His loyalty to the club was being tested. "Yes, they can. My dad told me that shooting somebody and killing them is a felony. Kids are tried as adults. In fact, all of us here, would go to jail for planning to do something bad to someone."

"I ain't done nothing." DeShawn said.

"Me neither," Billy chimed in.

"No, but talking about it is wrong. If something happens to her, and one of us did it, we're all in trouble. My dad has told me about kids that use guns. They go to jail for a long time."

Robby suddenly said, "Sorry, I've got to go. Piano, you know."

The boys all respected Robby's skill with the piano. They envied his talent and wished they could do something so cool. But they still didn't know what to do to help the angry adults in their families.

Chapter: 37

The next morning, the receptionist and I methodically called every employee requesting that they return to the dealership and report to work. Some calls went to voice mail and others agreed to return to work.

Customer cars were lined up outside the shop waiting for someone to write up their concerns. Slowly, one by one, most of the employees showed up for work. Customers complained about the wait, but they were eventually taken care of.

I was sitting at a desk in the showroom floor surrounded by salesmen who joined me for a sales meeting. I brought donuts, they brought chairs, we sat and talked until the meeting started.

I said, "You can see stacks of file folders in the conference room. Those are warranty claims sent to the car company for payment. Most were fraudulently stuffed with extra labor operation codes and parts. Your dealership was cheating the manufacturer for personal profit. The people responsible will be held accountable. You need to know this activity will no longer be tolerated."

"Okay, but are we still in business? I heard we were being shut down. Some say, it's your fault," Morton Chalmers said.

"The business is not being closed down. Your jobs are good. From now on, all car deals will be reviewed for errors and trades will be scrutinized. You'll get paid on the true margin. There will be no 'special deals'. We will build a reputation of honesty. Play by the rules, or you play someplace else. If something doesn't seem right, or somebody threatens you, come to me and let me know."

An older sales man chewing tobacco, spit into a cup and said, "You're just a kid. What do you know about car deals?"

His question amused me. "Thank you for the compliment. I'm an accounting CPA. I know exactly what goes into a car deal. I know when the company is getting cheated and I know when the customer is getting cheated. Mistakes can be made, but no one will make a dirty deal." I gave him a knowing stare.

"We sell mostly used cars because Eddie refused to stock very many new vehicles on the lot. We couldn't even dealer trade because we had almost no inventory to trade," Lou Chalmers said.

I said, "I agree! Eddie the shark, bless his soul, is no longer with us. He didn't stock cars. The car company rep will be sending new cars and trucks, starting this week. I want one of you to step up and become our new inventory manager, Lou? From now on, there will be no more than two of you in the sales tower at a time. The rest of you will work the phones and the floor for sales."

"Your pay plans will change and may again. Your pay will be based on what you sell and how you use your time."

"Dealership doors will remain open three nights a week till 8:00 PM and on Saturday from 9:00 to 7:00. Football and basketball games will be televised on the floor for you and the customers."

One of the salesmen shouted, "Oh yeah! We've got a new Sheriff in town!"

I laughed and said, "Sheriff Turnbull may not like that idea. I'm asking you to get out and sell more vehicles. Take orders for cars and trucks that customers want; we'll get them. Sales will be posted on a sales board. Last note, the car company woman, Terri Foster, is here to clean up warranty. Stay out of her way."

On the way out of the room, I could hear one of them say, "She sure is a feisty one, ain't she?" That made me smile.

Terri walked in as the salesmen were walking to their desks. She said, "They seem happy. What did you do, tell them you were leaving?"

"Very funny. Here's that list of things you wanted. The files you requested are on the table. Feel free to get more if you need them. You have full access to the copy machine. The conference room is now your warranty audit room."

"Very accommodating, Miss Dupart. Thank you." Terri said.

Chapter: 38

Leaving for lunch, I looked around the parking lot and didn't see anyone waiting to leap out and surprise me. Today, I found a bottle of Southern Comfort next to my car in the parking lot. I have no idea what it was for. So, I went to Wanda's to order a chicken sandwich. I kept my eye out looking for a blue 4-door pickup truck.

I walked out of the restaurant, with a vanilla shake in one hand and a bag of chicken in the other. Standing in front of me, I saw a boy about 4 foot tall next to my Camaro door. The youth appeared to be a boy of mixed race. He had a short afro hairdo. He wore a loose shirt over jeans that were too big for him.

I thought he was just hungry and wanted my food. That was before he pointed the gun at me. My Beretta 92M9 was in my shoulder bag and my hands were full. I don't care if he is 9 or 99. At 15 feet away he had a gun pointed at me. It was either me or him.

I quickly rejected evasive action, like throwing my food at him and ducking behind a car. Instead, I stood my ground and said, "You seem to be upset. Why do you want to shoot me?"

"You took my Uncle's job away and the jobs of all my friends families. Lady, you've got to pay."

You can never take an unsteady child with a gun for granted. More than likely, he will shoot me to see how it feels. Or he could accidentally shoot himself. I took a deep breath and said, "Everyone is back to work at Magnolia today. I didn't send them home. The factory people sent them home. I brought them back. If you shoot me, you are making a big mistake, and you will go to prison."

"That's what Mark said but it's too late now. I have to see this through."

"Its not too late. If you shoot me, the police and Sheriff's deputies will hunt you down. They'll shoot you first and you'll never be able to tell anyone why you're angry. That's what you want, isn't it? You want to tell everyone your family has been treated unfairly?"

"Uncle Lance, he's real mad. You sent him home and Miss Mandy, too. He and some men from the gun club want to take you out someplace where no one will ever find you."

Out of the corner of my eye, I saw Deputy Riley approaching slowly behind cars, his gun drawn. This was not going to end well.

"Keep talking." I thought. "So, you didn't want your uncle to get into trouble, and you decided to come after me yourself, right?"

"I suppose."

"Lance is back at work today. He'll be paid for the days he missed. Put the gun down, I'll buy you a milk shake and take you to him."

"I don't know."

"Come on! A milk shake and you won't get into trouble. We can talk about what's bothering you." I said getting ready to pitch the bag.

I was surprised when the boy lifted the gun and said, "I ain't going nowhere with you." He fired the gun.

I heard the loud crack of gunfire. I fell to the ground rolling away. I heard a scuffle and the boy yelling. I felt around on my body and didn't see any blood. The boy missed me. I slowly got to my hands and knees, stood up, dusted myself off and saw Deputy Riley holding the boy in both of his arms. The gun was on the ground.

I took a deep breath and said, "Thank goodness you were there, Mike. I walked over and kicked the gun away while Mike Riley cuffed the boy. I turned and looked to see where the shot may have gone. No one was lying on the ground. A crowd gathered. I loudly asked, "Is anyone hurt? Did anyone get shot?"

They all looked at each other, and everyone began to speak at once. I said, "Please, go inside and see if anyone inside of Wanda's is hurt. Come back out and tell Deputy Mike."

Two people ran into the restaurant. They came out and said no one was injured. I thought, *"Talk about dodging a bullet."*

The boy was cuffed then Mike bent over and picked up the gun. I said, "That's an antique."

Mike said, "Just as lethal."

"What will happen to him?"

"I'll take him in and he'll be processed. We'll call his mother. She works long hours at a laundry."

"Do you know him?"

"Yes, Lawrence is a friend of Mark's."

"He said he was mad because his uncle was fired from work. That didn't happen. All of the employees who want to work are back to work today, including the boy's uncle, Lance Butterfield. He said Lance and some men are planning to take me out someplace where no one would ever find me."

"You need to come in and make a formal statement, Annette. Are you sure you're okay?"

My hands weren't shaking. "Yes. My lunch didn't do so good. Tell Nathan I'll be in shortly. I'm going to reorder my lunch."

"Alright, Lawrence, let's go." The boy was put into the backseat of a Sheriff's SUV cruiser. Mike told me that he came to Wanda's for lunch, just like me and thankfully he took action. I have no doubt the boy would have pulled the trigger twice.

I was suddenly euphoric to be alive. There were no gunshot holes in me. At this moment, I was sad for the young, misguided boy being hauled off in cuffs.

I reordered my lunch at Wanda's then drove to the Sheriff's office. I sat at his desk, eating my lunch while giving my statement.

When I left the Sheriff's office, I returned to the dealership to meet the Hispanic techs about their status. None of them showed up. I wasn't surprised. I asked Jill to make sure cash envelopes were prepared for their pay. I wasn't able to tell them they could return if they could produce green cards. I asked her to put a note, in Spanish, in the envelope, telling them they could return, if they wanted to.

With no Hispanic employees, I focused on meeting with Sloan and Butterfield. I wanted to know how they planned to do work in the shop without technicians. Neither was in the building.

I returned to the accounting office and sat in my chair. I was now shaking, trying to compartmentalize nearly getting shot. What really happened? I was blaming me for being totally unprepared to defend myself. I kept reliving the look in the boy's eyes as he pulled the trigger. I wondered, *"Could I have killed him?"* That thought scared me even more than the near miss on my own life.

Instead of dealing with my near death grief, I chose to bury the experience deep inside me. I would deal with my emotions later. Secretly, I knew this was how PTSD could develop.

Chapter: 39

The next day, I settled down long enough to call Vivian Chalmers. I spoke to her a week ago, after Bucky's unfortunate murder, to offer my condolences. Today, she invited me to her house, a place I had been to before.

Up to this point, my time at the dealership had been quite busy. In spite of Bucky's death at the house, I went to visit Vivian. She greeted me warmly and offered me tea. I accepted and she said, "I've been following you and what you're doing at my husband's car business. Frankly, I'm glad you came to see me. I have a few things to tell you that I think you should know."

I was taken aback by her direct approach. I said, "Thank you Mrs. Chalmers. Let me know what I can do for you."

"Just call me Vivian. Bucky was fond of calling me Viv, a name I detested."

"Thanks, I think you probably know why I came to Columbus. I am auditing Magnolia Cars. Bucky asked my firm, LeDuc and Johnson, to do so. He wanted help with a warranty audit, and an audit of dealership's books. He knew numbers on the financials didn't reflect what was going on in the business."

"Yes. He knew employees were taking money out of the business and cheating customers. He suspected some people, even family, but he was unsure who was involved. He wanted proof. I must say, you were quick to find problems as fast as you did."

I nodded and said, "I came to this house the day he was killed. I wanted to ask him about certain people and to find out what he knew about the rapid drain of cash out of the business. I didn't get a chance. He was busy and I left."

"I get the picture. I think he invited you because he knew someone was coming after him. He wanted a credible witness, but he spared you the confrontation that resulted in his death."

"Yeah, about that. I noticed Bucky really wasn't a real healthy specimen. He was overweight with bad eating habits and I heard, he had a propensity for cocaine."

Vivian sighed and said, "He was a gregarious caricature of himself. He wasn't really the buffoon he led people to believe. He was top of his class in economics at Old Miss. It was his brain, not his position on the football field, or his family money, that I found compelling when we met. He was bright as a brand new penny and funny. And he was, up to the day he died."

"I don't understand! Why did he cover up his abilities? He could have done so much more with the business. It seems like he had lost complete control over the entire dealership. And why are there so many family members on the company payroll?"

"His father, Dean, was an overbearing ass. He wouldn't let Bucky have any important role in the business. He's the one that called him Bucky instead of Buck or Buckminster and it stuck. He called him Bucky to belittle him. Dean didn't want anyone to outshine him. He's the one who hired all of the family members."

"Dean. He's the man sent to prison for killing a cuckold husband at the dealership, right?" I asked.

"Yes. The prosecutor at that time claimed it was premeditated murder. A set-up to rid Dean of a bothersome husband so he could have the wife."

"Blanche. Right?"

"That's right.

"Did Bucky ever enjoy drinking Southern Comfort?"

"No! Absolutely not. He detested the stuff. Said it tasted like cotton candy. That bottle was a plant, a message of some kind."

"Bottles have been left beside my car. I don't know why or who left them." I took a breath. "You'll hear about this soon enough. A child, probably no older than 9, pointed a gun at me yesterday and fired the weapon. He nearly hit me."

Vivian put her hand to her mouth and said, "Oh, no! Are you okay?"

"I am not injured but I am shaken up over the incident. The boy, Lawrence Butterfield, was arrested. I have no idea what charges he will face." I hesitated again. "I came out here today to ask you about any succession plan Bucky may have made for Magnolia."

"My father and grandfather, both lawyers, insisted Bucky and I have separate wills. I have a family trust with a pre-nup that excluded Bucky or the Chalmers family from my assets. Bucky didn't care but Dean never forgave me. When Dean was arrested and sent to prison, Bucky sued the dealership corporation. All of Dean's shares were transferred into a trust. Bucky bought them over time. I'll show you a copy of Bucky's will if you want. I'm the sole heir of his Magnolia shares plus some personal things and his car collection. His children are each beneficiaries of life insurance policies."

"I need to know, because the car company has plans to close down the business and claim all of the assets. I need to know where *you* stand in this picture."

Vivian was taken aback, looked totally shocked, and had difficulty getting words out. "No! You cannot let that happen! Are you here to make sure that happens?" She gave me a piercing stare.

I threw up both of my hands and said, "No. Not why I'm here. I and my company are in the business of preserving dealerships and if need be, we offer them for sale. We find buyers who come in and take over a business by offering a fair price. We do not destroy and liquidate car dealerships."

"Then, please do what you can to save Bucky's business. Magnolia represents a substantial investment. Save it, so I can liquidate it at my leisure."

"You say you're the only heir to the business and you have the only will. Are you sure about that?"

"You mean does Bucky have a holographic will that could spring up someplace? I wouldn't know, but I doubt it."

"No, I was thinking about people like Blanche and Marcy."

"Blanche was taken care of by Dean. She was awarded shares of Magnolia stock. She's still in the business to protect her interest. Marcy, good lord! She is a widowed friend of mine. She was just Bucky's window dressing. I'm telling you this and will deny it if word gets out. Bucky was impotent. He couldn't get it up."

I nearly burst out laughing but held myself in check. Then reality set in. I said, "I agree, the Southern Comfort bottle was some kind of message and the poor woman he was with, was executed for being in the wrong place at the wrong time. Why am I getting bottles of Southern Comfort? A death threat do you think?"

Vivian was inspecting her fingernails and said, "I don't know about the Southern Comfort and I'm sorry that you're being dragged into his murder investigation. But I am happy you are doing your best for me with that car dealership. Keep it up."

Chapter: 40

After visiting Vivian I planned to confront the people performing the warranty audit. I marched to the conference room and heard lively conversation and laughing on the other side of the door. I stepped inside and the room instantly fell silent. Terri and her team were reviewing warranty claims. No doubt, they were chuckling about the amateurish attempt of Magnolia employees to load ridiculous labor ops and unrelated parts to repairs. Terri looked up and asked in a flat voice, "May I help you?"

"No, but I may be able to help you with things I discovered."

"We're busy here and would like to wrap this up before the next scheduled Olympics. Can you be brief?"

She was still playing the arrogant company employee who looks on dealership employees as underlings. "I'll do my best."

"Bucky Chalmers was not as dumb or unattached as it would seem. His wife, Vivian, confessed they had separate lives, but she admitted he was brilliant, clever even, and he knew something was wrong in the business. He wanted to turn things around."

"How so?" Terri asked.

"The information on the financial statements didn't add up. Vivian said he didn't approve of fraud. He knew the shop was out of control. People were undermining his authority. He made it known he was on to them, and when I came, they killed him for it."

"I inspected the warranty claims and spoke to Ezra about them. He agreed with me. The submissions appeared to be deliberate fraud to simply steal money and pocket the cash for their personal benefit. Yet others, were trying to sink Bucky's Titanic."

"Uh, they, being who?" Terri asked.

"Just my opinion but Mandy Sue, the office manager, and her lover, Lance Butterfield. There are others whom I am documenting in my audit report. Keep in mind, you're looking at an organized attempt to ruin the Chalmers family. Bucky admitted this to Vivian. He told her, before I arrived, the threat to his life was real."

"Why is that important to me?" Terri asked, semi annoyed.

"Because Vivian is now the majority shareholder of Magnolia stock. She's the person your people will have to deal with in order to liquidate, sell the operation, or if you attempt to close it down. She is from a family of Mississippi lawyers. She won't go away quietly, and she'll be a tough competitor. Do not close down the dealership."

"Why did you go see her?"

"I'm looking for a successor. Bucky and his brother were both murdered just before your factory audit. Bucky asked my company to come to Columbus and dig into his business. He wanted proof of who was doing the damage. He wanted answers about things he suspected, things that I quickly discovered. Mandy Sue is a relative he wasn't sure he could trust her. He needed someone from the outside to lay eyes on the books to get proof. That's me."

"So, you're saying there was some kind of conspiracy to destroy the dealership on purpose? That doesn't make sense. The business goes away, so do their jobs. Why would they do that?"

"I'm saying there were thieves and vindictive non-family members who hoped to take over the business. I believe two warring factions were working together against Bucky. One, the Chalmers family, and others who had a multi-generational grudge."

"Two warring factions? This is getting curiouser and curiouser." Terri spit out, like Alice in the rabbit hole.

"Yes. There's the Chalmers family for three generations and others who would do anything to destroy the Chalmers family and would even resort to murder to achieve their goals."

"Any idea who those *other* people are?"

"Not everyone in the family has a plum job. Could be jealous family who felt left out, and people not related to the Chalmers, like Lance Butterfield."

"So, what's that got to do with my audit?" Terri asked.

"It means you are really researching a criminal conspiracy. I have discovered proof that a lot of people will get punished for their crimes. They don't want to go to jail. They will blame you."

"Do you mean me and my team?" She asked challenging me.

"You, me, your staff here, and anyone who helps us."

"Are you saying, I and my staff are in physical danger?" Terri asked, looking incredulous.

"I'm saying it doesn't hurt to pay attention to where you're at and where you go. Please be careful while you're here!"

A middle aged man with graying hair stood up with a smirk on his face and said, "I've heard enough of this conspiracy BS. I'm not buying it. I think she is just trying to scare us off. If there's even a shred of proof to what this woman is saying, we just stick together and watch each other's backs." He stood there and glared at me.

I threw up my hands and said, "You're right! Do your work, do what you want, and go home, safe." I turned and left the employees watching me go, believing they had accomplished a win. I hoped they were right, but I wasn't taking any chances after today.

Chapter: 41

At the end of the day, Terri and her crew were told to leave the building by a maintenance man. Lights were turned off, and the doors were locked. She said, "Okay gang, pack up, leave the files, we're taking all of the photocopies with us."

One of the women told the older man who spoke up earlier, "You do know, I read a text that yesterday, Annette had been shot at. Some kid fired a hand gun at her and barely missed. The kid was arrested and taken to the county jail."

"She was shot at and she came to work?" The man asked.

"I know, right? I would be at home nursing a box of wine with the shakes for a week," a woman said.

"And she went to visit the dead dealers widow before she came to see us today? Who does that?" A young auditor asked.

"I think she's crazy as a loon. I've never met anyone like her," the older man with the graying hair said.

"Sorry, I've got to admire her. She earned her CPA, and she seems to know a lot about car dealerships," a young woman said.

"I think she's full of it. Come on. Let's dump our stuff at the hotel then get a good meal and relax. I hear there's a place called Thibodaux Charlies, just south of town. They have great Cajun food, live music and tonight is half price 'shot' night." The older man with the graying hair said while grinning.

Everyone said, "I'm in, let's go!"

Another one laughed and said, "What happens on the road, stays on the road, agreed?"

"You bet!" They all chimed in.

I sat in my car watching the jovial factory people leave in their Suburbans. I knew where they were staying. They felt safety in numbers. I didn't think they had any idea what they might be coming up against.

I called Sheriff Turnbull and told him, "I think we may have a problem with those warranty auditors folks from Atlanta."

"How so?"

"They didn't take my warning about dangerous people who may do them harm because of the audit at the dealership. I think they might run into some trouble tonight. I'm calling to let you know that I'm keeping an eye on them, from a discrete distance, to see where they go for supper."

"I can't let you take that risk."

"I don't plan to get involved with them. I'll just watch to be sure they don't do something foolish. I believe they're going to be drinking and making some poor decisions. The armed masked men who jumped me in the parking lot probably have friends who would get a hoot out of going after these people. I don't think those old guys seriously want to hurt anyone; they just want to scare them."

"Where are you at now?"

"Still at the dealership, watching them leave. I think they'll go to their hotel then drive someplace to blow off steam. Discretion is not on their list of things to do, for these people."

"When you know where they're going, call me. I'll have two deputies show up in a cruiser just in case you're right."

"There they go now. Okay, I'll call."

When they got to the hotel, Terri no longer seemed to be in charge of the group. The older guy was animated and urging them to hurry up and take their things inside then come back out. With my window down, I heard him shout something like "The 'shots' are waiting!" Whatever that meant.

Twenty minutes later I watched six people pile into a dark green Suburban and drive off. I followed just far enough back.

The party animal warranty auditors took a highway south. They pulled into a busy parking lot with a building that looked like a fishing shack next to a pond. The sign read Thibodaux Charlies.

I parked behind where I could see both the Suburban and the front door. I dialed the Sheriff and said, "Thibodaux Charlies."

"I'm very familiar with the place. It's a Cajun themed honky-tonk. They do zydeco on Tuesdays and Thursdays and country music the rest of the week. Since it's in the county, my department has been there to break up a few bar fights. It looks like your car people are looking for some dangerous fun. Are you going inside?"

"Nope! Thought I would sit outside and read emails. I do not want to run into any of those people. My mission is to watch for who's watching them and see if I recognize any of them. They could be Bucky's killers."

"Do you think you were followed?"

"No. I think they are following these car people. I'll tell you more later. I have a feeling these may be the guys who killed Bucky and Eddie. They want to scare them away."

"Would they kill them?"

"No. Just scare them. The guys who came after me are not the brightest candles in the box. I'm watching to make sure nothing bad happens when it starts to rain stupid outside."

"Deputies are on the way. They'll look for your Camaro."

"I'll be here eating pizza."

Chapter: 42

The knock on my Camaro driver's window startled me. I looked up and read the name badge. TJ Christensen was standing next to the car. I rolled down my window. We greeted each other and he said, "I think we need to see what's goin on inside."

"I'm not going in there unless I have to go to the bathroom. I ordered a single serving pizza, and I plan to stakeout their Suburban."

"You ordered a pizza? I've never heard of anyone doing that on a stake out. Now if it were a steak, I might join you."

"Ha, ha, TJ. So, are you just planning to stroll into the dinner club wearing your uniform and unobtrusive utility belt?"

"Not unless I have to. Lieutenant Mike and his wife Suzane are coming in civies to do that. Mike said Suzane was looking forward to a night out with him. Tonight is zydeco night. There will be music and dancing and a lot of hollering and hooting."

"TJ you sound like a prude. You don't approve of Cajun music?"

"Well, I guess I'm kind of a Lynyrd Skynyrd music fan."

"Snob, you mean. Don't get me wrong, Lynyrd created some of the best classics of that era. But you can't put down hootin' and hollern' and ay-eee. It just ain't right. Know what I'm saying?" I said laughing.

"Okay, I see where you're coming from. But…"

I cut him off and said, "Look at that over there."

"What, where?"

"See that blue 4-door pickup and the gray one following. I think that's who I'm looking for. You'd better get out of sight. We need to see what these guys are up to. Hurry, TJ! If they see, you they'll leave."

"Where?"

"Get in my Camaro if you must, but hurry."

"Okay, I'll call in my 10-20 location."

I watched as the two pickups cruised the parking lot. When they drove by the Suburban, both TJ and I scooted down in our seats, so as not to be seen.

I said, "I think that's the same blue pickup I saw near Bucky's house the day he was killed. I would bet on it."

"I'll tell my partner, John, to watch out for it."

Both pickups parked behind the Suburban, not far from where we were sitting. It looked like they were setting up a trap to catch the drunken car people by surprise when they came out of the restaurant. The position of the vehicles did not look good.

I watched men, dressed in blue jeans, step out of their pickups. They walked into Thibodaux Charlies two at a time to scout out their victims. I didn't recognize any of them.

TJ said, "I see Mike now, in that red SUV. I'll call and give him a description of the men who just went inside. Can you tell me what the car people look like?"

"He'll pick them out. They're a mixed group of six men and women, drinking shots, laughing, and having fun."

TJ waited patiently while I nibbled on my pizza and scanned emails. He finally asked, "I don't mean to be rude or pushy but are you seeing someone back in Tennessee?"

Surprised, I looked up from my phone with a smile on my face. I asked, "Why TJ, are you hitting on me?"

"Well, no, I mean yes, kind of." He stammered looking for an exit from his question.

Still smiling at his sophomoric approach I said, "I have no one in Germantown I'm seeing. I do have someone I see, now and then, who's with the FBI in Virginia. Are you asking me to go out with you?"

"Uh, well, kind of. Oh! There! I see men coming out of the restaurant. Those are our guys. I'll let John and Mike know."

"Yes, it's the same men from the pickups. Let's keep an eye on them and see what they're up to."

Five men left the restaurant and walked to their vehicles. They eased into their two pickups and waited, talking on their cellphones while watching the restaurant. After a few minutes, a black pickup drove by and parked beyond my line of sight. That made three pickups, five men and possibly more in the new truck waiting for their prey. I said, "We may need backup."

I believed the men were probably armed for intimidation. On our side, we had Deputy TJ, Deputy John Law, Deputy Inspector Mike, and me. If handled properly, we should be able to diffuse the situation rapidly without harm to anyone.

While waiting, I told TJ that I would enjoy going to a movie with him. He seemed delighted. People left the restaurant. We waited. At 10:30, I saw Terri and her group walk out of the restaurant. They were cheerfully boisterous and one of them was so drunk she was being helped along between two of the men.

Laughing, Terri used her key fob to unlock her vehicle. Just as the group arrived at the Suburban, the third pickup screeched to a halt in front of her vehicle. Men quickly jumped out, and the factory employees were immediately surrounded by eight armed men wearing black ski masks.

I said, "Oh-oh! This is it. Let's go."

TJ unstrapped his service weapon, and I was armed with my 92M9 Beretta. We had no plan, so we approached from behind the Suburban. TJ would take the lead, and I would be backup. I didn't see John or Mike, but I knew they wouldn't be far away.

The men wearing ski masks were roughing up their victims pushing the people toward a truck. Strange, it looked like they were trying to abduct them out of the parking lot. A night of horror had been planned for these folks.

TJ lunged forward. He took a wide stance with his weapon in front and shouted, "Sheriff's Deputy, drop your weapons."

The hooded man standing next to the Suburban held a sawed off shot gun. He simply turned and fired. TJ was knocked off his feet. I immediately shot the man holding the shotgun. And shouted, "You're surrounded. Drop your weapons. Now!"

Two men fired their guns wildly in my direction and I returned fire, hitting one of them. The other men scattered, running for their pickups. Gravel flew while Mike and John fired their guns at the departing vehicles. A 4 door blue pickup was in the lead.

I immediately ran to TJ. He was lying on the ground, bleeding badly. I saw a circular wound about 8 inches wide on his uniformed torso. I flipped my phone open and dialed 9-1-1 and demanded "Hurry, officer down and two more on the ground."

Mike rushed to the Suburban and was shocked to see TJ bleeding on the ground. He asked, "What happened?"

"TJ ordered them to drop their weapons. Instead, that one over there on the ground, turned and shot him with his shotgun."

John Law walked over to Mike and said, "One dead and one wounded. He's cuffed. There are no injuries to the car people. They're pretty upset, however."

"Thanks, John." Mike said.

I asked Mike, looking around, "Where's Suzane?"

"I told her to stay inside. Here she comes now! John, people are coming out of the bar. Establish a perimeter around this area. No pedestrians, understand? I'm calling Nathan now.

I slipped my Beretta back into my shoulder bag and put it inside my car. I then took over from Mike, applying pressure to stem the flow of blood from TJ's injury until EMT's arrived. Mike shouted, asking people to help keep the curious from getting close.

The factory warranty team sat inside their Suburban shivering and crying from their close encounter. Both the Sheriff and I would deal with them tomorrow. Tonight, we would see to TJ and fill out paperwork. I just wanted to know, *"Who in Columbus owns that blue pickup?"*

Chapter: 43

The next day, Lowndes County Prosecutor Emanual Jackson sat at his desk, drumming his fingers on his desk. Sheriff Nathan Turnbull sat across from him and listened.

Jackson said, "So let me get this straight. You set up a trap using civilian people as bait to lure out people who you thought may have killed Bucky and his brother?"

Sheriff Turnbull's face turned red and he said, "No! That's not what happened. Miss Dupart, our county 'friend of the court' at Magnolia, was concerned about the safety of the car warranty people. She followed them to make sure they were safe. I sent a vehicle to assist in case she was right."

"Deputy Investigator Mike Riley volunteered to help inside the restaurant by keeping an eye on those car people. We were taken off guard when the car folks left the restaurant and were suddenly assaulted by a group of eight men wearing ski masks."

Nathan continued. "Deputy Christensen followed procedure and announced himself. He told the men to drop their weapons. Instead, one of them turned and shot my deputy in cold blood with a sawed-off shotgun."

"Miss Dupart, deputized by me, fired her weapon killing the man who shot TJ. She wounded another who was shooting at her. This was not a trap we set up. We were protecting visitors to our county and none of them were hurt during the incident."

"Why did Miss Dupart think they might be at risk?"

"According to Miss Dupart, the car people were digging into fraudulent claims sent to their company. The people responsible for the fraud didn't want to be held accountable. I believe you would call that motive. Names were named and people's jobs are on the line. We believe they decided to go after the car people to stop the audit and make them go away rather than face jail."

"Where are these car people now?"

"They are staying at the Marriott Courtyard with orders to not leave the county until they make a statement to my department. I imagine they'll get on the highway to Atlanta as soon as they can."

"Now, the key question, who are those masked men?"

"The dead man is Bud Grove. The wounded man is Martin Fairbanks. We believe the others are all local, maybe Magnolia employees. The others probably farm in the area. We believe they belong to the same sporting gun club."

"So, we have random locals who decided to go after some people visiting from Atlanta? I can't wait to hear what the Chamber of Commerce has to say about this." Emanual said.

"The connection is the gun club north of town. Are they related to one another, I don't know? There could be family links. The wounded man has lawyered up and hasn't given us any names. Mike recognized a couple of the men. One is a tech at Magnolia."

"We've had run-ins with Bud Grove in the past. He was a devout anarchist and secessionist. He preached first amendment rights and gun ownership. He handed out leaflets about how it was time for a new Civil War."

Jackson rubbed his eyes before saying, "Good god! How many of them are out there? How's your deputy?"

"Not good. His wound is serious and there's a lot of organ damage. He may not make it."

"Is Miss Dupart in any danger for her participation in last night's gunfight?"

"That, I cannot fully answer. I believe she is back at the dealership. She may go back to Memphis for the weekend, I don't know. She's a strong willed young woman and can take care of herself," Nathan said.

"Those men are still out there, and they may come after her for revenge. I have a lead on a blue 4-door pickup and a partial tag number. Miss Dupart is still working on names of those in the dealership who profited from the fraud schemes. She will give that list to me as soon as it's done," Nathan said.

Emanual Jackson stared out his windows before he said, "Please, look after her safety. I'm not telling you how to do your job, but my office is encouraging you to do everything in your power to keep her safe and find out who these men are. This looks like another rebirth of the KKK to me. I want it stopped."

"Mark my words, my department will prosecute them to the full limit of the law. Should Deputy Christensen die, I will see that every one of them involved, will be charged with his murder, and I'll demand the death penalty," Emanual said.

Nathan Turnbull exhaled and said, "I couldn't ask for more. My department is on it, E-man."

Chapter: 44

I woke up groggy because I had a very restless night's sleep. The pizza snack I ate came back to haunt me but that wasn't what kept me awake. I was shot at on two different occasions, one day apart. I could feel my luck running out.

Pulling on my running clothes, I couldn't get the thought out of my mind, *"I'm still reeling from having a child point a gun and firing it at me. If my hands hadn't been full, I would have pulled my gun and killed the child out of instinct."* That made me ill.

My second encounter last night at the restaurant was automatic and decisive. Those men turned and shot a man without thinking twice. I just got to know TJ. He was bashful and kind of cute. If he had asked me to go on a date, I would have. Today his life is hanging on a thread. I am sad for him but not for the men I shot.

I planned to look in on TJ Christensen at the hospital before going to the dealership. When I returned from my run to the B&B, I sat down to a delightful breakfast of eggs, sausage, hashbrowns and fruit. While eating, I wrote out a list of those people in the dealership I suspected of being involved with last night's attempted abduction of Terri and her team. First on my list was Lance Butterfield.

The two certified technicians whose names and numbers appeared on fraudulent warranty claims were on my list. The back parts counterman. Then there was a burly salesman, Tom Law. Related to John Law the deputy, I wondered?

I believed Ralph Renard, a finance manager, was in up to his neck with shady deals. But one name on my list that makes the most sense is Blane Sloan, the service manager. He had to know what was going on with phony warranty claims. He couldn't be that dense.

I didn't know if any of these people were wearing masks last night, but they sure had a lot to do with fraud in the dealership. Could any of the people on my list have family or friends willing to commit assault and kidnap people in the middle of the night?

I went to the hospital to visit TJ. My visit was brief. He was still in a critical care unit, and no visitors were allowed. I left some flowers and a small teddy bear.

After my visit to TJ, I went to the Sheriff's office to see Nathan Turnbull. He was not in and neither was Mike Riley. Disappointed, I got into my Camaro and drove to the dealership.

When I got there, the employee parking lot was half full. It was Friday, but several people chose not to come in today. It would be interesting to see who didn't show up. I did see three green Chevy Suburbans parked next to one another. Terri was tougher than I thought she was. She was in the conference room.

Friday is a busy day. Operating the business with a skeleton crew might be beyond my ability. When I checked, only a handful of uncertified technicians came in today, with no one to do warranty work. Of course, none of the Hispanic techs were to be found.

I wanted to talk with Sloan. He was in his office with the door closed, head bent down reading something. I left him alone.

The parts manager, Troy St. Clair was on the dock, busy checking in a parts shipment. So, I let left him alone, too. A back counter parts man gave me a beady eyed stare as I walked through the department. I wondered, *"Where was he last night?"*

I went to the conference room to meet Terri. When I opened the door, paperwork was spread all over the table. It was Friday, I expected all of them to rush back home. I stepped inside and asked, "Is there anything I can do to make your job easier today."

Terri looked up and I couldn't read her expression. She said, "Yes. Bring me the people who signed these claims to the conference room. I would like to meet the technicians and congratulate them on their clever use of fiction."

I held back a grin and said, "I would like to see them too. They all seemed to have jumped ship today. Nearly a third of the staff has chosen to not come in."

"Because of last night?"

"Probably. I think people would rather not show up than to be arrested for their crimes. Most of the people who did not come in, I suspect, are complicit with stealing money from the dealership."

"So, what do you do now? Close shop?" Terri asked.

"Terri, I was hired to keep this business working. It's not working the way I planned but it's better than having the factory shut the business down and put a lot of people out of work."

"I don't agree. Sometimes you have to fish or cut bait."

"The cliché doesn't apply. My offer to help you still stands. Make your photocopies. Are you staying through the weekend?"

"I think we've seen enough of Columbus, thank you very much. We're just wrapping up."

"Where are your two helpers, George and Cindy?"

"He wasn't feeling too well this morning, and neither was Cindy. We'll pick them both up on our way home."

"Yeah, around here I think they call that a case of Southern Comfort Flu. Found another bottle by my car if you want it."

"How did you know? And while I'm on the subject, how come you were there last night when that Deputy got shot? You shot someone yourself, didn't you?"

I thought for a second and lied, saying, "Yeah, I was there with my boyfriend, the Deputy, who is now in critical condition."

Terri opened her mouth to say something but thought better about her response. She said, "We'll be out of your raven colored hair very soon. I warn you, our legal department is thinking about filing charges against you and Magnolia for putting our people at risk. They may come after you. You could have killed one of us when you fired your gun."

"Yeah, I saw you and your crew last night. Like they say, 'If you dance with the devil, your feet will get burned'. I'll be happy to testify at any hearing." I said with a half-smile on my face.

Terri looked at a co-worker and said, "What do you have on that claim, Josh?"

I turned and walked out of the conference room. Wolf told me that people like Terri are very common with the car company he used to work for while he was in Detroit. They're arrogant and would run over their grandmother for a positive performance review.

I sat in the accounting managers office, shut the door, and called Wolf. I explained everything in technicolor detail. He could tell by my voice that I was nearing the end of my tether. I was grateful there was no lectures, no admonitions. He silently listened and at the end he said, "I'm so sorry."

Chapter: 45

I didn't notice right away when I entered the accounting office and was shocked when I saw Blanche. She was busy posting invoices into the computer. I couldn't help myself. I said, "Blanche, what brings you in today?" I looked around and couldn't see any half empty bottles of booze.

"I work here, in spite of what you think." She said sharply.

"I see. Working on anything in particular?"

She put her invoice down, leaned on one arm at the desk and said, "Since Bucky's niece no longer works here, someone has to do the work. I don't see you doing any data entry."

She was right and I didn't intend to either. "So, you're here for the good of the company. Very noble. Maybe when you've finished with posting invoices, you can look over last month's payables schedule and help me understand why some people are getting Magnolia checks without supporting source documents."

"Look missy, you understand what you're looking at, you don't need my help."

I laughed at the "missy" comment, "Oh, I think your input would be very valuable. Knock before you enter my office."

"Your office?"

"For now, yes."

Later, Blanche came into the office with a copy of the payables schedule. We reviewed each line item one at a time on the schedule. I highlighted the ones that did not have a source document or a reference number. Blanche gave me a serious nod and she said, "Yes, I questioned those checks, too. I was told to shut up and just make the payments."

"I see five names on checks that are printed and sent out every month with no documentation. Who are these people?"

"I never really knew. Most of the payments began when Dean was still here. I think Dean felt like he owed these people."

"Okay, I'll print the names and addresses, and we'll find out who they are. Do you think any of them are local?"

"One or two names in the schedule surprised me, Georgia Davis, and Simone Sanders. There are a couple of Butterfields on the list. We have one working at the dealership, I think you know him."

"You mean Lance? But these payments predate his employment here?"

"You know, there's some old rumors about things that happened a long time ago. Things related to some kind of rift between the Chalmers and the Butterfield families."

"Like what kind of rift and what kind of things?"

"I don't have all the facts, but I remember Dean talking about his dad and uncles and how some of them died. He said there were people around here who held a grudge against him and his family."

"A grudge, going back how far?"

"He said it was when his father, Homer, was a young man. But he didn't give me any details."

"You mean a feud? Like the McCoy's and the Hatfields?" I asked with a grin.

I believe this was the first time I had ever seen Blanche laugh. She said, "Not exactly a shooting war but something happened back then. Homer was shot and killed when he was in his late 50's and that caused problems between the two families."

"So, the problem is just between the Chalmers and the Butterfields? Or are there other family names involved?"

"Yeah, it gets complicated. Daughters married and changed their names. I have no idea who all of the names are from either family anymore."

"Thanks for your insight." I said and I meant it.

Blanche actually smiled and I said, "As you can see, Magnolia is running out of people. I have a plan to bring additional people in to help the dealership, on a temporarily basis. I intend to keep the doors open. I would like for you to return as the office manager again. Hire whoever you need to make the office run properly. You'll be paid an office manager's salary. Can you do that while I'm headhunting for the other departments?"

"So, are you going to be the dealer?" She asked wide eyed.

"No, I am a court ordered caretaker. I'm working with the blessing of the majority stockholder, Vivian Chalmers."

"Vivian? That's a name I haven't heard in quite a while. So, has Bucky's will been read?"

"It will be announced soon. In the meantime, Vivian has all of Bucky's ownership stock in the business. Vivian didn't mention any other family members who could step forward."

Blanche looked disappointed and said, "I spoke to Dean, and he was heartbroken over Bucky and Eddie's deaths. He said his lawyer was working on an early bereavement release with parole for good behavior. The hearing is scheduled for two months from now."

"Interesting. The way things are happening around here, I think he would be safer where he's at, on the inside, rather than walking the streets on the outside." I said without irony.

"I told him that I was still waiting for him." Blanche sadly said.

I could see that Blanche was a faded rose, still nursing her love affair with Dean Chalmers. I felt sorry for her, and I hoped she would help me keep this sad boat full of miscreants afloat.

I walked to Blane Sloan's office and knocked on his door; he looked up and nodded. I walked in shut the door and took a chair across from him. He said, "It's a real mess, isn't it?"

I said, "If you mean the slew of fraudulent warranty claims submitted for payment with your name on them and not to mention crimes in other departments? Yes, it is."

"Honestly, I didn't really know what I was signing. I am not a trained service manager. I am a hired Chalmers nephew filling a slot Bucky wanted filled. I was working in a grocery store."

"Are you saying you didn't know about the fraudulent claims?" I asked, not quite believing him.

"I didn't know what I was looking at, it looked like Chinese. Of course, I knew something was going on. Lance and Mandy Sue never told me anything. Lance was the shop foreman, he knows all about auto mechanics. He went to technician school right out of high school. He's a Butterfield, and I don't know why Bucky hired him. Probably because Mandy Sue asked him to."

Blane continued, "I thought Lance was hired to replace me, but he never seemed to want the job. I have no idea how much he got paid. He's the one who managed all of the warranty claims. I don't know where he got them, but he hired all of those people from Guatemala. His dispatcher pushed work through the shop, but I think a lot of the work was shoddy at best. I had no say or control over what was done. I just sat in here and played solitaire on my computer most of the time. Do you think they will arrest me?"

I exhaled a deep breath after listening to his confession. I said, "I do not know, Blane. You may be able to bargain for clemency if you testify against those who created the fraud scheme. You need a lawyer. I want to make you aware that I plan to have some people come in to run the shop. You'll retain your position and salary as service manager and the person who comes in will be the assistant service manager, but he will run things. Understand?"

"Not much of a change from the way things are now." Blane said.

"They will be here Monday. Help them in any way you can. Who do you know that owns a blue 4-door Dodge pickup truck?" I asked.

"Blue truck? I wouldn't know one blue truck from another. I've seen Lance drive one from time to time. Why?"

"Nothing. Make valuable use of your time, get that lawyer."

Chapter: 46

A shocking series of events fell into place when Bob Carter showed up out of the blue at the beauty shop where Judy worked. He walked in and immediately thought she was going to come after him with scissors she had in her hand. She stood there, mouth open, staring at him, not believing what she was looking at. Her brother, Mike told her about Bob's second family in Australia. Early last week, using a lawyer, she filed documents demanding back pay for child support.

She finally blurted out, "Bob! Why are you here? What do you want?"

"Can we talk about this when we're alone and you're not holding a sharp instrument? I just came by to tell you I'm here." Every women in the shop was wide eyed and quiet. They watched Judy closely, wondering what her next move would be.

Judy looked at the scissors in her hand and said, "I'm in the middle of Maud's haircut. And I have another 'head' waiting. Meet me at Mike's office when I get off. We'll all sit down and talk about what's on your mind." She said with a frown on her face.

Bob knew Mike very well. They had gone to school together, hunted together, and he liked her brother. He said, "Okay, I'll meet you where Mike works at the courthouse. I'll be waiting there." He turned and walked out of the beauty shop.

Over at the courthouse, Mike Riley had Bob Carter on his list of 'persons of interest' for the death of Grace Dowd five years ago. He was astonished to see Bob walk into the courthouse and step up to the reception window. Mike couldn't believe his eyes. He walked over and told the receptionist, "Send Mr. Carter through. I definitely would like to see him."

Bob sat down with Mike in his office waiting for Judy to show up. Bob told a story about how he and Judy went through a rough patch five years ago. "She was always hounding me about what I did for a living. At the time, I was working at home building websites for customers on a contract basis. I admit that I wasn't earning a lot of money, but I was building my business."

Bob continued, "I just couldn't take the hounding any longer. She made me feel like a loser who couldn't support his family. I saw an online ad looking for computer jocks on projects with my kind of skills. I applied with three tech companies; one was in Australia. They called me one day and I had a skype interview. They hired me and I ran for the door and the nearest airport to get the job."

"You left your family behind. You didn't tell them you were leaving. You just disappeared," Mike said. "That's abandonment."

"I hated leaving my son, Robby. He was only 4 at the time and the baby was fussing all night. I figured they would probably do better without me. Robby needed someone who could throw a baseball to him. I'm not that guy," Bob said shrugging his shoulders.

Mike listened quietly while Bob blithered on about his unfortunate life with Judy in Columbus. He had little sympathy for the man who left his sister, son, and a baby with no support. Mike asked, "So, Bob, tell me *why* did you come back?"

"Last week, I was contacted by a solicitor in Melbourne. He told me that Judy Carter was filing a motion demanding support for herself, her 9-year-old boy and 5-year-old daughter. I panicked. I was applying for citizenship and now married to another woman in Australia. Judy and I never divorced. I needed to set things right. I have a good thing going in Melbourne. I'm a technical supervisor for a large tech firm and make good money. I hope to become an Australian citizen. Her coming after me would ruin everything."

Mike couldn't believe his ears. He slowly said, "And you never considered that walking out on Judy, with a baby in her arms and a 4-year-old, five years ago, might not ruin everything for her?"

"No. I'm truly sorry for doing that. When I left I had no money and no backup plan. I was barely able to pay for my airplane ticket. I slept rough in Australia for the first couple of weeks until I could earn a paycheck. I came back to Columbus to make up the child support I'm responsible for."

"Just that? The child support, no alimony? Is that the only reason you came back?"

"That and to help Robby with his piano thing." He said with a smile.

"Aaah! There we have it! How did you find out about Robby's piano playing ability?"

"I check happenings in Columbus on line, every now and then. I went to school here, you know. Just looking for names I recognize. I saw the post about Robby playing piano at a local concert and that he's a prodigy. I saw the video. The kid's good!"

Mike had so many things he wanted to say but he thought it would be better if said through the mouths of lawyers and the county prosecutor. Bob was a suspect in a murder, and he was a run-away-dad liable for a pretty good sum of money. He wanted Judy to get her child support claim settled first. Bob only came back because he thought he could cash in on Robby becoming famous. Bob would not leave the courthouse, and he would need a good lawyer.

Mike looked at Bob with sad disappointment and said, "Judy will be here soon. I have a baseball in my desk. Why don't you take it outside and practice throwing the ball against a building before she and Robby show up. You probably could use the practice."

He heard Bob mutter, "No thanks. I'm good."

Chapter: 47

Judy showed up at the courthouse with her son, Robby, and her 5-year-old daughter, Dotty. Robby was torn between loyalty to his mother and uncertainty about meeting the man standing before him. His mother told him his father came back to Columbus and wanted to meet him. Robby resented this intrusion into his orderly life with his mother, his piano, and his school buddies. Robby felt there was no room for this stranger, just like there was no room for Pete Baker's dad to be hanging around, showing up all times of the day and night. Robby didn't like either man.

"Come here, Robby. Give your daddy a hug." Bob said grinning. Robby stood frozen across the room with his arms folded eyeing the man who seemed shorter than he had imagined. He said, "Naw, I'm good."

Bob angrily looked at Judy and demanded, "What? Did you tell him lies about me?"

"I didn't really tell him much at all about a man who just left his wife, son, and baby one day. Get over it! He doesn't trust you and neither do I," Judy said crossing her arms.

Mike moved the Carter's into an interview room down the hall. They waited for Sheriff Turnbull and Prosecutor Emanual Jackson to come in and listen to what Judy and Bob had to say.

Judy turned and looked at the door, hoping someone would come in soon to prevent her from leaping across the table to attack her former husband. Bob didn't apologize, he didn't say, "Nice to see you!" He just reinserted himself back into her life. She was uncomfortable and had no idea why he was here or what he wanted.

Bob didn't appear to be nervous. He scrolled his cellphone, waiting patiently, so he could say what he had to say, then move on. He was unaware Judy had the marriage dissolved a year and a half earlier. She won her case for divorce due to abandonment.

The door opened, Sheriff Nathan walked in with the prosecutor, Emanuel Jackson, and a woman with a notepad. Bob stood up. Nathan introduced himself and the prosecutor. He didn't introduce the woman. Bob put his hand out, but no one shook it.

Nathan began, "Long time, Bob. I understand you've been living another life, down under. What brings you to Columbus?"

"I think that's pretty obvious. Jill is suing me in an Australian court for abandonment and child support. I flew back to the States to clear up this dispute." Bob crossed his arms and waited.

Nathan nodded and asked, "How do you intend to go about doing that, Bob?"

Bob sensed something was not quite right. He said, "Do I need a lawyer here? I contacted an old friend, and he said he would come to the courthouse if I needed him."

"That's up to you, Bob. Right now, we are having a friendly conversation that is being recorded. You have not been charged with anything. We're here with Judy to find out what *you* want."

"With a County prosecutor? That's odd." Bob said.

"He's a lawyer and we have some questions for you. But first, tell us please, how you intend to clear up your legal matters with Judy."

Bob exhaled, smiled, and said, "I am willing to offer a settlement agreement that will provide funds to cover missed child support payments. She just needs to sign the agreement, the funds will be transferred to her bank, and I'll fly back to Melbourne." Bob leaned back, crossed his arms again, and waited.

Nathan asked Judy's brother, Mike, not to attend the meeting. He was afraid things might get out of hand. He looked at Judy with arms crossed and she looked steamed. He was about to say something when Emanual asked, "May I see a copy of the agreement that you want Judy Carter to sign?"

"It's a document between a man and his wife. I do not think you have any authority to look at anything between us." Bob said matter of factly.

Nathan closed his eyes and said, "That's where it gets sticky for you Bob. Judy is no longer your wife. She filed for and received a divorce a year and a half ago. You're no longer married to her. You abandoned her and you failed to pay child support. So, the prosecutor has a right to look at what you would like her to sign."

Bob looked both shocked and relieved. "Divorced? I never signed any divorce papers. But if that's true, I am not a bigamist! The document was meant to annul our marriage so that my marriage in Australia would be legal."

"Good! Hand it over." Emanual said with a smile.

Bob reached inside his jacket and withdrew a document. He said, "There is a condition in the document that says she will agree to the amount mentioned, then she would file for an annulment."

Emanual said, "Thank you, the document, please." His hand still out waiting.

Bob handed the paper to Emanual who immediately handed the paper to the woman sitting next to him. She unfolded the document and read it. She looked up and said, "This appears to be a legal draft that took place in Victoria and filed in Melbourne, Australia."

Bob proudly announced, "It's legit alright."

The woman spoke up, "And redundant! As the Sheriff pointed out, you and she are no longer married."

"I'm sorry, who are you again?" Bob demanded.

"I am Delta Figg, Judy Carter's attorney."

"Well, my solicitor assured me that I could do so and my marriage in Melbourne would then be valid."

"You sir, are not in Australia. You cannot legally go back to annul a marriage from a woman you were married to in the US that produced two children, then be married to another woman for four years that produces two more children in another country. You, sir, are a bigamist and a law breaker. On top of that, I quickly did the math, and the amount of money you suggest as a onetime settlement falls way short of the amount you owe through the family court in Lowndes County. I repeat, you are a bigamist and a dead beat dad. Pay up!" Delta said.

Bob jumped up from his seat and said, "How dare you call me a law breaker. I'll sue you for slander."

Nathan sternly said, "Sit down, Bob."

Emanual spoke up, "You are being charged with failure to pay child support and alimony, for the past 5 years for Judy Carter and your children, Robby and Dotty. This was filed for in our county court. You will be held in the county jail, until such time as you can make the restitution applied for in the county court by Miss Figg."

"That's all. I want a lawyer. I came here in good faith to settle differences between my now ex and me. This is gotten way out of hand. I want justice!"

"That's not quite all, Bob." Nathan slowly said staring him in the eye. "We have another matter to discuss with you."

Now angry, Bob crossed his arms again and said, "What? Some parking ticket you want to blame me for?"

"No. And you may want to ask your attorney friend if he has time to come to the courthouse today."

"What?" Bob's face went blank.

"I must warn you that anything you say, can and will be used against you in a court of law. You are entitled to legal representation. I'll ask you one more time, do you want to call your lawyer friend?"

"Am I under arrest?"

"Besides holding you for money due in family court, you are now being held as a person of interest for the abduction and murder of Grace Dowd, five years ago in Lowndes County."

"What? You've got to be crazy. This is extortion for the child support, isn't it?"

Nathan quietly said, "You have one call, Bob."

Bob put his head in his hands and wrung his hair between his fingers. All he intended to do, was clean up an old marriage and see if he could get any future money out of Robby's music talent. He would return to his life in Australia. He thought Judy would jump at the chance to make a few thousand and say goodbye.

Nathan said, "Judy, you, and the kids can leave now. Thank you."

Judy, Miss Figg and Dotty stood up and prepared to leave. Judy said, "I feel sorry for your wife in Australia. I don't think she really knows what a prize she has in you, Bob."

Nathan and deputy Tom put handcuffs on Bob. They ushered him into the other room to have him processed and jailed.

Across the room, Robby Carter watched the suffering man squirm and cry. A cynical smile crossed his face, and his mind drifted to a Chopin piece he was working on. The man who left the room, meant nothing to him.

Chapter: 48

While Nathan Turnbull was busy in the interview room, Mike Riley was reading the ballistics report sent to him from the state forensics lab.

The gun obtained from the assault on Annette Dupart by 9-year-old Lawrence Butterfield was a match to four slugs removed from the cadavers of Reed Butterfield and Fats Donahue. They were the cold case victims shot and killed over 60 years ago on a piece of land at an oxbow lake where Robby Carter found Grace Dowd's detached finger bone. The bullet fired at the ballistics lab, however, was not a match for those found in Bucky Chalmers or the woman in his bed. Mike wanted to know who possessed that gun for 60 years?

Curious, Mike inspected the gun closer and checked the serial numbers on line. The gun was, indeed, a 1940's snub nosed 38 Detective Special. He grinned. His grandfather jokingly called those 38's a Mississippi Pea Shooter.

The gun was an antique. But what concerned him most, was why would Lawrence Butterfield be in possession of a weapon used to kill a Butterfield family member who was either a great-great grandfather or a great uncle? That didn't make sense.

Mike wanted to know where the gun had been hidden all of these years. Lawrence, a juvenal, could not be questioned any further without several lawyers from family services.

Instead, Mike decided to go back to the original crime scene with a metal detector. He would search the area again for any lead bullets fired from this gun and missed by the forensics team. So much was going on the day that the bodies were found. It would be easy to miss something as small as a bullet in the earth.

He would take Robyn Shoptau, a deputy, and a member of the forensics lab with him. He made calls to a forensic volunteers club. They would help him search for possible artifacts of a murder over 60 years ago. This time, he would tow the department motorboat making access to the building easier. The forensics team agreed to meet Mike at the Sheriff's department just after noon.

Mike looked at the door to the conference room. Nathan was still busy with Bob Carter and his sister. Mike decided to visit Annette Dupart at the Magnolia dealership before he left for the search. He asked Robyn Shoptau to come with him.

Annette shot and killed Bud Grove. Bud's buddies were still roaming the area looking for revenge. She was not safe. Mike wanted to know who had not returned to work today. These were the people he would look at for who were present at the restaurant last night to capture warranty car people and who shot his deputy, TJ Christensen.

Chapter: 49

I felt like I scored a goal with Blanche. She blossomed before my eyes as a new woman. Proudly taking charge of her office, she literally threw herself into her work. She seemed to enjoy being useful and she knew her way around the dealership's accounting office. The old girl was even humming her favorite song.

With Blanche managing the posting of source documents and temporarily handling title work, I was free to begin looking for temporary workers for the dealership.

I told Wolf about the number of people who failed to show up today. He said, "Our position as the county appointed caretakers of the business is to keep the dealership running. I'm concerned about the sheer number of employees who have failed to show. I'll find some replacement bodies, but I cannot fill such a large order, especially on such short notice."

"I realized that. What *can* you and Ezra do, then?" I asked.

"Ezra may be more help than me. He'll call a couple of his friends to loan us a couple of certified technicians for Magnolia on a temporary basis. I'll call one of our employees, Frank Carlson, he'll step in to act as a general manager for you."

"I'll also ask around to see who can fill some of your critical slots in the dealership. You do know what you're doing don't you?"

"Yeah, I think so. What are *you* thinking."

"I'm thinking you're trying to become a Dr. Frankenstein. You're trying to resurrect a dealership back from the dead."

I laughed and said, "No, I'm really a zombie killer. And today, the zombies have left the building."

"Zombies! You had a close call with that kid and again last night at the restaurant. You told me you shot two men and killed one of them. Annette, I'm coming to Columbus and help. I can even ask Chick, at Reliant, to provide protection for you."

"I told you, I am officially deputized by the Sheriff. He did so when he asked me to look for potential killers of Bucky and his brother while working on my audit report. As an official deputy, I'm carrying my gun and the Sheriff, and his department are looking over my shoulder. Just find people to help me here on Monday or Tuesday at the latest."

"I'm making those calls as soon as we disconnect. Seriously, cousin, please watch your back. Ezra just walked in and said he's driving to Columbus on Monday. He said he has a couple of people who will be coming with him. Are you coming back to Germantown this weekend?"

"I want to, but Saturday is a key car and truck sales day. Someone has to mind the sheep."

"Sheep or shop?"

"Both." I said.

I looked up and saw Deputy Mike Riley standing near Bucky's office door, grinning. I hung up and asked, "What?"

"Nothing, I thought I had just stepped into the war room at the White House. You sound like the chief of staff."

"Thanks, Mike. I suppose you're here to find out if I have any suspects for Bucky and Eddy's murders."

"That would be nice. Do you?"

"My first instinct is to say all of those guys who showed up at Thibodaux Charlie's last night. Did you happen to get the plate number on the blue 4-door pickup in the parking lot, last night?"

"I got a partial, Mississippi tag, last 4 digits, 6792. Why that particular vehicle?"

"I am pretty sure that was the vehicle I saw, partially hidden at Bucky's farm when I went to meet him that night. I strongly believe that whoever killed Bucky was in the house while I was there. Find the truck and you find Bucky's murderer. Blane suggested that Lance has a blue pickup that he occasionally uses."

"Lance, eh. We're looking for him. I came to tell you, as you know, our department is short of manpower. But, I have assigned Deputy Robyn Shoptau to you. I was going to use Deputy Law, but he's busy on another assignment with Nathan. You will go nowhere without her. She's going to shadow you everywhere you go. And before you say no, this is not a request. She and you will be like twins. She's just outside your office. She was going with me to look for bullets, but I thought her talents would be a better fit for you."

I was stunned. Of course, I didn't want anyone to follow me or slow me down. I'm a very private person and I do make impulsive decisions. Also, I didn't want to put anyone else at risk. I sighed and said, "Shoptau. That's an unusual name."

She is a half Choctaw native who grew up in the area. Her mother is a professor of English at the Mississippi University for Women here in Columbus. Her native father is a Professor of American History and Native Studies at the same school. Robyn is the only one out of three children who decided law enforcement was a calling she couldn't resist."

Curious, I asked, "Where is she?"

Mike turned saying, "Just outside, let me introduce you."

When I saw her, I was stunned. Her features and mine were very similar. She had longer black hair, like me, lighter skin, and was slightly taller than me. I smiled and said, "So, you're my doppelganger?"

"No ma'am. I am here to protect you." She said without a smile.

I was amused by the similarity between us and silently thought, *"This might work out well. I can be in two places at once."*

I said, "Welcome, Robyn! Follow me to the accounting office and have a seat. I am in the middle of trying to rebuild the Magnolia workforce. You're local and you may know some people who I could use. I have several open positions." I looked up and Mike waved goodbye.

Blanche gave me a half smile and slightly shook her head. I was warming up to the old gal. Who knows, we might even become friends one of these days.

Robyn sat down in a chair next to me, and I began going over critical positions where I needed people immediately. Robyn smiled and she began to come up with names of people she knew to call. Sometimes, all you have to do is ask the right question to the right people.

I might even have time now, with Robyn helping me, to go get that hair appointment with Judy. That would take something off my mind.

Chapter: 50

Saturday morning after my run and breakfast, I arrived at the Magnolia dealership at 7:30 AM. Blane Sloan arrived the same time. He opened up the shop and I went inside. I didn't expect to see Robyn Shoptau this morning, but I did see the two ASE certified techs who now do most of the work in the shop. With my new pay plan, they would do extremely well by closing open repair orders.

I have to admit; I was impressed with Robyn. Not by her close resemblance to me, but by her spunk. She was younger than me by 4 or 5 years, so we were very close in age. She and I hit it off right away and I looked forward to seeing her again.

I walked by the parts department and was surprised when Troy St. Clair actually smiled and waved at me. I wondered what caused his change in attitude. Now, salesmen needed to show up. By 9:00, most of them sauntered into the showroom. Jill came in and said, "Not too late to cut the week's payroll." I just smiled and waved.

Robyn arrived with a friend, Tonya Wilson. Robyn said she had been a title clerk for a used car dealer that went out of business a month ago. I said, "If you know how to do title work on new and used cars, you're hired."

I said, "Thanks, Robyn." She was wearing blue jeans and a loose top, not a uniform. "I didn't think deputies worked on weekends."

"Yeah, I thought the same thing about CPA's."

"I'm getting my hair done this morning. Will you be good here while I'm gone?"

"Yeah, I could use a 'do', too. Go ahead. See you when you come back."

I was just on time for my appointment with Judy. She took her time trimming and feathering my hair, then washing and drying it. Then she brushed my hair in a way that changed my looks in a pleasant sort of way. I tipped her well. She didn't talk about her ex husband and I didn't ask.

I returned to Magnolia, a new woman. I went into the accounting office and found Robyn and Tonya working. Robyn looked up and waved while making phone calls to people she knew, asking if they could use a job at Magnolia. She handed a list of people for me to expect on Monday morning.

I asked Robyn, "The title clerk is a good find. What do you know about Bobbi Jo, the former title clerk?"

"She and I never got along. She's from the side of Columbus that thinks Native people ought to go back to where they came from. I wasn't welcome in her circle of friends."

"Her circle may be getting larger. When Sheriff Turnbull and Emanual Jackson examined her title transactions at Magnolia they said an indictment would be forthcoming."

"I heard. She was taking money to change branding on car titles. That's a class one felony."

"She had a relative in Kentucky working this scheme with her to wash titles of theft, prior accidents, and mileage differences. Paperwork was shifted back and forth to make the branding disappear. How long have you been with the Sheriff's department?"

"Almost two years now. I'm studying for my Sergeants exam, and I tested good at the range. I understand you're a good shot. Maybe we can go and shoot together, sometime."

"Poking holes in targets always makes me happy."

I started to get up and Robyn asked, "Where are you going?"

"Coming back from the beauty shop, I left my computer backpack in my car. I've been using Magnolia's computer."

Robyn said, "Stay here, let me have your car key, I'll get your backpack. Can I get you anything else?"

"Thank you, that's very considerate of you." She smiled, waved, and she asked Tonya if there was anything she could get for her.

Chapter: 51

I was helping Tonya with a car deal and heard gunshots.

I immediately stood up, unstrapped my Beretta, and ran through the building toward the shop. I dashed past a couple of techs, out a bay door into the parking lot. I saw four armed men firing pistols and rifles making holes in a silver pickup.

It struck me like an electric shock; they were shooting at Robyn and had mistaken her for me. She was either wounded, dead or pinned down behind the silver pickup. From my vantage point I could see they were focused on the pickup, not me.

They stopped shooting and began walking toward the pickup. I ran into the lot and stepped behind a large truck and used that for cover. I took aim and began to rapidly pick off the gunmen, one at a time.

Alarmed at being fired upon from their flank, the men began firing their guns in every direction. I was well protected and only one of the men saw me. His shot hit the truck, and I wounded him in return. Another man went down. Finally, the remaining two men ran out of the parking lot toward their vehicles. Two were down and injured, for sure.

I watched two trucks speed away. My attention turned to the armed men I shot. One of them was severely wounded, I kicked his weapons under a car. The other one had a superficial wound, and I disarmed him. I said, "Take off your shirt now and apply pressure to that man's bleeding or he may die."

Securing the parking lot took time and I was worried about Robyn. A crowd of curious employees came out of the building. A technician ran over. I said, "Quick, get some zip ties, now."

"Yes, Ma'am."

When he came back, they zip tied the two men to vehicles. I ran over to the silver pickup afraid of what I would find.

Robyn was sitting with her back against another vehicle holding her bleeding shoulder. I said, "Oh, Robyn. How bad is it?"

"Pretty bad. I'm losing blood. I called dispatch and told them people were shooting at me and to send backup and an ambulance."

That was when I heard the whine of sirens getting louder.

Local police and Sheriff's deputies soon flooded the back parking lot. An ambulance showed up and another was called to assist. Deputy Shoptau was taken to the hospital in the same ambulance as one of the critically wounded men. Eventually, all of the wounded were rushed to the hospital.

Nathan Turnbull escorted me and my gun to Bucky's former office in the Magnolia building. An hour later, I was sitting in Bucky's office chair, staring at Nathan, Emanual, the local Police Chief, and the city Mayor. They were quiet and none of them looked happy. Neither was I waiting for someone to break the silence.

It was the Mayor. "Surely, this gunbattle will make news from here to Miami. We pride ourselves as being a peaceful community. We are the hub of local colleges and an Air Force base just north of town. People don't even lock their doors in Columbus. Then, all at once, people are getting shot at a restaurant just south of town and three people got shot here today. Nothing like this has happened until you, Miss Dupart, came to town."

Sheriff Turnbull was angry. He stood up and pointed a finger, "That's quite enough, Carl. You forget, the owner of Magnolia was shot and killed in his home. Then his brother Eddie was killed a few days later. And there's the cold case of Grace Dowd and all of those bodies found at that oxbow lake south of town. Miss Dupart had nothing to do with any of that. I hate to say it, but it's your local citizens causing all of this chaos. Miss Dupart simply defended herself and deputies who work for me."

"Yeah, I think you're part of the problem too, Nate. We'll see what happens during the next election." The Mayor snorted, self-assured.

Turnbull shot back, "Yes, we will Mayor. And you're up for re-election, too. I can't wait for the debates."

Emanual spoke up and said, "Gentlemen, none of this bickering will settle anything. I personally would like to commend Miss Dupart for coming to the aid of Deputy Shoptau. They surely would have killed her. I will see to it all of those men will be prosecuted for attempted murder of a law enforcement officer. This uncontrolled culture of gunslingers in our streets must come to an end. And I'm just the person to make that happen," he shouted.

The Columbus Police Chief spoke up and said, "There's no mystery as to why they began shooting at Deputy Shoptau. She's a dead ringer for Miss Dupart. At least she was. She looks different now. They were after her. The Mayor's right, she's stirring up trouble at Magnolia. How many people have left the business? Those people rely on those jobs. They're blaming this woman."

Emanual said, "They are taking the law into their own hands. There is no place for vigilante law in Columbus or our county. I know you recognized some of the men wounded outside, Carl. Trust me, they are not your friends. They're criminals. Help us clean up our community." The Mayor and Police Chief looked sullen.

"My office and the Sheriff's Department believe there was a criminal conspiracy of former employees at Magnolia. They killed Bucky and Eddie. They committed numerous acts of fraud in an attempt to steal money. The Sheriff is close to identifying all of those involved." Emanual said.

"Yeah, but what about her? She shot people. Are you going to prosecute her?" The Mayor asked.

"Miss Dupart is an appointed 'friend of the court' and a sworn in deputy, appointed by the Sheriff. Her role is to keep the business running with as many people as possible. Several bad apples committing crimes walked away from work. Not her fault. My suggestion to you is to go outside and paint the best possible picture on these events. Tell them their community is safe."

The Mayor gave Nathan a dirty look. He and the Police Chief stood up and glared at me. I exhaled and said, "Now what?"

Nathan said, "Bob Carter is scared. He's filling us in on things that happened around the time Grace Dowd went missing. Thanks to you and Reliant Security, I have a lead where Drew Dowd has been for the past seven years. Sharon, Drew's wife, was in Mobile. I hope to find out more about Grace's murder."

I said, "I think I'm done here today. I'm going back to Germantown and will come back on Monday. I'm asking you Sheriff, to make sure the doors are opened for business on Monday."

"I think we can meet Mr. Sloan here on Monday. Sounds like a good idea. We discovered an interesting fact when we looked into your title clerk, Bobbi Jo. She is a descendent of Fats Donahue. He's her great, great grandfather and she's also a Butterfield. Think that's a motive for fraud, or maybe a murder or even a conspiracy?"

"Could be. That's one more ornament on the Magnolia fraud tree. Thanks for letting me know," I said.

"I found out there were three babysitters during the time Grace was killed. You won't believe this, Mandy Sue, Bobbi Jo, and Grace were all friends at the time," Nathan said with a satisfying grin. "I do believe we have a connection."

"Well, I'll be. Things are making more sense." I said.

Before I left, I told Tonya and the remaining employees to go home early, depending on car sales and to come back on Monday. I asked Blane Sloan to shut the place up and lock the doors once all of the law enforcement people, reporters and the simply curious left the grounds. I told him to expect some help in the shop on Monday. He didn't seem to care.

I planned to swing by the B&B, pick my things up, then go to the hospital to see how Robyn Shoptau was doing with her shoulder injury. Then, I would check on TJ before leaving for Germantown.

When I got to the hospital, Robyn was patched up. No vital organs were hit and no bones broken. She was sore but would heal and be back at work in a couple of weeks. TJ had not fared as well. His injuries required surgeries to repair organ and colon damage. He was transferred to the University Medical Center in Jackson, the best level one hospital for this type of injury in the area. I feared for his survival while driving the 2 ½ hours back to Germantown.

Chapter: 52

Earlier, Mike Riley was at the oxbow lake when he received word about the gunfight at Magnolia Cars. A gunbattle that left one officer down and put two perpetrators in the hospital with gunshot wounds. He was told that I was okay and driving back to Germantown. He said, "This has got to stop!"

Mike was searching for lead bullets or fragments to match the 1940, 32 revolver in his office. He intended to do a thorough search of the area looking for bullets missed by the forensics team over a month ago. He planned to take just a couple of people and a metal detector. Instead, he was now supervising a team of fifteen enthusiastic forensics volunteers with metal detectors and archeology tools to comb through all of the known crime scenes.

The spot where the Corvette and three bodies were found was still a huge open gash in the landscape. The pit was considered a "Glory Hole" for the amateur volunteers. It was amazing how many pieces of metal they discovered with their sweep of the terrain. One person even found a Confederate belt buckle with a piece of lead shot stuck on it. Fragments of Civil War weapons were found. Iron pipes and auto parts were discovered. Everything would be tagged, numbered, and recorded, including a gold necklace with an angel.

Evidence was piling up and Mike still didn't have what he was looking for. He thought the Confederate relic would probably go to the local museum and the necklace could be a link to Grace.

Piles of dirt left over from recovering the car and the bodies, was sifted through. Searchers looked for the smallest detail. Everything was bagged and numbered for further examination. A couple of squashed lead bullets were found that may or may not reveal some ballistic evidence. Mike thought they could even be lead shot from Civil War guns.

The search expanded to where an outhouse once stood. Then they went on into the woodland. "This is the crime scene where the bear trap was that held Grace Dowd's bones." Mike said.

Bone fragments were discovered near a large tree and bagged. The metal detector sounded. A bullet was carefully extracted from the sandy soil. Using rubber gloves, the bullet was bagged. Underneath the bullet was more bone fragments. They were shown to Mike and his heart sank. He said, "That looks like pieces from a skull. Bag them. This could only mean one thing. Grace was alive when her abductor returned, found her, and did a coup d' gras by firing a gun into her head. No Grace, no witness."

In all, 6 bullets in various kinds of condition were discovered. One was found in the side of the wood building.

Chapter: 53

The rest of my weekend at home was wonderfully quiet. I notified Wolf that I was back in Germantown. Then I called my mother in St. Martinville and did not tell her about the people trying to kill people, especially me, in Columbus, MS. She told me my brother Bobby, and his wife Babette were expecting another child. Babette told her it was a girl. Of course, this information is a source of joy for the Dupart and LeDuc families around St. Martinville.

I stayed in my apartment tonight. I cooked food, did laundry and little things. This forced me to forget work and gunplay entirely. On Sunday, I made a list of meals and went to the grocery to purchase things that would make me happy. I even organized my kitchen utensil drawer. I was running out of things to do. Monday morning, I would get up early and drive back to Columbus in a clean shiny white Camaro with a red racing stripe.

My night hours, after watching my favorite streamed shows, were crowded with nightmares of two Lowndes County deputies who were shot while I did my best to defend them both. Still, they were casualties for my probing into crimes I discovered auditing books at a Mississippi car dealership. My career seems to be full of tasks linked to quasi law enforcement roles that get people hurt.

I haven't heard from my sometimes boyfriend, Hop Dickerson, for quite a while. He told me his career at the FBI cybercrimes division kept him busy. Too busy to call me as it turned out. Not long ago, he asked me to give up my career as a CPA with Wolf and move into an apartment with him in Washington. I don't know what he expected me to do all day, knit sweaters, I guess. I declined and now, I only hear from him, occasionally. On my way home, I shed a tear for TJ's offer of a date.

Sunday, I took my car to a hand wash facility and I detailed the interior. This was a labor of love for me. I took special care washing and polishing the wheels on my Camaro by hand. She now shines inside and out with pride. My brothers who made custom improvements on the car, would be pleased.

As my one exception to staying home alone, I treated myself by having dinner at the Southern Social Restaurant in Germantown by myself. I dressed up for the occasion in my new black dress and ate Grits and Shrimp along with Seafood Gumbo. I ate a Harvest Salad and enjoyed strawberry cake with a sparkling candle on top. I turned another year older today and celebrated the day alone with sparkling grape juice and a tear.

Chapter: 54

I returned to Columbus on Monday and dropped my things off at the B&B before driving to Magnolia Cars. I had a hollow feeling. I really didn't know her well, but I missed Robyn. She was shot because some terrible people thought she was me.

When I arrived at the dealership, I was greeted by a different Deputy. John Law who was TJ's partner at Thibodaux Charlie's. He was supposed to be TJ's backup. John Law, I shook my head thinking, what an ironic name.

I carried my computer bag inside and set myself up, this time in Bucky's office, not the accounting office. I didn't think Bucky would mind. The first thing I did, was call the Sheriff's department and leave a message that I was back at the dealership and that Deputy John was with me.

Blanche was already in her former office. I could tell that she was doing her best to prepare a reasonable facsimile of a monthly financial statement. I noticed two more women in the accounting office, besides Tonya and Jill. I gave Blanche a curious nod. She said, "Yes, they are working here now. I know their families, and they were eager to have the work."

I said, "Wonderful! You should know that last Friday, I called the Junior College and asked them to send any technician trainees they had in their Automotive program to us. They were happy to comply. Skilled or not, they can work part time here while they attend school. Make sure they complete the appropriate paperwork."

"Of course. I'm not a rookie, you know" she said with a half grin.

"I know. I'll never underestimate you again. My coworker, Ezra, will be here today. He hoped to recruit a couple of certified technicians to work here on a temporary basis until we can hire our own. They will be on LeDuc and Johnson's payroll and will be itemized on our statement for payment. I'm pretty sure Blane will get some help from Ezra while he's here, too."

Blanche put a pencil down and looked at me. She said, "So, you really are going to make this dealership work, aren't you?"

"That's the plan Blanche. I need that list for people receiving mystery monthly payments out of the payable schedule. I'll follow up with each of them to discover why they are getting the payments. If there are any contracts we need to honor, I'll be turning them over to Vivian's attorney."

The receptionist stepped into the accounting office and said, "Miss Dupart, there's someone here to meet with you. I told them to wait in Bucky's office. I hope you don't mind."

Thinking it was Ezra and his buddies, I said, "No, that's all right! Thanks for letting me know. Virginia's your name, isn't it?"

"That's right Ma'am. I meant to thank you for doing such a good job."

"By the way, I'm expecting someone from the local TV station to show up. Let me know when they get here," she nodded with a smile and left.

I asked Blanche, "Have you ever hired any students from the local Women's College?"

"Women's College? Not really. Never needed to. We've always hired family first. Besides, with Bucky and Dean, no young woman would be safe within three blocks of this place."

That made me laugh. I said, "I thought you and Dean were…uh!"

"We are, but he's a safe distance away right now. If you're thinking about hiring students, what would they do?"

"I don't know, filing, wash and detail cars, greet people in the showroom, schedule service appointments. Maybe they can even learn how to change oil and rotate tires or work the internet phones. Besides that, we need 'lot people' just to move cars around the lot."

"Not sure how dependable they might be, but I'll make a call to the school administrators' office and let them know the girls can get some part time work here, should they want it. Just keep them away from those randy salesmen."

"I hear that. I have someone in my office. Thanks Blanche."

I hurried to Bucky's office to meet Ezra. When I stepped inside I was surprised to see Vivian Chambers sitting at Bucky's desk. I said, "Vivian! You're the last person I expected to be waiting for me."

"I hope I'm not disturbing you. I wanted to come in and see how things were progressing."

"Progressing is the key word. I have some certified technicians due in today which will allow us to continue doing warranty work. The warranty audit was concluded last week. I'm expecting a formal letter telling me how much the fines and charge backs will be. It won't be cheap, but the business will have to bite the bullet and pay, if we want to keep the doors open."

"I heard half of your employees left the dealership last Friday. How are you managing with getting shot at and all?"

"Yes, not half, a third maybe. The guilty left. They were doing more harm than good and will not be missed. I suspect many of them will face warrants for their arrest in the next few weeks."

"We still have 75 good people on the payroll. Blanche has stepped up and so has Blane Sloan and Mark St. John. By the end of the day, I think we'll have a temporary sales manager who can act as general manager. LeDuc and Johnson will provide a good finance manager to help eager, qualifying car buyers secure a vehicle."

"I imagine your little gun battles with Bucky's enemies have managed to keep customers away." Vivian said.

"No Vivian. Just the opposite. People are morbidly curious about sensational things like that. All kinds of people are stopping by, including people who want to buy new and used cars. I have salesmen asking visitors to fill out a visit card with what kind of cars they have and how old. We promise to find what they want."

Vivian laughed and said, "I know, I was asked by three different salesmen to fill out a card when I arrived."

"Yeah, my fault. I have an incentive plan in place for who can get the most cards. Sorry about that."

"I don't come around here much. They don't know me from Eudora Welty."

I laughed and said, "No, I'm sure they wouldn't."

"May I have the receptionist get you something, soda pop, coffee maybe? Or wash your car while you're here?" I smiled.

"No, I have to go. After hearing about your run-in last Friday, I had to come and see how you were doing and tell you, well done! I admire spirit in other women, and you have that."

I said, "Like Robyn Shoptau, the young woman who was shot. That girl has grit and I miss her. You know, Vivian, I must say, you look good behind that desk. Are you sure you don't want a more important role in the business?"

"Lord no! I just came here to see you. Keep doing what you're doing. That's all!"

"Alright, but if you change your mind, I think my company and I can turn you into a savvy business owner of a car dealership, pretty easy."

"I know nothing about buying or selling cars. That was all Bucky's kettle of fish," she said with a wave of the hand.

"Believe it or not, you hire people to do all of that for you. It's about managing money, and I think you're a natural."

"From the woman who is saving Bucky's car store?"

"You bet! Thanks for your support."

Chapter: 55

I was expecting Ezra all morning. I was surprised to see Frank Carlson, our LeDuc and Johnson's field consultant from Destin, Florida, walk through the door. Frank travels anywhere we need him to consult. He coaches dealers on how to improve car sales and improve operational profits. With an honest smile, I said, "Frank, what a pleasant surprise."

He gave me a hug and said, "Wolf called me Friday and asked me to change my plans and come to Columbus for an emergency visit with you. He's on his way and should be here soon. He and I will analyze the car sales operation. We'll start with sales personnel compensation packages, then we'll study the Columbus market to see if vehicle inventory on the lot matches local need."

"Any word when Ezra might arrive?"

"No, none. Wolf wants me to serve as general manager and sales manager. My key task is to search for local talent to fill my shoes when I leave."

"I appreciate you coming. We've lost forty plus employees, some in key positions. I called the local bank to help with car financing, but I'm sure you'll have a better solution."

Frank nodded agreement and said, "I do and I understand you've had a rough time here with a couple of close calls."

"I did and I'm grateful for the help Wolf, Ezra and you are providing. Let me show you to the sales managers' office and introduce you to the salesmen on duty. What do you think? Could women be added to the sales staff, something they've never done here before?"

Frank grinned and winked.

Less than an hour later, Wolf arrived with a woman who appeared to be in her mid to late 40's. He introduced Cheryl Murphy and said, "This lady is an experienced finance and insurance guru. I've known her for years. She's currently between jobs and will be happy to fill in that slot here, for now. It would be great if you can set her up with computer passwords and introduce her to the dealerships F&I software. She'll need a rental car while she's here. LeDuc and Johnson is covering her salary and the car."

"Nice to meet you Cheryl. Wolf, you're free to use Bucky's office. I'll meet with you and Ezra in there later. Come on Cheryl, let me show you around the good ship gravy boat."

I spent almost two hours helping Cheryl get familiar with the computer and the finance programs. I didn't know it, but Ezra had been working in the service department since before lunch prior to Frank's arrival. When I found out, I went out to greet him.

"Ezra, how are you and Blane getting along?"

"Let's step outside." I thought, *"oh no, not again!"*

We moved beyond earshot of the shop and Ezra said, "I read your notes, and he is exactly as you said. He knows nothing about anything in a service department. He would be better suited in the parts department. I've brought in Bruce Folger. He's in his early-60's and when a public car corporation bought out his dealer, Bruce was let go because of his age. Their loss. He's one of the best service managers I have ever known. He was delighted to fill in here at Magnolia."

"What about technicians?" I asked.

"Magnolia now has two factory certified technicians performing warranty work. One of them is a diesel specialist. They are unloading their tool boxes now. I've had a chance to review the carryover work. They will work on that as soon as they're set up."

"That's amazing. The SAE Certified techs and the uncertified techs have been doing an okay job of doing simple work out in the shop. Troy has agreed to emergency order parts, for now, to get the work out of the shop. Have you called the manufacturer to see what they will do about a better warranty rate and the fines?"

"Not yet. We need to get the charge backs and fines out of the way first. Then, we invite Terri back for a shop inspection."

"Did you know her, before all of this?"

"I know her boss's boss in Detroit. We have some leverage especially after they received your audit report on the dealership's status. LeDuc and Johnson has risen in respectability with the factory and with dealer 20 group companies. We speak; they listen."

"Well, I know one thing, Ezra Johnson has a lot of 'swag' with the big boys in Detroit. Thanks for helping with this touchy situation in Columbus. How long can you stay?"

"I leave Wednesday afternoon. A couple more technicians should be showing up before I go. They want to remain as permanent employees and are ready to move to Columbus."

"Fantastic! I contacted the local Junior College and told them we could use some of their automotive tech students part time."

"I can make good use of them, to be sure. Still, I'm going over to the school this afternoon to talk to the department head of Automotive Technology. He may know of more ASE certified techs we may be able to tap."

"I even asked the Dean of Education at the Mississippi University for Women here in Columbus to send some students over. I was thinking they could be used to detail cars and even learn to change oil and tires," I said proudly.

Ezra gave me a double-take look. He chuckled and said, "Interesting. We'll see how *that* works out."

The next morning over breakfast, I told Wolf about being invited to Bucky's will reading later in the week. "I'm providing a current state of the dealership report for the heirs. It will not be pleasant for them. I think they are looking for a big pay-out, and the current net worth of Magnolia Cars simply does not provide one."

"Should the business even remain open?"

"I believe so. With the help you and Ezra are bringing, this business can be saved, at least long enough for you to find a buyer."

"Well, I'm working on that. In fact, I have a conference call this morning with an auto group who's shown some interest. You said the widow may be interested in the operation?"

"She says not, but I think she secretly is. She'll probably inherit the majority of stock. If she chooses not to sell, I believe she would make a wise choice for a leadership role in the company. I'll know more after the reading of the will in a couple of days."

Wolf thought a moment then said, "You know, in spite of what has happened, you seem pretty energized with rebuilding this store. I think you're cut out for this kind of work," he grinned.

I said, "You think? I have to admit; I am having fun running this business when I'm not getting shot at."

"Amen." Wolf said.

Chapter: 56

After a productive week, it was time to go to the reading of Bucky's will. I was glad that I brought several dresses with me this time. I chose to dress conservatively, with a gray jacket and skirt. I left my guns in my Camaro. My shorter hairdo was easy to fix with a blow dry and a few strokes of the brush, I looked pretty good.

Delta Figg asked me to read a statement concerning the current financial condition of Magnolia Fine Cars to the heirs. When I arrived, the sign next to the door read "Delta Figg, Esquire." I stepped inside and introduced myself to a woman with a name tag which read on two lines, "Donna Park, Administrative Legal Associate." She smiled and greeting me warmly, "Welcome Miss Dupart. Please go to the conference room. May I get you anything?"

The trip to the conference room was a short one. The large glass walled conference room held a sizable Brazilian wood table that had no fewer than ten chairs on either side. I figured the end chair would be where the lawyer would sit, depending if she needed the white board. I would sit in a chair at the opposite end. I planned my presentation to be brief and to the point with as few questions as possible.

I was early but five people were already sitting around the conference table. Not one person said hello. I chose to sit as far away from the door as possible. My only reason for being here was to announce the status of the business. I handed my documents to the Associate to be photocopied and distributed.

Vivian Chalmers had not yet arrived, and two of the five people were men dressed in business suits. Lawyers, I guessed. People began to filter into the conference room. I recognized a face or two. Delta Figg's Associate appeared and instructed everyone to sign a name tag and wear it for the reading. She had a stack of papers, probably the items I gave her to be photocopied.

I was checking my watch when Vivian Chalmers, wearing black, walked in accompanied by a good looking young man in a blue business suit. He appeared to be a little older than me. They took a seat across from me and closer to the front. Some people in the room acknowledged her and she said hello in return. She made eye contact with me, and I could detect a slight smile.

Besides Vivian and her escort, Bucky's cousin, Troy St. Clair, my parts manager, walked in and took a seat. His cousin, Blane Sloan, sat not too far from me. Blanche was wearing a black well-pressed dress. She sat with her back straight and didn't smile or look at anyone. She sat directly across from me.

Scanning the table I saw a tall college age man, Josh Chalmers. That name rang a bell as someone Sheriff Turnbull mentioned when talking about Grace Dowd's murder.

Then, I was surprised to see Deputy John Law in uniform, a few chairs away. He didn't look at me. Merigold Law was one of the names on my list to visit this afternoon. I would ask John about her.

I was especially curious about a strikingly attractive black woman, with short hair. She sat in the middle on the other side. She had a boy with her, who I guessed was Robby's age. The names on their tags was Sanders, a name on my go visit list. Simone Sanders, I presumed, DeShawn was her son. Hmmm, mentioned in the will?

Further down the table I saw an older gentleman with a nametag that read Dub Chalmers. Next to him was a younger man, Lou Chalmers and his wife, Jess Chalmers, Another boy was with them, Oron Chalmers. The same age as Robby and DeShawn.

I wasn't sure what other assets Bucky may have squirreled away, but my report would read that finances of the Magnolia dealership is on its last legs. The business had barely enough working capital to cover new hires and pay fines to the factory for warranty fraud, which I estimated as liabilities in my report. If all of these people are here to receive a share of the Bucky piggy bank, I felt that someone was going home very disappointed.

Chapter: 57

Delta Figg walked into her conference room straight faced, wearing a tailored suit, with an armload of files. She sat those files on the table opposite from where I was sitting. She remained standing and said, "Welcome to all of you here today for the reading of Buckminster Homer Chalmers, aka Bucky's, last will, and testament. Each of you have been invited because you are mentioned in his will. I especially want to thank Bucky's son, Andrew, for flying in from New York City, for the reading. I'm sure your mother Vivian is pleased to have you at her side."

Delta sat down and made herself comfortable. She asked, "Before we start, anyone need anything to drink, water, coffee?"

The older man, Dub Chalmers, spoke up and said, "Yeah, how about a shot of Southern Comfort. I think we should toast good ol' Bucky's memory."

Vivian saved Delta by saying, "Not now Dub. There'll be plenty of time for that later. I'm sure you can last that long without getting the shakes." There was a burst of laughter and Dub's face flushed red as a cherry.

I thought, *"Oh boy, it's going to be one of those readings."* Instead, Delta said, "Yes, let's move along."

Using a prepared script, Delta covered highlights of Bucky's life as a college football player, a handsome young playboy and student of the car business under his father, Dean Chalmers. Delta stopped and said, "Dean, Bucky's father was sentenced to the Central Mississippi Correctional Facility in Pearl, Mississippi. He is represented here today by his attorney, Morton Bassett. Morton, do you have anything to say before the will is read?"

Morton stood up and said, "Thank you, Counselor. Dean was doing fine when he and I last spoke. When Dean was charged and sentenced for murder, his assets were placed into a family trust. Bucky became the heir of Magnolia Fine Cars but not the stock. Dub, Dean's brother, got the farm and a grain elevator in town."

"Bucky used his personal resources to buy out the dealership's stock from the trust. During his lifetime, Bucky was able to acquire 72% of the stock in the car business. 10% stays in Dean's trust for his beneficiaries. The remaining 15% represents heirs in this room who received stock awarded by Bucky."

"Thank you, Morton. Any questions?"

"Yeah, my dad, Dub, gave some of his shares in Magnolia to me. Are you saying that stock is part of the 15%, the 72%, or the 10%" Lou Chalmers asked.

"Lou, yours would be part of the 10% of the current dealership's stock value and the value from when Bucky bought the stock from the trust. If any of you are a stockholder, you know where your stock in Magnolia Fine Cars came from. It doesn't matter where the stock comes from, the value per share is the same."

Troy St. Clair said, "So, that's it? Our stock is a percentage of a percentage. How much then, are the shares worth?"

"I will ask Miss Annette Dupart to answer that question for you. Before Bucky's untimely death, Bucky asked LeDuc and Johnson to clean up fraudulent warranty claims and conduct an accounting audit with their CPA, Miss Annette Dupart. He didn't trust his financial statement. I have the signed contract in Bucky's handwriting. It states, 'I don't trust financial statements given to me by my office manager'. He believed some employees were systematically stealing from him."

"So, Bucky was blaming family members? And Miss Annette was hired by Bucky before he died?" Lou Chalmers asked.

"That's right! And after his death, she was appointed by the Lowndes County court to keep the business running in Bucky's absence since no successor was named. Rather than declaring bankruptcy and laying off more than 130 local citizens, the county felt it prudent to keep those people employed. So, with that background, I now turn over the meeting to Miss Dupart for the current state of Magnolia Fine Cars financial position."

I stood up straightened my front and said, "I'm providing you with copies of the most recent monthly financial statement prepared by Blanche at the dealership yesterday. The copies have been distributed by Miss Figg's Associate to anyone who feels they may need one. Notice the line on the statement that says, 'net worth'."

"If you don't want to read the statement, a summary was also handed out for your convenience. For most of you, I think the critical bottom line is, how much Magnolia Fine Cars is worth as of this month and what is an estimate of how much your individual shares are worth."

"I do not determine the stock price, I can only estimate using a formula based on the dealership's net worth. As you may know, the corporate board of directors is guided by an accounting firm, hired by them, to set the value of individual shares based on profit, net worth and taking into consideration any cash reserves, debt to earnings ratio and potential earnings. LeDuc and Johnson is not that firm. That is a decision to be made by the board of directors."

"You say the value 'today'? How much were the shares say, two years ago?" Dub asked.

"Very good question, Mr. Chalmers." On page three of your hand out you'll see that two years ago the board of directors declared that a single share of Magnolia Stock was worth $450. Today, that same share based on the monthly statement, is estimated at $18."

The room burst into lively conversation. Delta Figg used her gavel to quiet the room. Lou spoke up, "I don't understand. Why so low? I remember someone saying a few years ago the shares were worth well over $5,000 each."

Delta spoke over the voices in the room. "That was before a stock split, then crooks happened Mr. Chalmers. People in the business robbed the dealership blind. Bucky was beside himself when he found out how much money was missing and he wanted to know why. I'm sure that had something to do with his death and also the death of his brother, Eddie."

"You're saying, somebody in the dealership killed Bucky because they were stealing money?" Dub shouted, not believing.

I ignored the question and said, "I told you what *today's* estimated value of Magnolia Fine Cars stock is worth. My short term goal is to improve stockholder share value so the stockholders will have a bargaining position with the car manufacturer for either the continuation of the business or the sale of the business to a prospective buyer. Once again, that's a decision for the board of directors. Given time, the business should be worth much more. My advice, don't cash in your stock, just yet."

There were no further questions from the shocked people in the conference room. I sat down to listen to the reading of the will.

Delta Figg said, "Thank you, Miss Dupart."

Chapter: 58

Delta Figg went on to read Bucky's revised will which was updated just a week before his death. Bucky's will was pretty simple. He gave all of his shares in Magnolia Fine Cars to his wife Vivian. He had the foresight to purchase substantial life insurance policies on himself for both of his children. Another smaller policy identified DeShawn Sanders as a beneficiary.

A modest trust was set up for Robby Carter's music education. Bucky wrote in his will that he was impressed with the boy's musical talent. Robby was the only heir not at the reading. Bucky's car collection was split between, his two children with a special car given to Dub, a 1937 Tecumseh, very rare.

A few bequests were made and that was the end of the will's reading. Everyone in the room was mentioned in the will either by shares of Magnolia stock or a small bequest.

Most of the people in the room were too stunned by the reduced value of their shares to talk. They could not understand why they were not rich beneficiaries of Bucky's car dealership fortune.

After the reading, I stood up, quickly gathered my things, and caught Mrs. Sanders in the hallway.

"Mrs. Sanders, I'm sorry to bother you but I have a couple of questions to ask regarding money being sent to you each month from Magnolia Fine Cars."

Her eyes glared at me. She said, "I thought a smart person like you would have figured it out by now. Bucky was paying child support for DeShawn."

"I didn't know. There is no documentation to that effect at the dealership. You do understand your claim for child support is a family court matter against Bucky's estate, not Magnolia cars, don't you?"

"I have no idea what you're talking about. Bucky told me that he was taking care of me and DeShawn. That's all I know."

"Mrs. Sanders, I am sorry to inform you that Magnolia will no longer be making those payments to you. You will need to get a lawyer and file a claim against Bucky's estate."

Simone looked totally incredulous. Then anger took over. I was afraid she might get violent. Before she did, I saw Deputy Law and said, "Sorry, I need to talk with Deputy Law."

I rushed over to John as he was walking out of Figg's office. I said, "John, just a moment, please."

He turned and said, "Yes, Miss Dupart, what may I do for you?"

"First of all, are you still my personal protection?"

"I've been asked to go with Sheriff Turnbull to Birmingham tomorrow. I believe another Deputy will be assigned to you."

"Okay. On another matter, Magnolia Fine Cars has been cutting a check each month to Marigold Law. Do you know anything about that? We have no documentation in our files as to why the payments are being made."

John looked stunned. He said, "Marigold is my mother. She fell in the Magnolia dealership parking lot a few years ago and broke her hip. That happened while Dean was still the dealer. Instead of turning the case over to his insurance company, he gave her a car, paid her medical bills, and agreed to provide her with money every month to help with her with Social Security. Why?"

I exhaled and asked, "Was there a contract signed for this agreement?"

John grew pale and said, "I don't know, why?"

"Like I said, there is no documentation in the files that explain why these payments are being made. Get with your mother and try to find a contract or a piece of paper that outlines why the payments go to your mother. I need that for legal purposes."

"What if she doesn't have any?" John asked.

"Get a lawyer," I said.

Chapter: 59

As I expected, the abysmal report on Magnolia's financial position disappointed expectant heirs. I saw Blanche rush to her car. No doubt, returning to the dealership to throw herself into work. She wants to improve the dealerships' stock value that Dean gave to her.

I hoped my report would have two results for heirs who still worked at the dealership. One, encourage them to work harder for their own benefit. The other, to keep them from hounding Vivian for money. Honestly, I had no idea what the stock value should be. The current financial statement would only support my summary, but fixing a stock price was not my job.

I've spoken to two of the five people receiving mysterious monthly payments from Magnolia Fine Cars. It looks like both the father, and the son were using Magnolia's piggy bank to pay for things they didn't want to go to an insurance company or the court system.

I have three more women yet to contact who were receiving monthly money from Magnolia. I called Georgia Davis, a woman on Social Security. She had no idea why she was getting the money, but she looked forward to receiving the check every month. It paid her rent. I didn't know what would happen to her.

Marion St. Clair, related to Troy, told me her dead husband had a payment arrangement with Dean to pay back a gambling debt. I wondered what Troy would say about that. Who had the gambling marker? I wondered.

The last woman was 70. Doris Butterfield. She admitted Homer was the dealer when Dean raped her. She was only 17 at the time, in high school. Traumatized, she never trusted any man after that. She became a locally famous painter and potter.

She said, Dean saw her art work at an art fair and he didn't recognize her. She angrily confronted him about what he had done and how it ruined her life. He was horrified and told her he was sorry. She didn't forgive him, but payments began to arrive shortly afterward and she never questioned them, she said.

Five sad stories of guilt and extortion. These woman have been receiving money for years. Cutting them off now would be cruel. But it was not the responsibility of a corporation to continue compensation for the personal obligations of prior owners.

I made notes in my computer for a report I would share with Vivian when we met. These cases would be for her discretion and the decisions of lawyers. I thought, *"This Magnolia boat is sinking faster than I can keep it afloat. I can't plug all of the holes fast enough."*

Blanche was now in charge of the office, and she was cleaning up the books. Every penny that passes through Magnolia Cars coffers is now being accounted for. New salesmen were added to the staff and car sales picked up. The shop was working better and business was brisk. The logjam of cars waiting for parts and repairs was cleaned up. Customers were showing up for advertised maintenance specials. Two weeks after the reading of the will, the dealership was showing signs of becoming self-sustaining.

I called Robyn Shoptau a couple of times. I felt responsible since she was mistakenly shot in place of me. When I checked, she was doing better. She expected to return to the Sheriff's department in a couple of weeks. I asked if she would like to have lunch. She was eager to get out of the house and have someone to talk to. She said, "yes."

We met at a local soup and sandwich shop, and she was effusive talking about her family. She told me she liked my hairdo and said she might do the same. I said, "Then they won't be able to tell us apart again. What have you heard about TJ?"

"Oh, that was so sad. The shotgun wound to his belly caused a lot of damage. His mother told me he may never fully recover or return to the Sheriff's department."

"That is sad. I met him just before he was shot. He seemed like a very nice man. Is he back in Columbus?"

"No. He's staying at a rehab center in Jackson. I understand the County is planning to put him on permanent disability pay. They're covering all of his medical expenses. I'm hoping he can eventually return to duty, even if it's only a desk job." She said.

"Robyn, I was wondering if you would like to work part time for me at the dealership until you can go back to full time work with the Sheriff."

"Work? What would I do?"

"You could be my administrative assistant. I can't always be in two places at once and you can take care of some of the things I do every day. You know a lot of the people in Columbus and can filter who I speak with, you can even handle some yourself."

"Let me check with the county, to see how that works with my medical leave. If it's okay with them, it's okay with me."

"We're talking about light duty work, phone calls and greeting people. You would be a companion to the 'friend of the court'. See what they say and let me know as soon as you can. I have a list of things we can do together."

"Kind of like twin sisters!" She said beaming at me.

"Yes, except your eyes are brown and mine are blue. You might need to get that hairdo, though."

Chapter: 60

Sheriff Turnbull and John Law drove to Birmingham, AL, where they had an appointment to meet with Drew Dowd.

Dowd left Columbus when Grace was only 12, a time when the young girl was very vulnerable. He packed up his bags, threw a few things into the back of his pickup, and drove away. He left Grace a note apologizing for leaving her with her mother. He knew they did not get along but he couldn't take her with him because he didn't know where he was going or what he would be doing.

Grace treasured that note and hid it from her mother. She would spend the remaining three years of her life listening to her mother's verbal abuse while putting up with her mother staying out all night and bringing strangers home to her bed.

When they arrived, Sheriff Turnbull and John Law met Drew Dowd and another man, Larry Harry. He said he was Dowd's attorney, but he didn't look like one. They met at a restaurant near Indian Springs Village in the southern outskirts of Birmingham.

Both Drew and Harry stood up to meet the two law officers from Columbus. Drew spoke first, "Please tell me you have some good news about Grace."

Sheriff Turnbull didn't know what Drew knew, so he sat down and began telling him about discovering Grace's remains. "I am sorry to report we found, DNA from the remains, which proves they belonged to Grace Dowd."

Drew appeared crestfallen. "Oh, I was hoping she was found alive someplace. What happened? Who did this to her?"

"Grace Dowd is a Lowndes County cold case, now five years old. A finger bone fragment was found on a piece of land next to an oxbow lake. We found additional DNA evidence suggesting she was a victim of foul play."

"Oh, my little girl. She must have been only 15 at the time. Who would do such a thing?"

"That's what we want to talk with you about Drew. Our information has you leaving Columbus when she was 12. We just need to get a timeline on who was where. Did you ever return to Columbus after you left?"

"You mean did I go back and kill my daughter? Hell no!"

"We just need to know if you ever returned to Columbus."

"Look, I had a brother who died and was buried in Columbus. I didn't even make it back for *his* funeral. No. I never went back. I didn't want to run into Sharon ever again. She was poison and a terrible person. I ran long and hard to forget her. My only regret was leaving Grace behind," he said with emotion.

"We would like you to search your memory before you left. Who did Grace know? Who were her friends? Were any of your neighbors particularly interested in Grace or Sharon at the time?"

"Sharon, heck yeah. Let me see? There were a couple of classmates in middle school that Grace seemed to hang around with. There was that kid who played basketball, Josh, Josh Chalmers. The damned Chalmers were all over Columbus, like pests. Yeah, she had two girlfriends, Mandy, I think her name was, and another one, Bobbi, something, I think. The girls all hung out together. They listened to the same music, and they had sleepovers."

"Those were her only friends?"

"Yes. I don't know what happened to any of them. They could be in prison or Harvard for all I know."

"Bobbi Jo Butterfield. Is that the girls name?" Nathan urged.

"Yeah, that's it. Odd, too. The Butterfields and the Chalmers never seemed to get along but all those kids were close."

"Including Josh Chalmers?"

"He was just a gawky kid who hung around. Harmless really. He would ride his bike all over town, I remember. I could tell he was going to be tall, and he was crazy about basketball."

"How about neighbors?" Nathan asked, making notes.

"Lots of nosey neighbors. More than one made it their business to make sure I knew that Sharon was seen with some man."

"Any man in particular?"

"You bet. That nosey neighbor who lived up the street, Baker, that's right, Joe Baker. The insurance man was always sniffing around my house and Sharon. He claimed he was only interested in selling us a policy. He was a smooth talker, always smiling. I knew him, we were in high school, in the old days. He started hitting on Sharon, I didn't like him, and I didn't trust him."

"Is that all?"

"Hell no! There was that evangelical preacher out near the Alabama line. Reverand Cal Brand. His idea about redemption was getting the panties off of women in his congregation. Sharon was a willing repentant. That was the last straw. She was making a fool out of me I couldn't take it any longer. I packed up my tools and left."

"I know this must be painful for you, but did Sharon ever have any contact with Bucky Chalmers?"

"The car dealer? No. What have you heard?"

"Bucky and his brother Eddie were both murdered a few weeks ago. Jealousy is a powerful motive for murder. I'm not saying you, but someone might not have liked the idea of Sharon taking up with the car guy and killed him for it."

"The Reverand would be my choice. She slept around and didn't care what I thought. I never had any reason to think she and Bucky had anything going on. After I left, anything was possible."

"Once again, I'm sorry to deliver the bad news about Grace. The address we have for you is somewhere north of Birmingham. Are you still living there in case we need to ask more questions?"

"I'm an auto mechanic. I work in a speed shop near a race track. Am I married again, no and hell no. Never happening again. I do have a live-in girlfriend, and we live in a double wide in the country. She likes horses. Anything else you need to know?"

"Just one, Drew. Has Sharon ever tried to get hold of you since you moved over here?"

Drew was quiet before he answered. "Yes, a few years ago. Someone gave her my phone number, or she tracked it down. When I answered and it was her, my heart stopped. She was absolutely the last person on the planet I wanted to talk to. I told her she had the wrong phone number and I hung up. I changed phones and got a new number and haven't heard from her since."

John Law said nothing during the interview. He was there as backup and witness. Sheriff Turnbull and he got back into their SUV cruiser and began the two hour trip back to Columbus. He was quiet and seemed to be preoccupied. Law finally asked, "What do you think about Dowd?"

"As a potential murderer? Probably not. As a man who was repeatedly cheated on? I feel sympathy for a man who just found out his daughter was murdered. He sure hated Sharon. I wonder what his relationship was with the 12-year-old girls."

Law said, "There were no tears, but he did want answers. To be honest, I think Grace was a neglected child who needed the love of her parents, which she never got. Her life and painful death was a tragedy. What do you think? Do we look for Sharon and give her the news about Grace's discovery? Could she have killed Grace?"

"The only reason to contact her would be to find out who she was sleeping with at that time. Maybe they had sex and the man wanted to do the same with the girl. The girl refused and paid with her life." Nathan speculated.

"What about Joe Baker, the insurance man? Didn't Mike say something about him bothering his sister, Judy, after Bob left?"

"Yeah, he fits the profile. Grace was sitting for their four year old, Pete, before she went missing. The thing that got my attention was, Mandy Sue, a Chalmers, Josh, a Chalmers, and Bobbi Jo, a Butterfield. Grace Dowd was neither one. Who else knew those four 15 year olds at that time? Josh is back from college for the summer. I think we need to talk to him again. He may remember something he forgot to tell us five years ago." Nathan said.

"You know, John, there's a question I've been meaning to ask you about," Nathan probed.

"Oh? What's that?" Law asked, staring at the road ahead.

"Your family name, Law. Mike did research into the ownership of that island where those bodies were found. The land was deeded to Shane Law before the Chalmers claimed ownership using a quit claim. Was Shane any relation to you and your family?"

John looked away staring at the passing countryside. He finally answered, "Yeah, he was my great grandpa."

"Okay. What happened to him? We don't know where he went or what he did after those men were killed on his property."

"It's something we don't talk about in my family. I learned a few things growing up though. You know, I was an inquisitive kid."

"You still are. That makes you a good Deputy."

"Great grandpa Shane was arrested while hauling a truckload of illegal whiskey while driving to New Orleans. All I know, he died while he was at Parchman prison. My grandpa, Shane Jr., married Grandma Susan. They had three children before Shane Jr. was drafted and sent to Viet Nam. He never made it back."

"Sorry. Your dad couldn't have been very old at that time."

"My daddy was the middle child. He worked as a salesman for the Chalmers at Magnolia. I went to the Junior College and received a two year degree in criminal justice before I went to the academy. You hired me and that's all the history I know."

"So, Shane didn't just mysteriously die after the murders on his property or disappear. He was hauling moonshine and went to prison where he subsequently died," Nathan asked glancing at Law.

"Do you think that's significant?" Law asked stone-faced.

"Yes. I think there's some connection. He was around when the men were shot and killed back in 1963. Fats Donahue was a known trafficker of illegal booze. He and two men in the Butterfield family were killed and buried on Shane's land. Was Shane just a moonshiner or did he plot to take over Fat's business?"

"If he did, none of that money ever filtered down in my family. My family have always been hardworking people."

"But what if Shane had help. Who in the county suddenly seemed to have a lot of money back in the 60's? How did Homer come up with enough money to buy a car dealership?" Nathan asked.

John sat up and said, "No! Do you think that Shane helped the Chalmers clan kill those guys to take over shipping of illegal booze to markets in the South? If so, why did they quit?"

"I suspect law enforcement was closing in on them, and they shut down their operation. Homer bought the car dealership with booze money. The Chalmers became legitimate business men and began paying taxes. Shane was left in prison to consider his deeds."

"Do you think that's why the Butterfields and the Chalmers have been at each other's throats all this time?" John asked.

"Yes, I think the Butterfield's blamed the Chalmers brothers for killing their missing family members and stealing their booze. It could be the Butterfields think the Chalmers cheated them out of moonshine money and they want their share. They've been at each other's throats for a very long time. Old grudges die hard."

"Is that what's going on at the dealership, do you think? Or is it just greedy Chalmers family members with their fingers in the dealership pie?" John asked.

Nathan grinned, "Either way, I think we have reason to believe the Butterfield family could be acting on a long held revenge against the Chalmers. They could be behind the fraud and criminal acts at Magnolia Fine Cars. That would also be motive for murder. Then there's that sporting gun club whose members show up to go after Annette. We need to look into their membership connections."

"Okay. What do we do, now?" John asked.

"All I have is speculation, John. We need absolute proof. We look for and find the proof," Nathan said.

"How are we going to find that?" John asked.

"I believe our 'friend of the court', Annette Dupart is doing just that for us. I think she's the key to everything we want to know."

Chapter: 61

The boys calling themselves, the 'Finger Bone Club', rode their bikes to the city water works. They met in a sheltered corner of three concrete walls. Pete was first to speak. "My dad went to see Lawrence's mom, Mrs. Butterfield. He said she's really upset. Lawrence shouldn't have taken that gun. It wasn't his to take."

"That gun belonged to all of us. We hid that gun together in a special place. It was our club secret. Lawrence shouldn't have taken it. I didn't think there were any bullets." Billy said.

"There wasn't any bullets. He found some," Oron said.

"What's going to happen to him now?" Robby asked.

"He shouldn't have gone after that woman," Mark said.

"She was taking everyone's jobs away. Lawrence was just trying to stop her." Pete said in desperation.

"What? By killing her?" Mark asked. "I don't think she was taking anybody's jobs. My dad said she's adding jobs."

"I bet it was just an accident. I don't think he meant to shoot her," DeShawn said.

"He's for sure in a lot of trouble, probably 'Juvie'. And so are we if anyone finds out we talked about hurting Miss Dupart. It's called conspiracy to commit a crime," Mark said.

Robby decided it was time to stand up to the other boys. He said, "Look, I think that woman is here to help keep the car store running. I don't think she's a bad person. My Uncle Mike says she is a very brave woman who can shoot better than anyone he knows."

"What? Like Annie Oakley?" Pete said laughing.

"Yeah, exactly like Annie Oakley," Robby returned.

Billy said, "I agree with Robby! That woman is not our problem. We need to regroup. Our friendship is our bond. We need to swear to never tell anyone the gun was ours."

"Oh yeah? That's not what Uncle Lance says. If she's not the problem then who *is* the problem?" Pete demanded.

"Look, we can't admit to having that gun. We *all* might go to Juvie. Our club has Chalmers and Butterfields, and *we* get along so don't let that divide us," Oron said.

Billy nodded agreement and said, "I heard my dad say, 'Old grudges die hard'. I say that no matter what our family's do, we remain friends and members of the Finger Bone Club forever."

"How are we going to do that?" Mark asked.

"We take a blood oath," Billy said solemnly.

"What's a blood oath? Pete asked.

"It's what the Indians did. They cut themselves and put their bloody arms together, their blood would mix, making them blood brothers, forever."

"There are six of us, not counting Lawrence. How are we going to do that?" Robby asked.

"All of you, get your pocket knives out. Then cut across your palm, like this." Billy sliced his hand open and blood began to flow.

The other boys watched in awe and they quickly followed suit. They each made a superficial cut across their left palm then they formed a six person fist by putting all of their hands together. Billy announced, "There, the deed is sealed. We are now blood brothers. We can never tell anyone else about our oath or the gun. We are bound by blood to secrecy."

The boys didn't have anything to stop the flow of blood except their dirty t-shirts. They wrapped t-shirts around their hands before getting on their bikes and rode to the ice cream shop.

Later, Robby's mother asked what happened to his hand. He lied and said, "Oh, I fell on some rocks."

She inspected the wound and became concerned. She said, "I think we need to go to the clinic, you can't play piano like this."

Chapter: 62

Robyn's shoulder wound was tender but healing. It was the physical requirements for her job as a Deputy that prevented doctors from returning her to work full time. She checked with the county, and they did give her the go-ahead to work with me because I was deputized and the work would not test her physical ability.

I was delighted. Robyn had Judy cut her hair, like mine. When people saw us together, they would do a double-take because we looked so similar. I often suspected there was some Native American blood coursing through my veins and besides, I missed having a sister while growing up. Having three brothers looking after me was great but talking and sharing things with a sister would have made things so much easier.

Robyn accompanied me everywhere I went. Wolf liked her and asked me if I wanted to hire her full time at LeDuc and Johnson. I said, "No, I think she's looking forward to continue working at the Sheriff's department and remaining in Columbus."

Robyn schooled me about local moonshine production. She said, "It's a local pastime for farmers in the area and source of undocumented income for many. Most of the sales take place on a farm behind a barn. I can get you some if you've never tried it."

I laughed and said, "No thanks. I don't drink alcohol. So, the Sheriff doesn't mind if they make the stuff?"

"Not his authority, that's the state. It's legal to distill for personal consumption. Generally, it's not sold outright, that's illegal. But they use it to barter for other things, like eggs, ham and even farm labor. It's a tradition that goes back to the first settlers on Native land around here."

"Where?" I asked.

"My grandpa still distills white lightning on his land."

"Native Americans distilling booze? I bet that makes the Feds crazy."

"My family is only half Choctaw you know. A lot of Irish and German blood in there someplace."

"Yeah, my Cajun family is a soup of many origins, too, but we are mostly French. So, if they were into moonshining, is any of your family related to the Chalmers or the Butterfields?"

"Neither one has anything to do with my Indian family. I think both of those families were part of the slave culture before the Civil War. Mine had nothing to do with any of that."

"Mine either," I said.

"In fact, around here, Native people were prohibited from owning slaves back then. My family just tried to stay out of the way. I was told they supplied fish, leather goods, and woven baskets for local markets." She laughed and said, "One of my Irish ancestors was hanged for stealing a chicken."

"Oh my! Hanged for stealing a chicken?" I said.

"Grandfather told me they didn't like Indians or Irishmen in those days. Grandma Guttenhausen was the family exception. She was an excellent cook, and she opened a bakery in the early part of the 20th century. My Grandfather Shoptau met her, fell in love, and became a bread maker. My father's generation went to school. My half Choctaw father joined the Air Force, came back, and married my Choctaw mother. So, I guess I'm actually ¾ Native American with lots of family living from here all the way to Tennessee."

"You're about the same age as that girl who was killed not far from here. Some boys found her remains before I came to Columbus. Do you remember her?"

"Grace Dowd. She was two grades behind me in school. I knew who she was and who she hung out with. None of them would associate with Native people. We weren't good enough."

"That was just five years ago. Was there outrageous racism against Native people then?" I asked.

"Of course. There still is. But I didn't want anything to do with those girls either."

"Why is that?" I asked.

"They were bad girls. They had a reputation. I didn't want to be a part of anything they did," Robyn said with scorn.

"Bad girls? They were just 15, right? What made them bad?"

"15 going on 30 you mean. All three of them liked to smoke, drink alcohol, and tease older men. It was no secret. Back then, they would go off with any number of men and do things I didn't understand then, but I do now. I know they were sexually active."

"Went with older men you say? Like who?"

"Yes, like the shop teacher at High School and a couple of the dads they babysat for. Bobbi Jo seemed fond of guys on motorcycles. The rumor at school was, they even did things with the Mayor back then."

"You don't mean, Carl, the current Mayor?"

"I think so. I don't know too much about our Mayor."

"Besides Grace, who were the two girls?"

"The former office manager here at Magnolia, Mandy Sue. She and the other one who worked here, too, Bobbi Jo."

"Oh, my. My two bad seeds in the accounting office. The best I can figure, Mandy Sue is a Chalmers, and Bobbi Jo is a Butterfield. What about the Baker's? Sally worked in the dealership accounting department, five years ago."

"I'm really not sure. I was told once that the Baker's are descendants of one of those men found murdered on that island, Fats Donahue. I think Bobbi Jo is related to him, somehow."

"The Bakers and Butterfields are related to the Donahue's?"

"There are no Donahue's living in the area that I know of. I only know about Fats Donahue because of what was written in our newspaper. The news article mentioned the Baker family as relation. Sally married Joe Baker. I don't know about the Butterfields."

"I can see how discovery of the bodies may have stirred up a lot of pent up feelings. Relatives of two families murdered, and another family that made a fortune. Apparently, these two families have had it in for one another for a very long time. I need to look at the familial relationship of the people who left work after the shootings. It's just possible, those who were coming after me and those who shot you, were all related to the Butterfields or the Bakers. Let's do a little research, what do you think?"

"I'm with you, if it helps to find out who shot me."

"Good. Let's get started," I said.

Chapter: 63

Wolf, Ezra, Frank, and Cheryl returned to Germantown for the weekend after spending two solid weeks working in Columbus. I feared my assignment was turning into a long term position, something I was not prepared to do. And I thought about all of the food I purchased two weeks ago, in my fridge, going bad.

Robyn and I gleaned through the list of employees of who left the dealership after my gun battle that left Robyn injured. She and I were able to identify family lineage for most of the absent workers and their relationship to either a Chalmers or a Butterfield and in two cases, we guessed, they were relatives of the Baker family. I matched that with a list of people who committed crimes.

Working together, Robyn and I formed a close bond. She confided in me, telling me about boys she had dated and one in particular who she had her eye on. I said, "I shouldn't ask, but is it someone in the Sheriff's department?"

She laughed and said, "No. His name is Hokta LeFore. I met him at a Pow-wow last year. He has an apartment in Olive Branch and works in Memphis. He's an intern at a hospital there and is working on his residency."

"Woah! A doctor. Very good! What's his specialty."

"It will be pediatrics when he's done. Baby doctor, but that's in the future. He cannot leave his residency, and I am happy with being a county Deputy here, at least for now."

"I think it's time to take what we know to Sheriff Turnbull. What do you think?"

"Yeah, I'd like to see my old boss again," Robyn said.

When Robyn and sat I in front of Nathan and Mike at the Sheriff's office, we organized 3x5 cards on a table with names on them. We laid them out in order of their family connection. I explained who they were and what they did at the dealership. I said, "Some of the cards in front of you are highlighted in yellow. On those cards, you will see where I have documented specific crimes those people committed. I have detailed proof for each crime. I'll sign a formal complaint against each of them for prosecution."

"Very good! That lays out the crimes so anyone can understand them. This will go before a grand jury," Mike said.

"Thanks." I said. "For the most part, the crooks were pretty sloppy. There were the enablers and the doers. Both schemed to steal money to line their pockets. It would, in effect, bankrupt Magnolia and Bucky."

"Who was behind the conspiracy?" Mike asked.

"I'm pretty sure the plan was hatched by Mandy Sue and Lance Butterfield, a couple of years ago. I think they planned to bankrupt the dealership then take over the failing company out of bankruptcy court using the money they stole from the business. Mandy apparently has no loyalty to the Chalmers family. Greed was her only motive."

Nathan chuckled and said, "In other words, the plan was to ultimately steal the company from Bucky's family and give it to the Butterfield family. Incredible! And you have the proof!"

"It might have worked, but they were inept and I think the plan would have ultimately failed," Robyn said.

Then she said, "I think you need to know the connection between Mandy Sue, Bobbi Jo and Grace Dowd." She explained how the trio worked a sex game with older men. "They did it for profit and for thrills," Robyn said.

Nathan looked at Mike and said, "We've been looking at those names, too. So, it was sex and all three were involved?"

"Yes, but I think they were all groomed by at least one man, maybe more," Robyn said.

"A pedophile sex ring, do you think? Who do you think was the key player for grooming those girls?" Nathan asked.

"All three of the girls babysat for families in Columbus during that time. One or more of the fathers probably engaged in sex with the girls. Robyn and I recorded the names of some of those Dads during that time frame." I handed the list to Nathan who studied the names.

Nathan said, "Yes. A couple of these names are on my list, too."

"What I don't fully understand, is why members of the Butterfield family, aided by the Bakers, went after the Chalmers. What did they ultimately hope to gain?" I asked.

Mike cleared his throat and said, "We think this feud goes way back to when men were killed on the oxbow lake property over 60 years ago. Nathan and I pieced together a theory for what we think happened on that island long ago, but we're lost for proof."

Nathan said, "What you've given to us is a good place to start. I'll take what you've provided to Emanual. We, with State Troopers, will begin to round up the people you have on the cards. I'll also begin focusing on men who were involved with those girls five years ago. Of the two girls, who do you think will break first?"

I looked at Robyn. She shrugged and said, "I think Bobbi Jo. She's tough on the outside, but I think she's the most insecure. She seems to favor the attention of bikers. I don't think she was into the daddy sex thing. I think that was just Grace and Mandy Sue."

"Okay. That's where we'll start. Mike, let's get deputies out to look for Bobbi Jo first thing in the morning. She's hiding or may have left town. We'll find her." Nathan said.

"By the way, I issued an interstate warrant to pick up Sharon Dowd in Mobile. I want to bring her to my county for questioning. I think her actions may have led to Grace's death."

Mike said, "I understand from a woman in town, that she has a four or five year old child. What will happen to him?"

"Child Protective Services. She may have family in Mobile, I don't know," Nathan said. Then he added. "I think there's a good chance Grace was groomed by her own mother to provide sexual favors to men. I intend to find out. If so, she will go down with the rest of them."

With Nathan's announcement, we were all in agreement. Sharon Dowd must return to Columbus and face questioning about poor Grace's miserable death.

Satisfied with presenting our research to Nathan and Mike, Robyn and I returned to Magnolia. I figured Robyn deserved a lunch paid for by the dealership. I personally felt no urgent need to return to the business. Everything there seemed to be humming on autopilot without me. And that made me happy.

Chapter: 64

Saturday morning, I woke up early, ready to run, then peeked out of the bedroom window and it was dark and pouring down rain. Disappointed, I sat on the bed for a moment then decided, rain or not, I was running. I put on my sweats and my older running shoes. I wore my Beretta Nano under my Frog Toggs rain slicker, just in case.

The sky lightened up a bit which made my run in the summer rain refreshing. I slogged through puddles and mini-rivers of running water along the way. By the time I got back to the B&B the rain had let up. I was careful to remove my running shoes at the B&B door and carry them upstairs. The B&B lady stepped out of the hallway to remind me breakfast would be served in 15 minutes. She offered to wash my wet things, including my running shoes, promising to have them in my room this evening. I thanked her.

While taking a shower, I had time to consider my time in Columbus. No one tried to kill me lately and no one has even looked at me in a strange way since Robyn was shot in the parking lot. The Magnolia business was running well and making money. Wolf and the rest of the LeDuc and Johnson employees would be back again on Monday. I was on my own.

A hot shower and a blow dry made me feel good. I was getting used to Columbus. I visited most of the restaurants and people were beginning to recognize me around town. They waved at me while I ran in the mornings or said "Hi!" while I shopped at the local stores. I think some saw me as a savior of the community by keeping people employed. Listening to gossip, no one seemed to understand who or what caused people to shoot at me. I was no longer news gossip for people to ask questions about.

The only threat I deemed notable was someone leaving the occasional bottle of Southern Comfort whiskey beside my Camaro. There didn't seem to be any pattern for when the bottles would show up. No note was ever attached, just the bottle. No one ever saw who left the bottles and, in Columbus, there was no video coverage behind the B&B, where my car was parked.

The Sheriff asked and I told him I saw no bottle of Southern Comfort when I went to visit Bucky the day he was killed. Sheriff Turnbull confided that an opened bottle was left on the night stand next to Bucky's body. Were these bottles connected? Why then leave a bottle next to my Camaro? Was it some kind of threat?

I now had several 750ml bottles of the whiskey lined up on the floor of my B&B bedroom. From my time working as a bartender in Lafayette, I knew Southern Comfort 100 was a blend of grain alcohol whiskey flavored with fruit, honey, and other extracts. I mixed cocktails with it as a bartender. The drink was a big hit with younger women looking for a good time.

Back in my drinking days as a college freshman, I tried Southern Comfort and gagged on the stuff, but that was me. I no longer drink anything at all. I have no idea who I would give my collection to. I know Wolf doesn't like flavored whiskey.

My day at Magnolia went well and I knocked off early to relax with a good meal and maybe a movie. I was coming out of the shower when my phone buzzed. I picked up and it was Robyn. "What is it Robyn, are you okay?"

"I am, but Robby Carter has gone missing. His mom, Judy took him to the local clinic because he had a cut on his hand that was becoming infected. She took him in for stitches, but some nurse said he needed an X-Ray. So, she waited in the waiting room. After forty minutes, she became nervous and went looking for him. Robby was not in X-Ray, the nurse was not there, and no one knew of any reason the boy would need an X-Ray for a cut hand. She called the police, they called the Sheriff, and he called me to make calls."

"Why call me?" I asked.

"I'm calling you because you are a deputy. I am just a part time phone volunteer. Mike Riley left the courthouse and rushed to the clinic. He called and said, a person at the clinic remembers seeing Robby and another boy who they described in detail. Mike thinks it's someone Robby knows. They saw the two boys leave with a woman who was posing as a nurse, out the back door. We don't know who or why or where they went."

Still wet from my shower, my hair dripping, I sat on the bed with the towel wrapped around me and said, "So, he knew the people he left with. Is there something I can do?"

"There was a note."

With some trepidation, I asked, "What did the note say?"

"*Ask the friend of the court to look inside her car,*" She read.

I suddenly became woozy. I said, "Okay. I'll go check my car and will get back with you."

"No need. I'm on my way to you now."

I quickly got dressed in jeans, a loose top, my better pair of running shoes, rain coat, and wet hair. I strapped on my Beretta 92M9. Grabbing my shoulder bag, I hurried out of my room, down the stairs and out to my parked Camaro.

I noticed my car door was unlocked. I never leave my Camaro unlocked. Cautiously, I opened the door and peered inside. Laying on the seat was a piece of paper with numbers written on it. On top of that was what gruesomely appeared to be finger bones.

I was about to reach in and pick up the bone when Robyn came to a grinding halt next to my car, splashing water. Wearing a rain jacket and a frantic look, Robyn rushed over to peer inside my car door.

"I found that thing on my car seat," I said pointing.

"Did you touch it?"

"Not yet. There's another note."

Robyn quickly whipped out rubber gloves from her back pocket, she put them on then picked up the bones. She said, "Damn! Another finger bone. I wonder who this one belongs to?"

"Maybe a museum. What's on the paper?" I asked.

Robyn produced a plastic bag and slipped the finger bones inside. She then carefully picked up the slip of paper. She read the numbers out loud. She said, "It's just numbers."

"Read it again, only slower. This is meaningless to me."

"Oh! Not meaningless." She said. "I believe those are coordinates and I think I know where they're at. Do you have GPS in your car?"

"Get in. I'll start my car." I said.

I put the coordinates into the navigation system and a blue dot appeared on the map. I asked, "Where *is* that?"

"Just south of here. It's where Grace Dowd's remains were found," Robyn said.

"Call Sheriff Turnbull," I said.

Chapter: 65

After I asked Robyn to call Sheriff Turnbull, I reconsidered. I said, "Wait a minute."

She had her cellphone in her hand and hadn't pushed her speed dial button. Her head tilted to one side waiting to hear what I had to say.

"Think! Breaking into my Camaro and leaving an obvious lure with the bone and giving me specific GPS coordinates. This is an obvious set-up that took time to plan. I don't think it has anything to do with Robby. I think these are two separate things. I think Robby leaving the clinic was a spontaneous act. A diversion. No one knew he would be going to that clinic. I think someone followed Judy to the clinic and managed to lure Robby out."

"Okay, I'm putting the brakes on. I'm with you. Two things. One, you walk into an obvious trap. The other, Robby is taken by someone he knew. Who would do that?" Robyn asked.

"Where is Robby's dad, Bob Carter, right now? Is he still in custody?"

"I'm not sure. I haven't been in the office."

"Robby's a bright boy. I don't think he would leave his mother behind and go with just anyone. Someone he knew encouraged him to leave the clinic without a fuss."

"What about the note left in your car?"

"Someone's has been playing me all along, teasing me, for quite a while leaving bottles of Southern Comfort whiskey. They've now left a total of 10 bottles of booze for me to find. I think someone is baiting me. But why leave Southern Comfort and now a note?"

"And why lure you out to that swampy lake where all of those bodies were found?" Robyn asked.

"Before we do anything let's consider our priorities. Finding Robby is our number one goal. Then something else just occurred to me."

"What's that?" Robyn wondered.

"When Bucky's will was read, I saw a lot of disappointed heirs sitting around that table. I believe some of them were angry at me for not getting an instant payday. I told them the value of their stock was nearly worthless. On top of that, I told five different women Magnolia cars would no longer be sending them a monthly check. Someone may be trying to get me to change my mind."

"So? What are you saying? Maybe someone in the Chalmers family killed Bucky for an instant stock pay-out? Or someone wants you to keep sending checks to family?" Robyn asked.

"Both crossed my mind. Families are upset; they could even be going after Vivian for money. I don't think she's safe out there on that farm. I'm going to call her." I said, picking up my cell.

"You said her son was with her and doesn't she have some farm employees out there?"

"Where were they when Bucky and his friend was killed?"

"Good point." Robyn said.

"We're spinning our wheels. You call Nathan or Mike and find out where Bob Carter is. Tell them about the finger bone and the note with the coordinates for the oxbow lake."

"What about those GPS coordinates? You're not going?"

"Whoever left the note is waiting for me at those GPS coordinates."

Robyn dialed Nathan, the call went to voice mail. She called Mike and he answered. She asked, "Where's Bob Carter, now?"

Her call was on speaker and I heard Mike say, "Bob's lawyer got him out on bail. He cannot leave the county while we investigate where he was when Grace was killed. And he needs to make arrangements to pay Robby's child support. Why?"

I spoke up, "Mike, Annette here. Could Bob have taken Robby? Could they be leaving for Australia?"

"We've thought of that. Bob is nowhere to be found. His attorney won't talk to us. We're holding his passport and Robby doesn't have one. He's our number one person of interest. We believe he's hiding someplace around Columbus."

"What about that note in Annette's car to lure her to the oxbow lake where Grace's remains were found?" Robyn asked.

"That *is* odd. I'm strapped for manpower, searching for Robby. I'll call you back. I may be able to spare a Deputy to check the oxbow lake and find out who's playing this hoax."

I sat on the wet front porch step of the B&B in my rain slicker, confused and wondering what I should do next. Robyn came over and sat next to me.

Robyn, said, "What a mess. If it were Bob, where would he go? And who is helping him? Mike said Judy had no idea that he was leaving five years ago. She told Mike that Bob was always secretive about what he did with high school hunting buddies, and computer gaming guys. He's a weird one," Robyn said.

"He had friends before he left. Those people may still be in Columbus. Maybe if we find them, we'll find Robby," I said.

"It's worth a shot," Robyn said.

I stared at the note with the longitude and latitude. Why there? I wondered, *"What's so special about that place?"*

Chapter: 66

I called Vivian to settle my curiosity about her wellbeing. She assured me she and her son were safe. "We're armed and we're safe. He invited me to New York to visit his wife and my granddaughter. His offer makes perfect sense. I'm glad you called. I want you and your firm to continue running the business while I'm gone, no matter what the county or the car manufacturer says."

"How long will you be gone?" I asked.

"I'm not sure. A week, maybe two. We'll see how things work out. My son is encouraging me to sell the business and walk away. I'm thinking that might not be a bad idea."

I was disappointed to hear this, but I couldn't disagree with her decision. I said, "Keep in mind, I still think you would make an excellent CEO once the dealership is up and running on its own. I don't think it will take long with proper management."

"I must say, you are quite the optimist. Give me some time to consider my options. We'll be flying out of Columbus on Tuesday."

"Bucky left a small endowment for Robby Carter in his will. Did you know he might do this?" I asked.

"I haven't been totally clueless as to what's goes on in Columbus. I encouraged Bucky to do something for the boy. Robby is very gifted and he needs further education to move on in music. I've been paying for his piano lessons to help Judy Carter. He sometimes practices on my grand piano here at the farm. That is precisely why Robby was included in Bucky's latest will."

"So, it was you? You do know Robby is missing? Someone took him from the medical clinic today. His mother is devastated."

"Took him? No! I've heard nothing. I had no idea."

"The Sheriff and the police department are looking for him now. They're searching everywhere."

"That's terrible, I can't imagine who would take him or where they might go," Vivian said.

"I'll call you once we know more. I'm glad to hear you're safe." I said and disconnected.

Robyn was preparing to leave for the Sheriff's office when my phone dinged leaving a text. I looked at my phone, it read, *"Had time to think? Where are you? I have something you want. Come alone, bring no one with you or it may turn out bad."*

I said, "Robyn, you should see this."

"Do you think that's him, the person who took Robby? Or is it the person leaving Southern Comfort bottles beside your car?"

"I don't know, maybe both. What do you think?" I asked.

"Whoever is sending the text is at the oxbow lake and getting impatient. This is a dangerous trap. Do not go." Robyn said.

"So, you agree, it's possible, this could be connected to Robby's abduction? Should I try to communicate with this guy?"

"I can't answer that or make that decision. Is Robby at that oxbow lake? Why on earth would someone take him there, then invite you? Still the message is cryptic. What do they want?"

I thought for a moment then made a decision. "To get at me. You go help Nathan and Mike. I'll deal with this problem on my own. If they want me, they may get more than they bargained for."

"No! You can't face this is by yourself. I'm calling Mike."

I said, "I threatened to take away monthly income from five women. This is not setting well with the families. Whoever sent the texts has plans to take me out of the picture and prevent me from cutting off the flow of cash. This seems to them like a better solution than hiring a lawyer and going to court to win a case against Magnolia. They just want me to back off."

I said goodbye to Robyn, then returned to my bedroom to change into more appropriate clothes to face my antagonists.

Chapter: 67

I didn't think the people I planned to face were stupid. I also didn't think they would to listen to reason either. Were they the same people who murdered Bucky? Are they the same people who left Southern Comfort bottles for me? I would find out.

I wore my green hooded Frog Togg slicker because a mist was beginning to fall and clouds made the late afternoon dark as night. As I drove, I watched the blue GPS dot on my navigation screen. I still managed to drive by the road that went to the location on the screen three separate times.

I found the blacktop road. It was dark and hard to see with lights reflecting off the wet pavement. I drove carefully avoiding pot holes and deep puddles. The road finally ended at a large turnaround circle. If I wanted to drive to the blinking dot on my GPS, I would have to drive down a murky and muddy two-lane track.

I sat in my car with the lights on studying the illuminated miserable quagmire in front of me. I decided the Camaro would definitely get stuck in the mud. I had my Beretta 92M9 sitting in the console and was considering my options when I heard a sharp metal tap on my car window. I jumped. A flashlight shined in my eyes through the glass. Someone said, "Roll down your window."

I was shocked to see Deputy John Law standing next to my car, flashlight in hand. He wore a full length rain coat. I had no idea where he had come from. I saw no other cars around me.

I finally said, "John, what on earth are you doing here?"

"I got word that someone sent a message for you to come here. I don't think this is a good place to be on a rainy night."

"Me either. Where did you park? I didn't see your cruiser?"

"Just behind those trees over there." He said pointing. "I don't think you want to drive this hotrod into that muddy mess, do you?"

"Not really. Have you seen anyone else out here? Someone I was supposed to meet?"

"This is the road to the oxbow lake where those people were killed. I can take you in my SUV. I don't think we'll get stuck."

"Yeah, I was warned to not bring anyone with me. That might not work."

"What are you going to do? Walk there in the rain and mud?"

"Doesn't sound very appealing, does it. No. I think I'll call it a day and drive back to Columbus. Thanks." I started to push the up button on my window and John said, "Stop what you're doing."

I swiveled my head in his direction and was staring at the barrel of his Glock. *"Damn!"* I thought. *"I sure had him wrong."*

"Get out of the car. Leave your cannon where it's at. Don't touch it or I'll shoot you where you sit."

I thought, *"What? And use your service weapon?"* I opened the door, grabbed my shoulder bag and he said, "Leave it, and your phone, too. Turn off your lights."

I sighed and slipped out of the Camaro, shut and locked the door. He said, "Walk toward that copse of trees over there."

I was mad, mostly at myself. I knew better than to be caught in a situation like this. I needed a distraction. I asked, "So, you're the one who sent those texts, aren't you?"

"I am. Keep walking."

"And I suppose you're the one who left all of those Southern Comfort bottles for me, too?"

"Southern Comfort? No. I have no idea what you're talking about. My SUV is right over here."

"What is it you think I would be looking for, in your text?"

"You'll see."

"Look. If you're taking me someplace just to shoot and kill me, get it over with now. The suspense is killing me."

"Very funny. Keep walking and shut up."

"You know, this is not going to end well for you, no matter what you do to me. Somebody will figure it out and you'll spend the rest of your life behind bars instead of putting others behind bars."

We arrived at his SUV. With his gun trained on me, he opened the vehicle door and told me, "Get in."

Sitting inside and glared at him. Using the hand without a gun, he freed his handcuffs and cuffed my right arm to the grab bar handle above the passenger door. He walked around and got into the driver's seat. He actually smirked at my restrained position. Then he started the engine, put the truck in gear, and moved slowly along the slippery, muddy road winding through poplar trees and long grass.

We drove slowly for 10 minutes. When he stopped I saw two blue pickup trucks parked in front of a body of water. Light reflected off the rain pocked water in front of us, which was a pond, a lake, or a river, I couldn't tell. I could barely see light spilling out of a building. John Law got out and walked around to let me out into the rain. I mocked, "So, is this where the local KKK meets on Saturday night? I hope they brought donuts; I'm starved."

He pushed me forward and said, "Move." We approached a good sized metal boat with motor. Law said, "Get in, Dupart."

The boat rocked as I boarded. John pushed the boat into the water, then hopped aboard. He used a paddle, not the motor through the fog toward the dimly lit building.

Law reminded me of the Greek ferryman, Charon, paddling across the river Styx. Sadly, I didn't have any coins for my passage. When we arrived at a small dock, another boat was tethered to a rope which played out across the water. I looked up, misty rain was lightly coming down and collecting on my green Frog Togg.

When we docked, John secured the metal boat to a post before he got out. He said, "Careful getting out."

"The irony. He brought me here at gunpoint. Was he really concerned about my safety?" I wondered.

We slowly walked up a sandy, muddy path, toward the building in front of us. Light was glowing out of three windows and a half open doorway. As we approached, I heard nothing from inside. I gave John a sideways glance and he grinned. I took a deep breath and stepped through the door.

I didn't really expect a surprise party. My birthday was over two weeks ago. I prepared myself for the worst, but I was not prepared for what I found inside the building.

Chapter: 68

"Where did you say she went?" Nathan Turnbull nearly shouted.

"The property where Grace's remains were found."

"And you just let her go, without you?"

"She seemed to think some people were going to confront her because Magnolia Cars was cutting off undocumented payments being made to some older women in the area."

"For what?"

"That's just the thing. There was no documentation and no accountability for the payments. She was visiting the recipients to find out why. She told me Magnolia would no longer honor those payments without documentation."

"So, you think a bunch of angry old people lured her out to the oxbow lake just to, what? Kill her? Force her to keep the payments going? Good god Shoptau, the oxbow lake building?"

"Call Riley! Get him in my office. We need to check this out." Nathan shouted.

Another Deputy by the name of Tom who had been searching for Robby said, "I got a call from Mike a few minutes ago. He said his son, Mark, is missing, too. He's out looking for him now."

The receptionist walked over and said, "Sheriff, I've got 3 mothers demanding we look for their sons. Each said, its rainy and dark and they shouldn't be out this time of night."

"Who?" Nathan asked, guessing the answer.

"Billy St. Clair, Oron Chalmers, and DeShawn Sanders. All of them missing," Tom said.

"With Robby and Mark, that makes five. What on earth are those boys up to?"

"They have some kind of club, don't they?" Robyn asked.

"I know about it. They were on that land together when Robby found Grace's finger," Nathan said.

"Who else was with them? I'll check and see if any of them are at home." Nathan gave her a list and Robyn began calling. She said, "Mrs. Baker, said Pete was with his father, Joe, someplace and she didn't know where."

"I checked Blane Sloan's son, too, but he was home. Lawrence Butterfield of course, is in Juvenile custody." She looked up and shook her head and said with frustration, "Boy's clubs."

Nathan announced, "This is beginning to look like Robby wasn't abducted and neither was Mark. I think the boys called a meeting and I think they want Annette to come to them, for what, I do not know. Let's get some deputies out to that oxbow lake and find out what they're up to. Lawrence is a member of that group. He fired a gun at Miss Dupart. They could be blaming her for him getting arrested. Her safety may be at risk."

The dispatcher said, "On it. I think we can get about six deputies to go out there."

"Call Mike and tell him where we think Mark is at?"

The dispatcher said, "A couple of hours ago, you told me to send a deputy out to the oxbow lake. I dispatched John Law."

"Law? He called in about two hours ago and said he was home sick," Said the receptionist.

"When I saw him, he didn't look very sick, only mad and he wouldn't tell me why," Deputy Tom said.

Turnbull turned to Robyn and said, "You, too, Deputy, suit up! You're coming with us tonight."

"Yes, Sir!" Robyn said bright eyed, with a wide smile.

Chapter: 69

The old wood building had no electricity. All light in the room came from two Coleman lanterns and an overabundance of candles. Smoke from the melting candle wax stung my eyes when I walked into a large room. It took me a moment to adjust my vison. I scanned the room and saw six serious looking boys sitting on folding chairs behind a fold out table. They were solemn as museum statues.

I saw three adults besides John Law in the room. I recognized Lance Butterfield and Mandy Sue Chalmers. There was another man behind them in the shadows I didn't recognize. John stood behind me in case I should decide to bolt for the door.

I had a half smile on my face when I said, "So, what now, are you planning burn me at the stake?"

One of the boys said, "Sit! And be judged."

I looked around and John pulled a folding chair over for me. I sat down, crossed my legs and my skort parted slightly. I waited silently thinking, *"I have access to my Nano, but could I shoot one of these children?"* I didn't think so.

The biggest boy picked up an old claw hammer and brought it down on the table with a loud "bang!" Which startled me and everyone else in the room. He slowly said, "We are the court of the Finger Bone Club."

He glowered at me and said, "We are here to judge you for arresting one of our members. What do you have to say for yourself?"

I'm sitting in front of six 9-year-olds. They have used a member of law enforcement to have me sit before a mock trial for what they considered a crime. I have two choices, play along, or get up and try to walk out. I figured the second idea would only end in defeat. I asked, "If this is a fair court, who are my accusers and who will stand for me in defense?"

The boy with the hammer looked confused. He looked at the other boys. They just shrugged their shoulders. Billy mustered some courage and said, "I am Billy St. Clair, and I accuse you. We know you had Lawrence Butterfield arrested. We know that you are responsible for having him jailed." Billy said matter-of-factly and nodded at the other boys. And they nodded in agreement.

"I see. You know? How do you know? Were you there?"

A boy spoke up and said, "I'm Pete Baker. No. We weren't there, we were told by Mark."

"Mark?"

"Mark Riley. His dad is the Investigator for the Sheriff."

I nodded in agreement and asked, "Mark, were you there?"

"No. His dad told him." Billy said.

I nodded accepting the answer. "So, Mark wasn't there, you weren't there and I doubt whether any of you at this table were there. Am I correct? Not one of my accusers were there! Right!"

"No. We were told by Mark what his dad said."

"In any court of law…" I hesitated and stared at the boys then continued, "What you are telling me, and accusing me of is called hearsay. That means you got your information from someone else. You heard about Lawrence's arrest, then you put 2 and 2 together to make up your mind why he was arrested. Am I right?"

"No. You told the Sheriff to arrest him. That's all."

"Mark, did your dad tell you what Lawrence did to get arrested?"

"No. Not exactly."

"So, you don't know what happened. Do any of you?"

They boys were dumbfounded. I said, "Your Finger Bone Club brother was arrested for pointing a loaded gun at me, and firing it, nearly hitting me. Mark, your dad was there. He saved my life. He arrested Lawrence and took the gun, not me! I was the victim."

"He had no right, to take that gun. It was mine." Pete stood up and shouted.

"So, that's where it came from. And where did you get it?"

"That's enough of this BS. The gun was mine. It's a war relic from the Second World War." Joe shouted from the back.

"And who are you sir?" I asked staring at the irate man.

"Joe Baker, but that's irrelevant. The boy didn't know the gun was loaded."

"That's right!" Lance stood up in defense of his nephew.

"So, it was an accident? But I was almost killed. The boy wanted to kill me because you, Lance, were mad about losing your job. Isn't that right? But you weren't fired, you quit!"

"Things were going well until you showed up," Lance sneered. "Yeah, I'm still mad. And I guess Lawrence wanted to make me feel better."

"Okay. I get it. You and your little theft ring stealing money from the shop, and filtering cash through Mandy Sue over there was cooking right along until someone found out what you were doing. Boys, you must be proud. You are hanging out with criminals. These people systematically stole money from Magnolia Fine Cars. They kept it for themselves. They are crooks, pure and simple. They lied to you."

The hammer came down hard on the table. Billy shouted, "Enough of your lies! My dad's not a crook. Most of the people in this room are related to each other. No one is going to call them crooks."

"No, your dad is not a crook. In fact, he's helping me now."

I exhaled and said, "tell me about who is related to whom. Who is a Chalmers and who is a Butterfield. How come you can get along so well and your parents can't?"

Joe Baker said, "You have no idea what any of this is about. Tell her John."

John Law stepped forward, backlit by candle light, he looked down at me and said, "Let me give you a little history lesson Miss Dupart. This land you are sitting on was owned by my great-grandfather. He and some of Mandy Sue's family came out here one day and they shot and killed Joe's great grandfather. They also killed two more men, who fought in the Korean War. They were the grandfathers of the Butterfields."

"The Chalmers boys took what rightfully belonged to the Butterfields and Joe's grandfather to buy that car dealership. They called the law on great grandpa Shawn, and he rotted in jail while the Butterfield's lived in poverty scratching out a living on poor farmland. The Chalmers took everything and lived like kings, leaving nothing for the rest of us. We are taking what belongs to us."

"Wow! No honor among thieves. Sounds like Dickins."

Everyone in the room simply looked at each other. Mandy Sue asked, "Who?"

I said, "Never mind, another county, another drama. So, I have to know, what created this unholy alliance between Chalmers, Butterfield, Laws, and Bakers to take down a car dealership?"

Mandy said, "Bucky was an ass. He spent money right and left. At least his father, Dean, felt a little family guilt and began to pay-off some of the Butterfields with checks and jobs."

I said "Mandy, you were besties with Bobbi Jo who was a Butterfield. Lance, your boyfriend, is her brother, right? And friends with Grace, who as it turns out is a Dowd? How did she fit in?"

"You don't get it do you?" Mandy whined. "We didn't care about what families had against each other from way back when. Just like these boys here," She said gesturing at the table.

"Yeah, about that. You babysat for some of these boys fathers, didn't you?"

Mandy shuffled her feet then said, "Yeah, what of it?"

"I think Bobbi and Grace babysat too."

Mandy became suspicious of my questions. Her eyes narrowed and she said, "So what?"

"So, you did everything together, didn't you, with men?" I asked.

"Not everything." Mandy mewed smiling.

Joe stood up and shouted, "Enough. I've heard enough! Are you club members going to pass judgment on this woman or not?"

I quickly said, "Before you do that boys, consider this. You have no proof I did anything wrong. You have no clue that I actually managed to save the Magnolia dealership to keep people, your family members employed, in spite of what you've been told. And I don't think any of you want to do something tonight you will regret for the rest of your lives."

The boys all looked confused and indecisive. Up to this moment everything was theater and amusement for the boys. Now they had to make a mortal decision. They floundered.

Joe Baker sneered and said, "See! Just like I told you Lance. They don't have the balls to pull the trigger."

I shouted "Like Lawrence? What did that get him? Don't listen to him. You have the rest of your lives to think of boys. Be friends, do good and put this behind you."

"Enough with the speeches. Lance, you and Mandy Sue, take her out back and serve the punishment we discussed," Joe demanded.

Chapter 70

Lance and Mandy Sue stood up. Lance grinned and said, "With pleasure."

"And watch where you step, there could still be some traps out there," Joe barked.

I thought, *"Really? I thought the area was cleared of traps."* Once I was outside with Mandy Sue and Lance, I knew that I would have a chance, even in the rain.

Lance shoved me with a gun and he said, "You're coming with me." He carelessly pulled me to the door, while Mandy Sue followed with a gun, grinning like a crazy monkey.

We stepped off the porch; it was raining harder. Lance pushed me hard in front of him and said, "This way!"

I've done a lot of night walking in the bayous of Louisiana both in and out of the rain. I knew to be careful watching where I stepped while keeping a keen eye on the surrounding terrain. You can't be too careful about what you might step on.

I stepped over a one foot drop in the ground that looked like a trench of some kind. Lance wasn't so lucky. He tripped, then slipped and fell into the muddy hole. Mandy reached down to help him. I took off running toward the nearest tree line. I heard him shout "Ouch!" behind me. I turned and glimpsed at him in the hole. By the time he recovered all he saw of me was a fragment of my green slicker between trees. Mandy helped pull him out of the hole and he asked, "Did you see which way she went?"

She pointed and said, "That way, I think!"

"Come on. Lets go. She can't get too far. It's an island after all." He pointed with the gun. And they began running.

Inside the building, the boys were complaining. Joe tried to mollify them. "Quiet! Listen up. Lance isn't going to hurt her. He's just going to rough her up a bit. He may even fire his gun to scare her. She'll run back to Tennessee. You'll see. She'll be alright."

The boys were scared. John heard enough and said, "Not good enough, Joe. I'm taking Mike's boy. We are no longer part of any of this. You told me it was just going to be a club meeting and a mock trial. This has gotten way out of hand."

"I'm going with Mark," Robby said.

"Me, too," Billy St. Clair chimed in.

Soon it became apparent that all of the boys had enough and wanted to go home. They were scared they might be in trouble.

Joe Baker was outnumbered. "Okay, run you cowards. But I warn you, never repeat what was said here tonight. You heard nothing. Telling anyone could prove deadly for you."

"Joe, threats like that are uncalled for," John said.

"Look Law, you don't you tell me what to do. That threat stands for you, too. Don't forget, you're in this as deep as I am." His eyes narrowed and he put his hand on his sidearm.

John Law saw Joe put a hand on his holstered gun. He turned and said, "Come on boys, Y'all come with me. You too Pete you can catch up with your dad later."

"What are you doing with that woman? We want to know!" Billy asked Joe.

Knowing the answer, all Joe would say was, "Yeah, she'll show up later. Go on now. If anyone asks, I was never here."

John closed his eyes for a moment, then urgently made the boys move faster. They needed to separate themselves from whatever Joe had cooked up with Mandy Sue and Lance.

The six boys piled into the metal boat and John started the engine. They motored across the oxbow lake. John herded the boys to his SUV. As he load the boat on the trailer, he heard the gunshot.

Chapter: 71

Joe Baker watched John Law shepherd the boys out of the building. He shouted, "Y'all be careful out there crossing the lake."

John got all of the boys on board his metal Sheriff's department boat. He pushed off and started the motor, leaving the tethered boat to those remaining ashore. Once on the other side, the boys watched while he loaded the boat onto the boat trailer.

Joe watched the boat and the boys leave with some concern. Things had not gone as he wanted. There was still time to clean up what he and Lance had planned for that nosey Dupart woman. He looked beyond the building into the woods wondering what Lance and Mandy Sue were doing. He heard Lance shouting something he couldn't understand. Then he heard the ear-splitting "Bang!" of a gunshot through the fog and the scream of a woman. Joe grinned and said, "Got her!"

In the woods, Lance heard Mandy fall, then the gun discharge. He stopped, looked back, and saw her screaming and crying on the ground. He didn't understand staring at her agony. He realized in stunned horror, her hands were gripping the jaws of a large rusty bear trap. She was trying to pull the massive teeth apart. She kept yelling breathlessly, "Help me! Help me, Lance."

Lance ran back and said, "Mandy! Oh, Mandy Sue, baby. What have you done?"

"Get me out of this thing. It hurts bad! Please do something."

Lance fell into the mud and grabbed the trap and tried pulling the jaws of the trap apart. He strained and swore. Nothing worked. Joe Baker suddenly pushed his way onto the scene with Mandy. He looked at Lance and asked, "Where's the Dupart woman?"

Lance pointed and said, "She went that way. Oh, Mandy Sue. I'm sorry. I need to get you help to pry that thing open. I can't do it."

Joe bit his lip. He said, "No phone service. Lance, go back to the lake and get help. I'll stay here with Mandy. He looked at her saying, "You know I'll take good care of you, don't you Mandy?"

Mandy tearfully nodded enthusiastically. Joe said, "Go Lance. Get going and if anyone asks, I wasn't here tonight. Got that? I wasn't here at all. Tell John, the Dupart woman set the trap for Mandy. Now, go on, get! I've got her." Lance ran toward the lake.

Joe slid down into the wet mud and leaves next to Mandy. She was in excruciating pain and was beyond crying any longer. Mandy kept begging him to do something. "Joe, please, Joe! Help me, please," She begged. "It hurts bad, Joe, do something."

Joe had been here before with Grace. His voice softened and he said, "You and I had a lot of good times together Mandy. Remember that? You never said no. We had so much fun."

Mandy wiped the tears from her eyes using her rain coat. She said, "Yes, I remember Joe. You were always very kind; you gave me presents and Southern Comfort. Oh! It hurts, Joe."

Joe chuckled and said, "You sure were fond of that Southern Comfort, weren't you?" Mandy wasn't crying any longer. She was descending into shock. She could barely form a word.

Mandy Sue barely laughed and said, "That Dupart woman took my dream away. She doesn't know I left those bottles of Comfort, or why. I heard she didn't drink. It was my death threat, my joke on her, eh!" She closed her eyes as she fell into shock.

Joe, still in the past said, "Bobbi was good, but not as good as you. Grace was just a big tease. I think I loved you, but that couldn't work out. People can't ever find out about us. You were only 15 and people wouldn't understand our sweet love." Mandy's glassy eyes were half closed when Joe put the barrel next to Mandy's temple and pulled the trigger. Joe put a hand over her wet eyes to close her eyelids and said, "Good bye, sweet girl." Joe walked to the lake, recovered the rowboat, then got to his truck and took the back road out of the nature preserve. Leaving, he said with vengeance, "Miss Annette, you're next. You'll pay for Grace and Mandy Sue."

Chapter: 72

When Lance fell, I escaped, running fast looking at the ground and looking for potential hiding places. I knew it wouldn't take long for Lance and Mandy Sue to continue hunting me. I stopped beside a tree, reached down, and removed my Beretta Nano from my thigh holster. I wasn't going down without a fight.

I thought about setting up a trap, but that would take time. My only option was escape and to lose them in the rain and fog. I knew Mandy Sue was armed and so were Lance, Joe, and John. If they joined the hunt, they would find me. I needed to put distance between me and them.

Behind me, Lance and Mandy Sue were not very stealthy. They noisily crashed through the overgrowth. Lightning flashed and something caught my eye. I almost stepped but withdrew my foot when I saw a length of chain beneath a pile of leaves. I knew what it was and carefully moved around the area and continued to run.

I tried to be as quiet as I could. I reached a rise in the landscape and tried to see through the pouring rain and fog. Down the hill, I saw a four foot wide creek of running water and a tall rise of land on just the other side. I could make it, I decided.

I ran down the hill and splashed into the creek. I heard Lance yelling something behind me. Just as I landed on the other side, I heard the loud crack of a gunshot, then a miserable scream.

I scrambled up the steep hill using small trees to pull my way up. When I got to the top, I was standing on a levy used to hold back flood waters from an engineered channel. Rain water was filling the channel fast. It was on flat ground, and I could go either way.

I stopped to make a decision about which way to go. But just as I prepared to move, the blood curdling screams became desperate. Not far away, I could hear Lance was franticly yelling, "Mandy, Mandy oh, Mandy baby." I think I knew what happened, but I couldn't wait to find out. I needed to escape; it was my only option.

With my hunters distracted behind me, I felt safe enough to orient myself to where I was at. The rain let up, just enough, that I saw the city lights of Columbus illuminating the sky in front of me.

If I stuck to the levy, I could get to Columbus, but lord only knew how long that would take, especially in this rain. With the glow of ambient light and the rain subsiding, I looked toward my right. I could see marshy landscape that stretched out before me. It appeared to be flat and swampy.

I worked my way down the slope of the levy and into the field. I slipped and fell while trudging through wet long grass and shallow puddles of water. That was when I heard the second gunshot. *"Were they signaling for help?"* I wondered.

My mind drifted, *"When I get back to my B&B, my good shoes would surely be toast. I'll have to throw them away."* My plan now was to keep forging ahead, with gun in hand, until I reached a paved road and help.

When I finally arrived at pavement, I looked left and right. Was this the road I arrived on or not? Looking toward the right, I saw the reflection of red and blue lights illuminating the sky and the trees. I thought, *"Robyn came with help."* I holstered my gun and put one foot in front of the other slowly trudging ahead, determined. I kept moving toward the distant lights, in squishy shoes.

When I arrived, I saw several Sheriff's SUV's, some cars, trucks, and couple of ambulances. The colorful lights made the scene looked like a carnival. I couldn't wait to get to my Camaro and drive home.

I walked toward the crowd, and no one paid any attention to me. They were too busy with people talking and tending to young boys. Walkie talkies chattered. I heard someone say, Mandy Sue had been injured, and the Dupart woman did it. I had my eyes peeled looking around the crowd for John Law, Lance Butterfield, and that Joe Baker. They were responsible for my misery.

At this moment, however, all I wanted was a warm bath and a soft pillow.

Chapter: 73

I think they mistook me for a weeping mother in my green rain slicker. My newly coiffed hair was now a mop of black strings hanging around my face. People were moving around me in every direction, most of them in a hurry. I saw Mike Riley talking on his cell, His boy, Mark, was standing next to him. I walked up behind him and said, "I'm sure glad to see the boys all got away safely."

Mike's eyes got wide he turned and said, "You! We've got the whole county out looking for you. Where have you been?"

"Escaping from people trying to kill me. I ran along the levy, in the rain, from Lance and Mandy. They were trying to kill me. What happened to her?"

"Lance and Mandy were chasing you? How could that be?"

"They both took me into the woods at gunpoint, I'm sure they wanted to shoot me. Lance lost his balance and fell into a hole and I took off running. I ran to the far side, away from the building. I jumped a ditch then climbed to the top of a levy. I heard a gunshot and heard Lance yell 'Mandy, something'. Then, maybe twenty minutes later, I heard a second gunshot."

"How did you get away?" Mike asked.

"I ran along the levy away from the noise then came down into the swampy field and walked out to the pavement. Oh, the second gunshot. Is that how you found them? A signal?"

"Ur, no. Lance, and John were with the kids when we arrived."

"What about Joe?"

"Joe who?"

"Joe Baker. He was with his son at that building."

"No, Joe is nowhere around here. Lance is saying you set a bear trap for him and Mandy. When she was caught in the trap, you came back and shot her."

"Uh, where was Lance at that time? He and Mandy were armed and coming after me."

"Lance came back to make sure the kids were okay and to get help for Mandy."

"Wait a minute. He was armed and coming after me, but ran back for the kids, but he was there to supposedly see me shoot Mandy Sue? That is absurd. You say Mandy was caught in some kind of trap? When would I have time to go into the woods, find, and set up a trap? None of this makes sense."

"I'll call Nathan and tell them to stop the search for you. Are you armed?"

"Your son, Mark, right?" I addressed the boy, "You and your Finger Bone Club had John Law bring me to that building at gunpoint for a mock trial. Mandy Sue Chalmers, Lance Butterfield, and Joe Baker were there. Your friend Pete was there with his dad. Where's Pete? Ask him where Joe is."

Mark looked at the ground and said, "I don't know what you're talking about."

Frustrated, I began to look around frantically for Pete. "There he is. Mike, get him and ask him where his dad is."

"I'm calling Nathan. As of now, you are being accused of the murder of Mandy Sue Chalmers. We'll work all of this out at the Sheriff's office." Mike made his call to the Sheriff, then he began organizing everyone to pack up and prepare to leave.

I surrendered my Nano and was placed in the back seat of a Deputy's cruiser. I wondered how I would recover my Camaro. My first call, if I get one, would be to Delta Figg. I would have her explain to Emanuel Jackson, the Prosecutor, exactly what happened at the oxbow lake. I was certain one of the boys would eventually break their silence. At least I hoped they would. Anxiety built up in me while I sat in the Sheriff's SUV, waiting and watching while another rain cloud passed through dumping more water on an already soaked landscape.

Chapter: 74

I was sore and stiff waking up in the county holding cell. I used the toilet and sat on the bunk pondering my fate. I was still wearing my damp skort and top. My soggy wet shoes and sox had been replaced by jail slip-on footwear, and my green raincoat with my car keys was missing. I had no idea how long I would be in here before I was allowed to make a phone call. It was Sunday, the devout went to church and I was just hoping for a hot cup of coffee.

What Mike told me last night kept going over and over in my head. None of what he said made any sense. And how did Joe Baker simply disappear? I knew the boys were covering for one another because they thought they were in trouble for kidnapping me. Now that Mandy Sue was dead, they wanted no part of my abduction.

John Law could clear everything up, but he was angry thinking that I was taking away his mother's Magnolia pension money away. When he told me that story, he admitted he was deeply tied to the feuding family drama. How deep, I didn't know.

I wondered if it was Lance or Joe who killed Mandy. And why kill her? Mercy killing, maybe, if she got caught in that trap? When I started asking questions about Mandy's babysitting gig five years ago, Joe exploded and shut me off quickly. Her lover?

I lost track of time. The jailer finally slipped a tray with an orange juice cup, black coffee, a paper plate with French toast sticks and a syrup cup to dip them in. No plastic utensils. I did have a paper napkin in case I wanted to do bodily harm to myself. The meal helped to improve my spirits but was far from satisfying. I needed a friend and I needed help, but who?

I knew Sheriff Turnbull would interview me. Whether I would be allowed legal representation or not was yet to be seen. I could tell by the sunlight streaming through the glass window high above, that noon was rapidly approaching. I thought, *"What's taking so long? Were they looking for volunteers for the firing squad?"*

My dilemma, I was caught in a classic clash of two large local families'. The Chalmers and the Butterfields. Law and Baker were in the mix because their families were also part of the conflict and my abduction. I only have my word against a whole bunch of people. I would be tried and forgotten. No one would care because I was a stranger from Tennessee, Louisiana actually, but no one would know the difference. This was enough to make me want to cry. But I couldn't let that happen. I needed to reach into my inner reserve and remain strong until I could prove my innocence.

One thing kept nagging me. When John Law pulled up to that lake, two other vehicles were there. It was dark but both pickup trucks were newer and they were both blue. One of them was there when Bucky was killed. My jailer appeared. "Time to go, Miss Dupart. Someone here to see you."

Chapter: 75

The jailer led me to a room and when the door opened I saw Delta Figg sitting at a table waiting. She said, "Come in and sit down Miss Dupart. This room is used as a secure legal conference room. I've used it before. How are you being treated?"

"The thumbscrews weren't too bad but the Iron Maiden kind of got under my skin." Figg didn't flinch or crack a smile. I guess my sense of humor didn't hit the mark.

She gave me a boring exhale and said, "You've been arrested on suspicion for the murder of Mandy Sue Chalmers. What do you have to say about that?"

"I didn't kill Mandy Sue. Ballistics will prove my two guns were not used in her death. I was abducted at gunpoint by Deputy John Law. I was forced at gun point to face a mock trial held by a bunch of boys, who had been fed false information by their elders."

"Joe Baker and John Law were both there. Joe seemed to be engineering the trial. As punishment, Mandy Sue and Lance marched me out of the cabin at gunpoint into the woods with the intention of murdering me. When Lance stumbled and fell, I took my chance and ran into the woods escaping along the levy."

"Rain was coming down in sheets. I managed to climb on top of the levy to get away. That's when I heard a gunshot. After I was maybe a quarter mile away, I heard a second gunshot. I found Deputy Mike Riley and told him what happened, then he arrested me."

"So, you are denying you had anything to do with the death of Miss Chalmers?"

"Yes! I did not! I was escaping from them at the time. It was Lance, Joe or John that killed Mandy and decided to blame it on me. I had no time to plot and kill anyone. I was running for my life."

"Lance is claiming Joe Baker wasn't there at all. John said he wasn't anywhere near the building or the oxbow lake."

"Well, John had a boat and they are obviously covering for one another. Check my phone. Law used text to lured me out to that place last night. Why would I leave my gun and phone in my car? Law told me to leave both. They put fear in those boys telling them to keep quiet. Their mock trial was almost comical."

"The boys are claiming they never saw you."

"If you can get one of them to tell the truth, the others will follow suit. They will tell you that Pete's dad, Joe, was front and center in that cabin and so was John Law. Surely, Mike's son, Mark or Robby will tell the truth."

"Alright, sit tight. I'll see what I can do." Delta said.

Two hours or more, I stared at bleak walls. Finally, the door opened and Nathan Turnbull walked into the conference room and said, "Okay, Miss Dupart. You're free to go. A deputy will help retrieve your things. Your car was towed to the courthouse. The key, a small gun and holster is at the desk. We locked your car and brought your purse, phone, and your other gun inside. We found a bottle of Southern Comfort rolling on the back seat floor. Yours?"

"I do not drink. That bottle along with several more were left for me, by whom I do not know. I have nine more in my room. Kind of a sick death threat, I think. You're welcome to all of them. What happened? Ballistics didn't match?"

"I can't talk about what *did* happen, but you are no longer suspected of murdering Miss Chalmers. I have reassigned Deputy Robyn to your protection. She's waiting in the outer office."

"I need to know, did someone finally confess that Joe Baker and John Law were both in that building?"

Nathan looked uncomfortable with my question. He finally said, "That is part of my investigation. I cannot talk about it."

Robyn Shoptau, reading her computer screen, looked up, smiled, and said, "Welcome back into the world of the living."

"Glad to be here." I said and I meant it.

Chapter: 76

I got up Monday morning and peeked out of my bedroom window. This time, the sun was just clearing the horizon in a beautiful orange hue. I dressed in my clean running outfit, slipped on my older running shoes as they are now my best running shoes. The others would be donated to the dealership dumpster today. Slipping on earbuds, I strapped on my Nano and began my morning run through the streets of downtown Columbus.

I still didn't know what changed the Sheriff's mind about charging me with Mandy Sue's murder. It didn't matter. I was glad to be out of the slammer and free to run this morning. I fully expected Wolf, Ezra, Frank, and Cheryl to return to Columbus today.

I figured Wolf would overreact and take over running the dealership himself when he arrived. I vowed to not put up an argument. I've already dealt with too much stress with crooked former employees, crooked Sheriff's deputies, and a group of 9-year-old children who belonged to some finger club.

I dodged a few remaining puddles from the early summer rain that soaked Mississippi over the weekend and listened to a Chopin piece through my earbuds while thinking of Robby.

He was there last night with the other boys. I don't think they intended to be cruel; they were just confused. Was he my savior?

I was sorry to hear that Mandy Sue suffered before she was killed. I did see that trap and chose not to do anything. In a way, maybe I contributed to Mandy Sue's death, I don't know.

When I finished my five kilometer run, Robyn Shoptau was sitting in her Subaru behind the B&B. She was busy scrolling on her cellphone when I knocked on her window. She rolled down her window and said, "You scared the daylights out of me. Do you always go out and run this early?"

"I do. Come on inside and share a breakfast with me. The lady here always prepares a wonderful meal."

"I know her, she's a friend of a friend."

At breakfast Robyn asked, "So, what are your plans today?"

"I checked, no Southern Comfort bottles beside my car."

"That's a good sign, isn't it?" Robyn asked.

"How did John explain his presence at the nature preserve?"

"I'm not supposed to tell you this, but Turnbull had him in his office for a long time yesterday. Each of the kids was questioned at length, with a family member. They finally confessed to the mock trial. It was all Joe Baker's idea. His son recruited the boys."

Robyn sipped coffee and continued. "Law, Butterfield, and Chalmers were all mad because a relative stood to lose monthly income from Magnolia. Nathan knew something wasn't quite right about the stories Lance and John told to Mike. Nathan spent most of yesterday sorting through murky details to get to the truth. Delta Figg helped with additional information that was later corroborated."

"So, what's Nathan going to do next?"

"I can't say because I don't know. But I know there's an order to pick up Bob Carter, Drew Dowd, and Sharon Dowd for questioning."

"Interesting. Did Bob, Drew and Joe all use the three girls, Mandy, Bobbi Jo, and Grace for sex, five years ago? It will be interesting to see how all of that plays out." I said.

"Yes, it will."

"John Law told an interesting story while I was being held in that old building, about events that took place on that very spot 60 years ago. He confessed the crimes of his great grandfather and those in the Chalmers family against the Butterfields. He said the Chalmers stole the land and booze. The same booze stolen from Donahue, from his great grandfather while he was in prison. Somehow this multi-generational feud needs to stop." I said.

"I can't disagree with that."

"I'll change clothes and come back down." I said.

We arrived at the dealership before most of the employees and definitely before Wolf. I had several things to accomplish today regardless of what Wolf might tell me about leaving.

I was pleasantly surprised to see four technicians lined up at the service door waiting to talk with a service manager. I introduced myself. Ezra told them if they came to Columbus they would have a job. He offered a high wage. If Ezra recommended them, they must be worth it. I said, "Unload your tool boxes."

Three lawyers were waiting in the customer lounge when I walked in. I invited them into Bucky's office. They challenged me for cutting off money for women who needed it to get by. I told them I wasn't cutting anyone off, yet. The women would continue to receive their monthly checks. I would set each of them up properly in the accounting system with paperwork. They would receive a 1099 and pay taxes, like everyone else. Satisfied they had won, the lawyers left to inform their clients.

Paychecks had been issued to three employees using fake names. Addresses didn't exist. After checking, direct deposits went to bank accounts for Mandy Sue and Lance Butterfield. They had been double dipping every week. I told Robyn. She took cellphone pictures of my records that she would share with the Sheriff. I stopped those fraudulent payments to Mandy Sue and Lance. They had been stealing using the payables, too. I had no idea how many phony invoices were submitted over three years, but it stopped now.

Ezra, Wolf, Cheryl, and Frank strolled into the building at the same time. I told them that I ordered lunch from Panera and it would be in the conference room by noon. Wolf greeted me without a smile and said, "We should talk."

I suspected what he wanted to talk about. I said, "I know, and we will, after lunch."

At the courthouse, Sheriff Turnbull discovered where Bob Carter had been hiding at a farm. Bob was brought to the Sheriff's department for questioning. He agreed to pay all back child support but no alimony, hoping the child abuse charges would be dropped.

Nathan requested the Alabama authorities to serve papers on Drew Dowd. They would drive him to the Mississippi state line where Nathan's deputies would take him into custody and drive him to the courthouse and the Sheriff.

Nathan didn't suspect either man of murdering Grace five years ago. Their alibi's were good. Those two, along with Lance and others, would face a grand jury for child sexual exploitation and child endangerment. Two of the babysitters in the sex ring, were now dead. Bobbi Jo was still alive. Nathan felt he could get her to testify. There were others, too, who would face evidence of child sex abuse. All of the men would eventually be indicted.

I didn't know at the time, but John Law turned in his badge and gun. He was suspended for abducting me.

Chapter: 77

John Law called Joe Baker and told him that the Sheriff wanted to talk to him. Joe became so angry that he swept things off his desk in his insurance office. A coworker ran in and asked what was wrong. Joe regained control and said, "Sorry, one of my longtime insureds cancelled and took all of their business to someone in Tupelo. It was a big account."

He shut his office door then slouched in his chair mumbling, "That damned Dupart woman again. She's ruining everything. I have to put a stop to her meddling. I can get a lawyer and get out of anything Nate thinks he has on me, but that woman keeps stirring up the pot. Damn that Lance. He should have just put her down."

Joe opened his top right desk drawer and pulled out his Ruger 40 caliber handgun. He ejected the magazine, reinserted it, pulled the slide, and chambered a round. Thinking back, he was relieved that he got out of the nature preserve in time using the backroad. That way, he didn't have to surrender his gun. His son, Pete, swore he never said a thing to anyone. Joe believed him. It was now his word against anyone else. *"Any good lawyer ought to be able to handle that."* He thought.

He prepared a travel kit early this morning. The kit had everything he needed to disappear, including camping gear. He knew places in Alabama, where no one could find him.

Nate Turnbull was coming for him. He had just one more thing to do before he left. He had to put down that Dupart woman. He would complete this last task before he disappeared. He carefully cleaned and oiled the Ruger. Since his time as a boot in the army, he always took special care with his guns.

Joe loved to hunt and hang out with his gun buddies. Many had moved on. But he still went to the firing range with his sporting gun club of likeminded men. The gun club and the girls were his passion. He needed that outlet. His wife hadn't let him touch her for years. He feared his manhood was leaving him.

It was women like Dupart who sought to emasculate men. He would punish her. She was surrounded by people, but he would catch her alone, somehow. He missed his chance when he shot that female deputy by mistake. He missed her three times. She killed one of his best friends and wounded several other friends in his gun club. She was everything he despised in women. Women ought to stay home and not challenge men in the working world.

He called his sporting gun buddies and rallied them to help put her down. They would follow her and help Joe set a trap. They would use every weapon in their arsenal to kill the she-wolf who killed their friend, Bud Grove.

Chapter: 78

When Wolf and I met, he was circumspect about my staying in Columbus. "You have done a damn fine job more than anyone else could have done under the circumstances. I spoke with the car factory general field manager this morning. I told him what happened so far and how we, I mean you, have turned things around. He gave me a stay of execution."

"And?"

"He told me, if the dealership could get a fresh infusion of working capital injected into the business, he would see to it the business would remain intact. Otherwise, they'll close the doors along with the dealership point in Columbus. They plan to reinforce nearby dealers inventories to pick up the slack."

"How long have we got?" I asked.

"Three weeks."

"How much?"

"An investment of 15% of net worth."

"That's a tall order." I said.

"I asked him about bringing in an outside buyer, if I could find one, would he allow time for that?" Wolf said shrugging his shoulders.

"What did he say?"

"He said, 'Get the buyer first then send a proposal and he would consider the deal'."

I sighed and said, "At least, let me speak to Vivian Chalmes about making the investment. If that doesn't work, do you have any candidates in mind?"

"One or two I know of. Yes."

I said, "If you need financial records, I have them."

"Yes. I need the last valid statements before things went sour. And a current summary of things you've put into place. That way, I have something to talk about with potential buyers."

"So, am I relieved of duty, so to speak?" I asked.

"I believe so. Frank Carlson is very capable of running this dealership until a solution is found. Our firm needs your accounting expertise with our other clients." Wolf said.

"Well, that's it then." I stood up, gathered my shoulder bag, and began walking out of Bucky's office.

"Don't be mad. This is a business decision and a personal one for your safety. Where are you going?"

"Target shooting. This is my way of blowing off steam. You know that, Wolf. I'll ask Robyn Shoptau to come with me. She could use the practice. I'm not mad at you, Wolf. Just tired."

I left Wolf making phone calls in Bucky's office and walked to the showroom. Robyn was busy working on her laptop. I told her I wanted to go target shooting and asked if she would like to come along. She looked bashful and I ask, "What?"

"I kind of left my service weapon at the courthouse. I didn't think I would need it."

"So, let me get this straight, My personal protection is not armed?" I said with a grin.

She meekly said, "No."

I burst out laughing and asked, "Can we go get your gun at the courthouse?"

"Yes." She said, warming up to going with me.

"While you're there, tell Nathan what we're doing. He may have a Deputy or two who needs to recertify."

Chapter: 79

Robyn walked out of the courthouse, grinning. She carried a backpack that I was sure held her service weapon and several rounds of ammo. When she got into my Camaro, I asked, "What's in the backpack?"

"I brought my service weapon and my personal handgun along with ear protection. I also brought a couple of boxes of cartridges."

I laughed and said, "You have two guns and you didn't bring one to protect me. Robyn! Robyn! What will I do with you?"

"I'm not officially released from medical to go back on duty, yet. I didn't know whether I should be armed or not."

"I think Nathan would forgive you. I know you're on paid leave, but you know, you will receive a stipend check from LeDuc and Johnson for serving as my personal protection in Columbus. I could have used you, however, Saturday night for backup and protection from John Law."

"I know. I should have gone with you. Nathan has him on suspension for now." Robyn said.

Neither Robyn nor I noticed an older red pickup following behind us. The driver was on his cellphone. We were busy chatting away about cooking and I foolishly was not paying attention.

Robyn navigated me to the shooting range. She said, "Columbus police and the Highway Patrol use this range for practice. The Columbus Air Force base security service also uses this range for practice and qualifying. The range is not exclusive to law enforcement. It's a public range, too, used by local gun enthusiasts and farmers. This is Monday, and I don't expect too many people to be shooting at the range today." Robyn said smiling.

We paid our firing range fee and got range advice from the attendant. He handed me a pair of ear muff headphones for sound protection. I didn't bring a lot of ammunition so I bought two extra boxes of 9mm cartridges and would practice with both the Nano and the 92M9. Robyn was prepared with her own ammunition.

We walked to handgun range #3 and set up loading our magazines at a station. We were the only shooters. A few minutes later, I was surprised to see John Law, in civies walk to a stall. He said, "Ladies. I got word you were shooting out here today. It's a fine day to come out and fire a few rounds, don't you think, ladies?" He posted a target then slipped on yellow shooting glasses and adjusted his ear protection. When the red light came on, he turned, grinning at both of us, took a firing posture, aimed, and began shooting his gun.

He smiled at me like nothing happened Saturday night. I sure had a ton of questions, but this was not the time. After a short while, two more men arrived to use the range and a pickup parked nearby.

At the range, a video camera records the shooters for safety. A range light was clearly visible with a red and green lights for everyone to see. When a light turned green, the safety buzzer alerted us that we could walk out into the range and set up our paper targets at whatever distance we chose. I chose 50 yards.

When the green light came on, Robyn, I and other shooters carried targets to replace targets on the range. I used a smaller, circle target with a black center. We pinned them up and walked back and prepared to shoot. Law posted a body target, and he gave me the strangest smile. The other shooters posted their targets as well. We walked back to our shooting stalls and waited.

We put on shooting glasses and ear muffs. We checked our weapons. While we waited, two more men showed up at the range and posted their targets. Finally, the buzzer sounded and the red light came on. The range was now open for use.

Even with safety precautions, accidents do happen at firing ranges. A shooter cannot be so focused on firing their weapon that they are unaware of what other shooters are doing. I aimed and rapid fired five rounds, then picked up my spotting scope to see what my target pattern was. I was a little off with a couple of shots outside of a quarter sized pattern at 50 yards.

Out of curiosity I checked the other targets. Robyn's pattern at 25 yards was not tight but most of her rounds hit the black body image on the target. A few went wide. She had fired through her magazine and was reloading. I continued shooting the first magazine in my 92M9. My Nano was loaded and holstered at my waist.

I changed magazines, then using the spotting scope, I checked targets of the other shooters. My mouth dropped open when I saw the word Dupart written on three of the seven targets. I suddenly realized that I was surrounded by armed men who planned to do me harm. I picked up my 92M9 and slowly backed up. I peered to my left. Men were busy firing handguns. I looked to my right. John Law was firing on the other side of Robyn.

While I was still out of my stall, Law slowly backed out of his while slipping a fresh magazine into his handgun. He was totally focused on me while taking the step back out of his stall.

He swung his gun in my direction. I purposely fell backward and fired, the shot hit him in the head. He wildly fired his gun twice falling to the ground. His wild shots nearly hit Robyn's feet.

I rolled and swung my gun to the left. I wanted to see what the other shooters were doing. They were still in their stalls, not noticing or hearing the gunfire that killed Law. I looked to see what Robyn was doing.

Robyn was instantly aware of gunfire behind her. She peeked back then swung her gun around and fired twice at two men on the other side of me while I was still on the ground. I watched as she fired. They had taken a squatted firing stance, and Robyn managed to hit both men putting them on the ground. I rolled over and when one wounded man raised his gun to fire back at Robyn, I shot him in the chest. The other man Robyn shot was critically wounded.

I rolled over, got to my feet, and stood next to Robyn swinging my weapon back and forth, looking for more shooters. I said, "Robyn, call this in."

She picked up her cellphone and dialed dispatch. "Robyn Shoptau. Shots fired, Deputy down. Shooters firing at us at the range. Hurry!" As she disconnected more men showed up. I immediately recognized Joe Baker and Lance Butterfield.

I noticed the two wounded men in the shooting stalls, were going into shock. Two other men in stalls 3 and 4 now turned around to see what was going on. As they ripped their ear protection off, Lance and another man armed with AR15's swung their weapons up and opened fire.

They were shooting from the parking lot. Robyn and I dove out of the way from flying bullets and rolled onto the range. One of the men in stall 4 turned and said, "Lance, what the…" and he was instantly hit by AR15 rounds. The other man in stall 3 also rolled onto the range, like us, to protect himself.

Robyn and I had little protection in the range, but we were out of the line of fire from the parking lot. We crawled next to the shooting stalls. Bullets continued to fly around us, hitting everything in sight. It was a miracle we weren't hit while we crawled.

On hands and knees, she and I scrambled toward the tree line at the side of the range. We sought shelter behind two large oak trees. While the men with AR15's were busy reloading, I peeked around the trunk. I aimed and fired, taking one of them down. The other one slammed home his magazine and began firing wildly at the trees around me. I ducked behind the oak tree.

I said, "Lie flat on the ground. Shoot from a prone position."

Robyn laid down and began returning fire in the direction of the AR15 gunfire. I chanced another peek. The shooter had taken up a defensive position behind a blue truck. I saw the recreational shooter on the ground in the range. He was slowly crawling along the line of stalls seeking shelter. I couldn't see Lance or Baker.

Gunfire ceased, temporarily. Robyn put in a fresh magazine and I was out of ammo in my 92M9. I heard a twig snap behind me, and I rolled over grabbing for my Nano. Baker stood there grinning. He said, "Gotcha, She-Wolf! Drop that gun."

Robyn started to move and he fired; the shot hit the ground next to her head. I lifted my Nano and rapidly fired three rounds hitting him in the chest and belly. He stood there stunned. He staggered before he fell face down, 10 feet away.

I whispered, "Don't get up. Not yet. Others are still out there." I stood up and ventured a peek. I saw shooters crouched behind the hood of the blue pickup waiting for a target.

I squatted back down and said, "They're well hidden." Then I heard a familiar voice shouting from the truck in the parking lot. "Baker, Baker, did you get em? Baker, do you hear me?"

It was Lance. I whispered again, "We can wait them out until help arrives. What do you think?"

"Help is on the way but there could be more." Robyn said.

She was right of course; we couldn't risk being surrounded again. I holstered the Nano and loaded a fresh magazine in my 92M9. I stood up, crouched, gun facing the shooters direction and made a dash for cover into the woods. I was hunting Lance.

The AR15 shooter saw my movement and he began firing. Bullets hit trees and leaves around me. I managed to work my way out of the woods and back to the paved road next to range # 3.

I crouched and ran toward my Camaro. Two men were standing in the road talking and waving their hands animatedly. Both of them armed with AR15's. Surprised, the two saw me, lifted their weapons, and opened fire. I rapid fired hitting both with body shots. I knew there was still another man behind the blue truck. With nothing behind me but open parking lot and no place to hide I walked toward the blue pickup ready to fire, once I saw the shooter.

When I got to the pickup, no one was there. I quickly looked around. Where was he? I walked back toward the shooting stalls and heard sirens approaching from behind me.

I stepped onto the range and saw a man standing next to the tree where Robyn and I had been hiding. He was holding her as a shield with a handgun to her head.

Lance grinned at me and drawled, "Drop your gun, Dupart. Your day in Columbus has come to an end."

I shouted back. "Why are you doing this, Lance? Baker killed Mandy Sue, not me. I think you know that. What's in it for you?"

"I ain't going to prison for some Chalmers BS. You're their trained dog hired to bring down my family. I ain't letting you get away with it. I may die, but so will you, sweetheart."

I was in the open, Robyn was in the way, I didn't have a clear shot. Lance pointed his gun taking aim it in my direction. I closed my eyes and heard the gunshot "Bang!" Was I hit? I felt around. I wasn't hit. I ran to the tree line. Robyn was on her knees crying.

Lance was laying on the ground with a red circle in the middle of his forehead. I asked, "How did you..." She shook her head. I turned around and watched as another shooter stood up and walked toward us. He said, "Man, that was sure a tough shot, but I made it." He grinned.

When the Sheriff and several Deputies arrived, they swarmed out of their SUV's with guns at the ready. Robyn, the shooter who saved my life, and I, dropped our guns and placed our hands on our heads. We were very relieved that help had finally arrived.

Ambulances arrived shortly and news crews rolled in. So did Air Force Security Service personnel. This was going to be a media rodeo without cows. Robyn and I sought shelter in my Camaro and we waited.

Sheriff's deputies rounded up four more men in two pickup trucks who were armed with AR15's. They admitted belonging to some local sporting gun club and their leader, Joe Baker, told them they needed to come to the range and seek revenge for killing one of their members, Bud Grove. One of the men arrested was the Reverand Samuel Brand. He was on Nathan Turnbulls list of child sex abusers, and he had a lot to answer for. I guessed he would be preaching from a different pulpit.

Chapter: 80

I called Wolf from my Camaro and told him what happened at the firing range. He called Delta Figg. They both showed up to the courthouse. I didn't really need the help. Mike and Nathan were busy talking to reporters, local police, Air Force Security officers and State Highway patrol officers.

The gunfight on the range was over and so was the reign of terror surrounding the Butterfields vs. the Chalmers family feud. The man who shot Lance was sitting by himself. I walked over to introduced myself and said, "That was one heck of a shot. Thanks for saving my life."

He stood up and smiled. "Technical Sergeant, Air Force Security Corps, Mike Rimel, Ma'am. Yeah, I was at the range when all hell broke loose. I had no idea who was shooting who or why. When it began, I hit the ground rolling away and just kept my head down."

"When I heard the automatic pop, pop, pop of AR15 gunfire I knew something was wrong. We were at a pistol range. Then I saw you in the open and the man had a gun at the head of that woman, I could see this was a hostage situation. That was when I took my best shot. Are you local law enforcement?"

"No. And thank goodness you fired when you did. I didn't have a clear shot. Robyn was in my line of fire. You saved both of our lives, Sergeant."

"Yes, Ma'am. You and that woman did a fine job in a fire fight against overwhelming odds. I'm not sure how you did it, but the shooters all went down."

"Sorry you were put at risk, Sergeant. They came to kill us."

"I'm not clear on the details as to why, but it'll all come out in time. Glad I was on the side of the good guys. I let the base know what happened. A Jag lawyer should be here shortly. You know, my Colonel would be pleased to meet you at the base sometime."

"I think I would enjoy going there to meet him, too. But right now, I have a lot of explaining to do."

"It doesn't look like they are very upset at you. Are you a local?"

"Uh, no, though I have been deputized. When this is over, I'll be going back to my home in Germantown."

"Germantown? That's where my wife's from. Do you know any Thompsons? They live there."

"Maybe. I haven't lived there all that long and I travel with my job quite a bit. I'm actually a Certified Public Accountant."

"Wow! An accountant who can shoot like Annie Oakley. I can't wait to tell my security buddies at the base." He said laughing.

"More like Lillian Smith. She worked for Buffalo Bill, you know." I said grinning.

My two guns and Robyn's two guns were collected for ballistics tests. All of the guns used by Baker and his friends were sorted and tagged. All of the shooting victims were identified and transported to the Columbus Hospital.

Of those shot in the gunfight, three were mortally wounded, including John Law, Lance Butterfield and a man Robyn shot. Law was killed with a single shot to his head by me. Joe Baker was critically shot with three of my bullets. His prognosis was that he would survive and face a long list of criminal charges, including charges for the murders of Grace Dowd and Mandy Sue Chalmers, along with charges for child endangerment of 15-year-old girls.

The recreational shooter who was shot by Lance had two flesh wounds and was released from the hospital. The remaining attackers had severe gunshot wounds. They were arrested and placed under guard. The rogue gun club was under FBI investigation.

I told Sheriff Turnbull that I would no longer be working as a friend of the court, and I didn't know how long the car company would let the dealership keep its franchise. He said he was sad to see me go. He told me that he had become accustomed to having me around. I took that as a compliment.

Before I packed up to leave, I called Vivian Chalmers. She said, "I heard about it and still can't believe that such a thing could happen where I live. So, who killed Bucky and his brother?"

"Bobbi Jo told Sheriff Turnbull, that Lance and Mandy Sue plotted to kill your husband and his brother. She left Southern Comfort bottles to tease the authorities. Baker killed Mandy Sue and Grace Dowd and he shot deputy Robyn. It's unknown how many others he may have killed. He and other men were part of a sex club that used teenaged girls across three states. Baker was getting rid of those who could accuse him. I believe Bobbi Jo, was next."

"My son and I are leaving for New York. Will your company keep the dealership running while I'm gone?"

"LeDuc and Johnson will do so without me. I called to ask if you would be willing to make an investment into Magnolia for working capital? It would serve to improve your stock value."

"I understand, but at what cost? I've talked with my children and Bucky's banker cousin. They agree, it's time to walk away."

"What does that mean?"

"I'm not sure. Just close it, I guess."

"My cousin Wolf thinks he may have a buyer for you. Let him work his magic. You'll walk away better off with blue sky factored in and so will the stockholders."

She said, "Do it. When I return, I'll be selling the farm. Too many bad memories. I may move to California to be near my daughter or near my son in New York. That has yet to be seen."

"Vivian, it's been a pleasure knowing you. You are a woman I can admire. I'm sure your help with Robby will launch him into a musical career." I said.

"A pleasure knowing you, too, sweetie! You know, I think you need to keep a sharp eye out for some handsome Southern gentleman to come along and sweep you off your feet."

I laughed and said, "Don't worry, my eyes are peeled."

Epilog:

I returned to Germantown without my two favorite firearms. They were eventually returned later. My life is not quite as exciting as it was in Columbus, but I am happy to simply be auditing car dealership accounting systems. Every once in a while, I think about the offer made by the Deputy Director of the FBI, to enroll as a new FBI agent. I would be doing good work for the government, and I would be near a man I miss, Hop Dickerson.

Unfortunately, Hop's interest in me is lukewarm. And I don't think I would enjoy living someplace like Washington, DC. It's too far away from my family in the Atchafalaya basin of Louisiana. I don't live there now, but I can be there in a few hours and that's close enough for me.

I hear from Sheriff Turnbull every once in a while. I think he took a shine to me, even though he was nearly double my age. He hinted that Mike Riley would run for Sheriff as his successor in a few years, and he was good with that.

Nathan told me that Mike's son, Mark, severed ties with some of the Finger Bone Club members. He remains friends with Billy St. Clair, Robby Carter, and DeShawn Smith. They all play on the same baseball team and the three began guitar and drum lessons.

The aftermath of the gunbattle at the shooting range resulted in the Sheriffs Office releasing a formal statement to the press.

"Sheriff's deputies, who were using the Lowndes County firing range for required gun qualification, were attacked by armed men believed to be a domestic terrorist group using automatic gunfire. All of the gunmen were subdued and arrested. The Lowndes County Sheriff's department is saddened to report that during the exchange of gunfire; Deputy Johnathan Miles Law bravely came to the aid of deputies under fire. He was shot and killed while defending fellow deputies. He will be honored with a Law Enforcement Protocol Funeral. A medal of Valor will be awarded to his mother, Marigold Law, of Columbus."

I read the release and was not surprised. What actually happened would be difficult to explain to the public. I was delighted that there was no mention of me in the release.

Deputies searched through Mandy Sue and Lances' house, and they discovered tons of stolen items. They had stockpiled mechanics tools, office equipment and four new trucks on the lot, including the blue one I saw at Bucky's house. Cases of Southern Comfort whiskey were found. The most shocking find was several piles of cash hidden in two old refrigerators in the garage.

Faced with years of prison time, Bobbi Jo broke down into tears and told Nathan everything. When the girls were 15, Grace was the leader of the girls' sex club. She tutored the girls with tricks her mother had taught her, things they could never have learned on their own. Bobbi Jo revealed the names of men they had sex with. The city mayor was on that list, along with Joe Baker, Bob Carter, and others. The men were all arrested. Because Bobbi confessed, she and her cousin in Kentucky were placed on probation and warned to stay away from the car business.

Bobbi Jo's statement exonerated Drew. He was never part of the circle of men who used the girls. He returned to his girlfriend in Birmingham. Sharon Dowd, the groomer of Grace for sex with men, left Mobile and is believed to be living under a different name in Florida. Authorities are combing records to find her. Bobbi Jo, fingered Mandy Sue, and Lance for Bucky's murder.

Mandy Sue rightfully saw me as a threat. She knew I didn't drink, so she taunted me with the bottles of Southern Comfort, her favorite beverage. Joe Baker gave her the first sip. I gave my Southern Comfort collection to Sheriff Turnbull, who shared the bottles with his staff at a year-end Holiday party.

Bob Carter paid the back child support but was still tried and convicted for child endangerment. He would never return to Australia. As a footnote, Judy Carter married the music teacher from Lithuania. Vivian gave them her grand piano as a wedding gift. Robby is destined to become a serious pianist.

Bucky's nephew, Oron, began working at the new dealership detailing cars. He loves working around cars and hopes to one day attend technician's school and work his way into management at a car business. I believe his father, Lou, is proud of him.

Lawrence Butterfield remained in Juvenal Detention for a full year. He was sent back to his mother on probation. They moved to Memphis, where he attends school and she got a job in hotel management. I heard she may be getting married.

Joe Baker's son, Pete, and his mother Sally, moved to Atlanta where her family was from. She's a trained bookkeeper and was quickly hired. She told Judy Carter that she didn't know how she would ever move beyond the horror of living with Joe Baker. He owned fifty guns which she sold to finance her move.

DeShawn Sanders and his mother continue to live in Columbus. He's a typical 10-year-old boy. He listens to music, play's video games, and enjoys basketball. Bucky's life insurance policy and cashed in shares of stock will provide for his future education. His mother, a nurse, is very proud of him.

There is no single conservatory of music in Mississippi. Instead, there are several. Wherever Robby choses to get an education, Vivian Chalmers' trust will help him get there. She named it The Trust For Robby's Music.

The Finger Bone Club became a footnote in the coming of age saga for each boy. They would all retain different memories of this period in their lives, the golden age of boyhood. They have a scar on their left hands as a constant reminder of their experiences. But life goes on, memories fade.

Wolf presented a package deal for the buyout of Magnolia Cars to the car manufacturer. A dealer friend in Huntsville, AL leapt at the opportunity to expand into Mississippi. Based on the dealers financial liquidity, the factory quickly agreed to the sale and awarded the franchise. The business name, Brandise Automotive has as its motto, "Brandise, The Guys You Can Trust."

Months after the sale, Vivian met with Magnolia stockholders in Memphis at the Peabody. They cashed in their shares for $1250.00 each, making Bucky's heirs very happy and Vivian very rich. She and I enjoyed a pleasant meal after her meeting.

Vivian sold her farm and moved to Orange County, California to be near her daughter and grandchildren. She vowed to raise them with old fashioned Southern charm and social manners.

My doppelganger, Robyn Shoptau, passed her Sergeant exam. She specializes in domestic dispute de-escalation. She vowed to visit me in Germantown. I figured she would come, just to be with her 'intern' love interest, Hokta LeFore. I knew it would be a hoot to have people see us walking together and get their reaction. The only difference, her eyes were brown and mine are blue.

I'm satisfied with what I accomplished in Columbus by cleaning up a corrupt and contentious workplace at the dealership, pulling it back from a precipice of total disaster to save it for the stockholders. I found most of the people I met in Columbus, joyful, pleasant folk who go to church and like to help their neighbors.

I have no regret for the people I shot but I see their faces in my midnight dreams. I still shake my head thinking about a mock trial by a group of boys who called themselves, The Finger Bone Club, who gave me a chilling case of finger bone club bluz.

end

www.ingramcontent.com/pod-product-compliance
Lightning Source LLC
Chambersburg PA
CBHW061514020726
47502CB00006B/2062